Paddy's Day
in
TRUMP TOWN

Paddy's Day
in
TRUMP TOWN

Steve Corbett

AVENTURA

Cover Photography and design:
James Callahan for Camp Rattler
instagram.com/camprattler

Model: Eugene Pavlico
Author photo: Scott Kucharski

9781936936182

Published by
Avventura Press
133 Handley St.
Eynon PA 18403-1305
www.avventurapress.com

First printing July 2020
Printed in the United States of America

As always, for Stephanie

BLAME THE IRISH

Pug Mahoney worried he'd blow his brains out before Election Day.

Nothing mattered more in his moldering mind than casting his first vote for President Donald Trump whose expected 2020 re-election offered eternal life to Pug's psyche, a resurrection for countless people in the fatherland who hated themselves as much as they hated everybody else. Trump signaled redemption, a drive to reclaim territory pale middle-class natives saw as their bitter birthright, turf that validated their blurred narrow minds.

Because of pure, white-hot bigotry, 18-year-old Pug's Irish-American coal town tribe would thrive. Clannish family and friends would prevail no matter how abysmal their luck or belief in the unholy underbelly of a dangerous faded identity. Trump embodied white power, harsh authority and salvation. Trump tempted more souls than Satan, winning more willing converts in the process.

Pug lived to sin.

Trump sinned to live.

All hail Trump.

Naked except for scuffed tan work boots he ripped from the feet of a homeless Afghanistan war veteran he mugged that morning near Public Square in Wilkes-Barre, Pennsylvania, Pug interlaced his long fingers into a bony web of tension. Squatting, he shivered on the roof of the skeletal hulk of a rusted building next door to the shuttered historic Stegmaier brewery that developers turned into a federal government office building.

Today was Pug's birthday yet he fought to hold back tears. Would suicide hurt? Would he scream? Would a soft collage of friendly faces drawn from his past come to mind in a flurry of nostalgia while he abruptly succumbed and disappeared? How did such grim thoughts of end days arrive to plague his youthful bloom? Who twisted him into such a cold American citizen and first-time voter? What evil created the deviate he had become?

Blame his hometown, the human animal shelter his Caucasian

neighbors saluted as their "almost nigger-free" refuge, now known coast-to-coast among FOX News viewers as "Trump Town." Blame wandering ghosts from Northeastern Pennsylvania's immigrant coal-mining culture that curled bloody fingers tightly around Pug's throat. Mostly, blame the Irish.

Green glass shards touched his balls as he crouched in deep contemplation. The jagged neck of a broken beer bottle tickled his pink-pimpled ass cheeks. When a frigid gust of early March air blew up his butt, Pug imagined his funny bone and let go laughing until he peed himself. Grinning like a ghoul in a low-budget horror movie, Pug felt the warm dribble of urine and slowly straightened to full height.

At six feet even, gangly and gawky at 172 pounds, Pug wore a pale face full of rusty freckles. With a long-ago broken nose and runny sky-blue eyes, his shaved white head resembled a cracked hardboiled egg or skull fracture x-ray. Small cuts crisscrossed his scalp from hacking with a disposable plastic razor he found near two bare young saplings that grew through holes in the vacant building's roof. Gone was Pug's thick, unruly crimson mane that once glistened as bright as a spicy happy hour Bloody Mary served in an unwashed pint glass. When an imaginary gold harp had flashed before his eyes a few weeks earlier, a vivid hallucination drawn from harsh Irish cultural indoctrination that defined his childhood, Pug dyed his matted hair green for the upcoming Paddy's Day parade. Just a few weeks away, the sacred march was closing in fast. Now his shaved skull throbbed with hate.

Pug loved hate.

From his perch, he stared at a rainbow of neon business lights flickering in the inky night above his grim birthplace. Wilkes-Barre, pound-for-pound the unofficial national underbelly of Irish America, endured a steadily decreasing population of about 40,000 people. As one of America's bleakest small cities, the town survived on broken memories, cheap beer and stubborn, family-tied provincialism that sired endless self-absorbed bigotry. Out-of-town journalists during the 2016 presidential election regularly called the place gritty, a rust belt coal town even though coal was dead. Gritty meant shitty. And shitty was nothing to be proud of unless you were Irish, pig shit Irish and proud of it.

Zonked on lime vodka and generic cleaning fluid he huffed from a wet rag, higher than Jesus ascending into heaven to sit at the right hand of God, Pug massaged the base of his head near the brain stem where he wore a green shamrock tattoo. For the first time in his life Pug had finally sculpted an identity all his own. Waves of emotional terror swept over his frontal lobe like swells crashing against the rocks below the Irish Cliffs of Moher.

Pug began to cry.

Fragile mental stability imploded whenever he did his best to resist increasing anxiety and erratic mood swings. Brooding and dark, Pug cried too easily. When anger grabbed him, he went silent quickly, suffering an evil need to get even, to do unto others before they did unto him. Drying his tears and going deathly quiet, he did as much damage onto others as he could whenever he could.

On this morning of Pug's total breakdown, his mother's monthly supply of fresh prescription opioid painkillers disappeared. So did the last bottle of Jameson whiskey he lifted from his old man's stash in the cupboard under the kitchen sink. Since leaving home a few weeks ago, Pug burglarized the house twice for supplies. No way could he go back to live there. No longer would his mom slur her weak reassurance that everything would be all right. Still, Pug knew he would rise again. This time, even if it took his funeral to do it, Pug would make his enemies come to him, preferably on their knees.

On the run now and on his own, Pug looked west toward the Susquehanna River. A bright digital billboard shined blue and orange in the distance, advertising "DONALD TRUMP 2020." Taking a long pull of whiskey, Pug swallowed a couple Oxycodones. Reeling and glassy-eyed, he unconsciously started playing with himself. The chemical imbalance that sent him careening through the day still energized him. Pug thought about masturbating but, embarrassed as always, slapped away his hand and balled his fingers into a tight fist. Allowing his mind to wander, a woman's face took shape in the sky. Amid black swirling clouds her lips shined emerald green. As she wept Pug heard a keening song made of tears take shape in his head. He knew she was forecasting death. The question was whose. Maybe she just wanted a favor.

"Anything," he said. "I'll do anything."

The woman's refrain turned to a ghostly melody that gave Pug goosebumps. Enchanted, Pug felt guilty, like he was cheating on Binkee, that sexy little dirtball girl he met about four months ago and screwed in the McDonald's dumpster, the runaway who smelled like honey mustard sauce. Where was she when he needed her? Little bitch wasn't even old enough to vote. Where were those who were supposed to love him? With his heart beating in his throat, Pug slammed his fists against his head and chanted.

"Trump, Trump, Trump."

The banshee's song turned shrill, catching Pug's attention, grabbing his mind like a dog whistle piercing the eardrums of a rabid homeless cur. Cocking his head to listen to the roar behind his eyes, Pug heeded the howl accompanied by a mad symphony of pagan war drums that laid down a beat between his ears. Accompanied by a fantasy tin whistle, an unreal squeezebox, and the mournful wail of phantom uilleann pipes, Pug imagined himself standing tall as a brave Celtic warrior refusing to run from migrant invaders. But Pug's heroic visions went blank as quickly as they appeared. Realizing he would never live the life of an Irish freedom fighter, as his father wanted desperately for him and for himself, the scrawny failure teetered on the edge of insanity.

After years of depression, panic and high anxiety, Pug decided to destroy his unholy existence. This once lovable sad lad turned maniacal bad boy simply wanted peace of mind. With nowhere to turn, Pug decided to give everybody something to remember him by, one last gala St. Patrick's Day parade march and a couple of search and destroy missions to get warmed up. Like his neighbors, family and friends, Pug loved and hated being Irish, a lousy contradiction destined to take root and explode, confusing the town and turning Pug into a barbarous martyr of white teenage pain.

Looking at his hands, Pug picked at dried skin that covered

his outstretched fingers and made them resemble skeleton bones in the moonlight. Sobbing now, Pug did a sloppy jig. Holding his hands straight at his sides, he bounced on the balls of his feet, keeping his back straight, lifting first one leg and then the other the way he had seen his grandfather dance before the old fellow keeled over for good from the black lung he got breathing coal dust in the coal mines. Out of breath in less than a minute, Pug surrendered to fatigue. Reaching for his jeans, he pulled them on, catching and tearing pubic hair in the zipper.

Cast forever from his race, Pug pulled on a cracked black leather motorcycle jacket with rusted silver snaps, his prize piece of clothing onto which he recently spray-painted "irish" on the back in green lower case letters. Digging his hands deep into the pockets, he felt the dead weight of a new steel and brass Buck folding knife. Climbing down from his sanctuary, he hunched sloping, bony shoulders and prepared to lay siege to the soul of his city. This desperate first-night patrol would take him deep behind the enemy lines of his own DNA.

Opening the knife with a deft flick of his thumb and wrist, Pug laid the wide side of the silver blade against his forehead. Pressing cold steel against his skin as he walked, he turned the blade cutting edge down. Slowly but surely he began to slice, not too deep but just right, leaving a thin one-inch vertical cut on his head. Turning his wrist, he cut again, this time a matching one-inch horizontal cut. The letter "T" for Trump dripped blood. Scrunching dry lips into a contorted pucker, Pug slobbered and slurred.

"It's Paddy's Day in Trump Town," he said.

A REAL CHARMER

After dragging their prisoner from Public Square, five beefy out-of-breath cops fought to restrain Franny Finnerty as he struggled and squirmed on a patch of broken concrete sidewalk outside Wilkes-Barre police headquarters.

Dressed in blue silk pajamas and an unraveling stained white turban that made him look like a dirty vanilla ice cream cone with rainbow sprinkles melting in the sun, Finnerty wrapped his arms and legs around a yellow wicker basket with a splintered straw top.

Detective Brendan "Bop" O'Brien recognized the flailing costumed character as a city native with whom O'Brien attended Meyers High School, a feminine type O'Brien heard left town years ago to seek fame and fortune as an interpretive dancer in one of the casinos on the boardwalk in Atlantic City. Finnerty now lived under the radar in seclusion in a rented South Main Street room, surviving as a disabled alcoholic recluse and mental health patient.

An agitated rookie cop tried to catch his breath. "He's carrying snakes without a license," he said. "Cobras and shit."

O'Brien fingered the butt of his gun and stepped back two giant steps.

"In the basket," the young cop said.

Prepared to shoot, O'Brien pried Finnerty off the basket and carefully lifted the lid. Instead of real snakes and shit, O'Brien saw eight rubber garter snakes with turquoise painted eyes and red forked tongues. Finnerty bought them at a dollar store to mimic the fake reptiles he used in his act at Trump's Taj Mahal.

A show business career at the shore really seemed possible when a bored choreographer chose Finnerty to swing and sway to exotic Indian music in an extravagant revue based on Trump's life had the real estate mogul been born a maharaja and lived in the real Taj Mahal. Finnerty played one of 1000 elephant slaves (50 of which danced on stage) used to construct the majestic structure. Pleased with Finnerty's pachyderm portrayal, a gay former Bollywood director promised him a chance to try out for the Mahatma Gandhi part in the production, but the dumbest of Trump's two sons intervened with news the show was failing.

"Dad says we need snake charmers, not elephants," he said.

For the next few months Finnerty sat cross-legged playing a flute outside the high roller men's room, slowly pulling from a basket fake dancing cobras attached to the flute with an invisible wire. Although Franny was pretty good at playing traditional Indian flute music, in bed at night in his tiny rented room on Atlantic Avenue he cried as his legs cramped from sitting all day in full lotus position. Eventually his barely-rising star flamed out over the ocean horizon, incinerated in the glitzy Trump-infested nest of excess. When a Boy Scout troop with a couple of sharp 11-year-olds from New Delhi detected the snake hoax, Trump assembled the team of oppressed charmers for an emergency meeting.

"You're fired," Trump said.

To the surprise of nobody on the Trump payroll, the garish casino decayed faster than Tandoori chicken left unattended over the weekend on an all-you-can-eat buffet. Trump went on to destroy bigger and better things.

Back in Wilkes-Barre the once-flamboyant Finnerty looked like an authentic Bombay beggar. The average Calcutta black hole held the same promise as Finnerty's life. Numerous personality disorders germinated in his psyche after working as long as he did at Trump's Taj Mahal. Finnerty slid deeper into his sickness. For a few weeks he even spoke English in a scandalous imitation of an Indian, sounding like a bigoted semper fi Marine Corps veteran mocking immigrant doctors at the Wilkes-Barre VA Medical Center.

And on this fateful day, the heat of psychosis sent him swishing silk scarves and pantaloons to Public Square where he planned to play his Indian flute and charm the fake snakes one last time before ending it all in a swan dive off the Market Street Bridge.

A flirt and a natural-born dancer who once instructed at the Arthur Murray studio downtown, Finnerty no longer performed slick samba, tango, waltz or disco boogie in perfectly timed steps. Once he twirled with happiness and measured abandon, wrapped in the world of art and finesse.

O'Brien ran in little circles around the body slapping his forehead in frustration with both hands. Tightening his grip on Finnerty, the rotund cop tugged his prisoner toward the police station's front doors. Franny struggled to hang on to his basket and what was left of his sanity. Looking into O'Brien's eyes, Finnerty saw the same evil he saw when he last saw Trump.

"You are finished, Mr. Finnerty," Trump said. "Turn in your turban."

Within a year of moving in with his sister in the East End section of town, she discovered him sitting naked in full lotus in the closet playing his flute by a wicker wash hamper loaded with rubber snakes and soiled underwear. After doctors diagnosed him as suffering from a severe nervous breakdown (he played the flute for them, too) he received a dozen shock treatments and eventually spent a month in a locked ward at a local hospital that accepts indigent patients. When released, Finnerty rented a small central city hovel, collected meager government checks, and stayed to himself.

Trump's 2016 election put him over the edge. Nightmares started. Finnerty's beer intake increased. He tossed his meds down the toilet. Working for Trump taught him how reality is sometimes too hard to take for the weak, infirmed and vulnerable. Finnerty prayed for strength, but his prayers went unanswered.

Then life got worse.

About eight o'clock on the morning in question, Franny Finnerty stepped into the same flashy costume he wore in his "glory" days. Dragging the stolen costume from the shelf where it lay in a nest of cob webs, he smiled and patted his rump because the outfit still fit snug around his waist, making Franny happy with his figure if only for a second. Mustering courage for one last enchanted flute-playing stroll around Public Square, reliving his past before he ended it all, the 58-year-old paranoid schizophrenic sat alone in his rented room all morning drinking can after can of warm Stegmaier Gold Medal beer he kept in a case under his bed.

When he heard the church bells peal at noon, Finnerty turned his back on the fire trap flophouse and stumbled down three flights of stairs to the street. When he reached Public Square, Finnerty tripped on a loose brick near the fountain at the center of the square, took a header and immediately lost consciousness. In a vivid dream he returned to Atlantic City on a pleasant summer day, snug in the first saloon off the boardwalk on Kentucky Avenue where he sat pounding down highballs at Eddie's Shamrock Bar with two male French-Canadian acrobats who were performing that week at the Million Dollar Pier. Excusing himself and rising from his stool, Finnerty strutted to the toilet where he stood before the urinal with all the confidence of the head judge at the Miss America Pageant. Sighing, Finnerty unleashed a forceful stream.

Instinctively struggling to his feet punchy from drink and groggy from the fall, Finnerty had no idea he was now in the act of publicly spraying the carved stone memorial dedicated to the late, great Dan Flood, Wilkes-Barre's most beloved crooked congressman who, despite his dishonesty, would always be revered by locals as St. Dan. Catholic nuns would tell you, "If he stole, he stole for us."

The subsequent arrest affidavit noted that Finnerty staggered across the park, continually turning to point his "gushing member" and unleash a urine stream with all the power of a geyser in a national park. The carved image of the late congressman caught the full force of Finnerty's flow right in the kisser, according to the police report that supported the assault charge. It mattered little that Flood was long dead and disgraced after a guilty plea for public corruption. Nobody cared that state law prohibits a sculpted stone bust from receiving living victim status. Political party affiliation aside, in this part of the country, even dead lawmakers receive courtesies withheld from the average living taxpayer.

Aroused by the prospect of gratuitous violence of any caliber, Detective O'Brien breathed in the short, heavy pants of an obscene phone caller. Many years had passed since this rogue cop from a shanty Irish background raised his hand and took an oath to protect and serve. That he did, too. O'Brien protected bookmakers, crooked elected officials, illegal after-hours club owners and other lawbreakers while digging into generous servings of cash bribes, kickbacks, shakedowns and assorted payola. O'Brien expected all people to obey all laws at all times unless he personally instructed them to do otherwise.

For a price, of course.

For this demented Ali Baba dipshit to even think about challenging O'Brien's authority forced O'Brien to consider he might be going soft. Grunting, O'Brien grabbed Finnerty by his skinny ankles. Flipping the poor soul onto his back and spinning him around, O'Brien dragged the pathetic, wriggling creature through the police headquarters doorway and toward the interrogation room.

Working his first shift since being named the city's first minority detective (actually the first detective of color because the first minority was Polish) Paddy "Duff" Duffin was coming from the criminal investigation office when he spotted the ruckus.

"Stay cool," he said out loud, hating that he was so concerned about what the white cops might think.

Duff watched O'Brien continue to play with his prey now curled into a grotesque defensive posture. No matter what Finnerty had done or why, Duff felt sorry for the poor fellow whose sobs echoed throughout the building. Looking at O'Brien, Duff spoke in his most non-threatening voice.

"C'mon, O'Brien, let's call it a day," Duff said. "What do you say, man?"

Turning to the dozen or so officers huddled nearby snickering and nudging each other, O'Brien straddled the beaten prone figure, looked up at Duff, and spit his response.

"No, we will not call it a day, man," O'Brien said.

Embarrassed, Duff looked to other officers for support. No one returned his gaze.

"A gypsy snake charmer pulls his dancing penis out of his pants and defaces our congressman. That's what's wrong with this country. That's why we're making America great again."

O'Brien pushed off his captive, grunted his way to his feet and, glaring, pointed at Finnerty.

"This ain't the giggly Franny Finnerty I remember from high school when he played piccolo in the band and danced in the senior class play. This snowflake is one kinky libtard loser if there ever was one."

Spinning to face Duff, O'Brien's voice rose to a shriek. Doubled over in spasms of hilarity, the assembled cops tried to keep from fainting from laughter as O'Brien's voice rose to the level of a dentist's drill.

"Walk Swami Salami over to meet the first graders at St. Nick's, why don't you. Let the boys and girls shake hands with the dancing snake. How about that, Paddy, me boy?" O'Brien stressed the word, "boy."

"The boys will be waving their little snakes around because this A-rab freak did it and nobody stopped him. Taking snake selfies and sexting them to their second grade Valentines. What do you say, man? What do you say, man? Still want to call it a day?"

Astounded, Duff stared at the panting, gasping cop. Did O'Brien really believe his own rant? Did the younger cops nodding in agreement sense truth in his incoherent tirade? Tunnel-vision time warps like Wilkes-Barre only got worse. Duff sometimes felt like giving up, turning in his badge and starting a boxing gym.

Gently taking over from maniac O'Brien, a desk sergeant led a frail Franny Finnerty toward the holding cells. With his unrolled turban trailing him, he plodded disheveled and defeated toward an uncertain future. Thinning dyed hair the color of black licorice saltwater taffy lay wet and tangled against his skull. Hives erupted on both sides of a bulbous nose inflamed with a map of broken blue blood vessels. Keeping his head down, Finnerty's face registered pain, shame and turmoil too deep to gauge.

A female officer wearing long fake eyelashes carried the basket of rubber snakes and the flute to an evidence room. She heaved the hamper and musical instrument adorned with purple rhinestones into a corner. Walking away, she laughed so hard she squeezed her legs together and picked up her pace to the ladies' room before she wet herself. Unlike Finnerty's accident, had that happened, nobody would have beaten or berated her beyond degradation. She would have merely changed her uniform pants and headed into a city where too many people still viewed female cops and male nurses as ass-backward human mutations beyond comprehension. A male nurse or female cop fit their definition of transgender, abnormal and scorned.

Guys like O'Brien considered their class to be genetically perfect male human specimens.

Forget about equality and diversity. Life should be simple. Why complicate existence by thinking?

SORRY FOR YOUR TROUBLES

On Thursday, February 27, 2020, at 10:04 a.m., solidarity and alcohol abuse brought three founding fathers of the Irish Guys social club together at the Coal Hole for their first blessed drink of the day. Members of the Irish Guys brotherhood always represented themselves well in their neighborhood headquarters, a dank, musty dive bar and center of their cultural universe, that hosted them damn near any time of the day or night. Real coal holes resulted in deadly cave-ins and explosions, but at least work in the mines paid off. Laboring at two-fisted drinking in the Coal Hole took a far greater toll on the purse and liver and we're not talking about the Thursday night kitchen special with fried onions.

Mostly men from the old neighborhood gathered at the beer garden, sometimes around the clock (forty-six hours without leaving was the record), to drink copious amounts of whiskey, beer and stout, watch sports of every kind on TV, place illegal gambling bets, and otherwise engage in a misplaced communion of manhood that forever fused the most intimate rituals of their Irish Guys existence as working-class white men, at least when they were working.

They still called Italian Americans "colored" and the only time they might find common ground with other white ethnic tribes occurred when their whiteness was attacked. Let's say they attended a hall of fame sports banquet of some kind and spotted an Italian table over here, a Polack table over there, and a German table in the corner. When a Black table appeared (which never happened), the Irish Guys would immediately cast their lot with the Krauts, Dagos and Roundheads in unity against "the niggers." There is no other way to say it. That's what they said. That's what they saw. That's what they felt. Wilkes-Barre feudalism bubbled worse than boiling oil dumped over the castle walls during war in the European Middle Ages.

Their East End neighborhood was changing fast and, to hear them tell it, not for the better. Nothing they did could stop the onslaught of diversity and devolution. But they could try. So try they did. The Irish Guys invented burning the village to save it. And they never ran out of matches.

"I'm sorry for your troubles," Bop O'Brien said to Patrol Sgt. Daniel "Danny Boy" Duggan. "I just heard the news."

Looking into the overflowing foam that topped his small draft beer, O'Brien leaned both elbows on the bar and crossed the arms of his emerald green satin warm-up jacket. "Irish Guys" stitched across the back in large orange and white thread shined in smoky light filtering through the cracked bar window. "Bop" (as in a severe blow to the head with his nightstick) appeared in white thread across his left breast, embroidered in the middle of a stained lime green shamrock.

"Our Danny will bounce back," Duggan said. "Junior's a natural."

Duggan's nickname had faded on the breast of his well-worn club jacket. Still, he donned the green cloak each morning with as much symbolic dignity as the Pope showed when he put on his house dress each day, a garment name that would give fits to the Irish Guys if only they knew.

Duggan and O'Brien worked as city police officers and union officials. Duggan had served as O'Brien's first partner, breaking him in and sharing the secret nuances of police work in Wilkes-Barre, a lost civilization in what fewer and fewer people called "the coal region."

In uniform except for his club jacket and on duty, Duggan swallowed his beer and motioned to bartender Mikey Hoyle for the guaranteed free refill. When O'Brien, on the overtime clock as a plainclothes criminal investigator, made a two inch gesture with his right thumb and forefinger, Mikey poured him a healthy shot of Jameson.

"I can't believe they gave Danny's job to a Wop," O'Brien said.

"They work cheap," Duggan said.

"How can an Italian do the job of the walking pint of Guinness in the Paddy's Day parade? You need to be an Irish Guy for that."

"That's the whole point," Duggan said. "When Danny started the public appearances last year he was a perfect fit. All the sports teams were using them furry mascots like the Phillie Phanatic and the Nittany Lion so Danny applied to be the first walking pint of Guinness in the Paddy's Day parade. He wanted to make history."

Mikey Hoyle's face went pale as peeled shrimp left overnight on the bar in a bowl.

"Remember how we all rooted for him when he put in the application? We said to use us as references."

"He had just started dating that Eileen, the beer distributor's daughter," Duggan said.

"I can see the scene like it was yesterday," O'Brien said. "How proud his mother, Peggy, would have been, may she rest in peace. How proud you were when they offered Danny the position and he accepted. How proud we all were. Lining up outside the bar here on parade day to cheer him on like he was Bobby Kennedy walking up the street."

A dreamy look clouded O'Brien's eyes that normally appeared half-closed and puffy, like a punched-up drunk after a bad night at the Coal Hole. An Irish Guy's son getting the nod as the walking pint of Guinness in his own hometown Paddy's Day parade was better than getting a full Penn State football scholarship. Of course, the boy was a thick lug who couldn't accurately count his change on the bar, let alone add up the receipts for the Guinness deliveries he had to make at the distributorship. But young Danny beat the odds. Not only did he represent the international Guinness company and his girlfriend's father's business by marching in the parade for a couple of years, he branched out on his own and did special guest appearances at children's birthday parties, wedding receptions, wakes, christenings, Notre Dame Club meetings, you name it, working enough as the walking pint to call himself an entrepreneur on the business cards he paid Eileen's brother to make up at the high school print shop. Nobody in town even noticed the misspelled word "entrepreneur" with a couple of "a's" where there should have been "e's." Anything seemed possible for Junior then, even one day running for state representative. Bigger shitheads in the coal fields have been elected to the legislature and even Congress.

But now Duggan and O'Brien worried about the future, and not just for the kid but for other coal field bogtrotters like themselves. Mikey Hoyle wiped his face with the filthy bar rag and looked like he was going to break into tears.

"What are we going to do about it?"

Reminiscing about past Irish Guys victories (high school sports, bowling leagues, dart teams, etc.) shaped a big piece of each club member's way of life. So, too, did plotting revenge for their defeats. Losses outnumbered wins, so Irish Guys carried grudges almost lovingly, sometimes nurturing them for years before acting on the emotional venom that fueled their warped personalities usually for life.

"We got to do something," Mikey Hoyle said.

Duggan held up his hand with the authority of a patrol sergeant directing traffic at an anti-abortion fundraiser.

"I already arranged another position through the motorcycle officers' political action committee. The lad's been feeling bad the past couple of months, drinking at home and adjusting his nerves to the down time. Even let his hair grow so nobody would recognize him. Just this morning, though, he posted his new position as president of "Bikers for Trump" on his Facebook page."

"My neighbor's wife saw his picture and told me," O'Brien said.

"I saw his page yesterday," Mikey Hoyle said. "With the hair and all, he looks like Cher."

Duggan gave Hoyle one of them how'd-you-like-me-to-break-your-legs looks.

"Sorry, Danny." Mikey Hoyle said.

"Eileen's dating that meatball weight lifter from Pittston her father hired as Danny's replacement," Duggan said. "Muscle-bound steroid head just like you'd expect from up there. Last summer he worked off his DUI community service slicing pizza at the tomato festival."

Twisting the sopping bar rag with both hands, Mikey Hoyle gritted his teeth.

"This grease ball stole Danny's job and Danny's girl?"

"Eileen told her father Danny was drunk all the time. OK, so he's got a lot on his mind, waiting for the results of the city police exam. Living at home isn't easy for him. He's got his pride, you know," Duggan said.

O'Brien seemed puzzled.

"How old is Junior now, Danny?"

"In his thirties."

"Jesus, his First Communion seems like yesterday."

"We got a lawyer," Duggan said. "Smells like a federal civil rights lawsuit to me, a clear case of discriminating against him because he's white."

"Them Ginzos pull that affirmative action shit all the time to get on the police department," O'Brien said.

"Typical liberal bullshit," Duggan said. "Cater to the colored."

"Who's the judge?"

"Don't know yet."

"That should be easy enough to fix," O'Brien said. "Almost all the judges in federal court in Wilkes-Barre and Scranton are Irish. Those who aren't wish they were or took bribes from us who are."

"We'll load the jury with our own, people just like us," Duggan said.

"Irish lives matter," Mikey Hoyle said.

O'Brien cracked thick knuckles that looked like the pickled pigs' feet floating in the fat glass jar by the cash register.

"You don't think the jurors or the judge will hold it against us because we're Trumpsters, do you?"

"Nah," Duggan said.

He drained his beer and signaled for another.

"So are they."

TRUMP DIGS COAL

"That was some show the other day," said Wilkes-Barre Mayor "Spuds" McAnus. "I never knew the Finnertys had Indian blood in them. What are they, Apaches?"

Uncomfortable in the mayor's presence, Detectives Duffin and O'Brien fidgeted. About the only thing the two had in common was their firm dislike for McAnus. Incompetent and dictatorial, the mayor held onto his job through intimidation, graft and various levels of extortion which made him a traditional Wilkes-Barre Democrat.

Three generations earlier, somewhere along the long line of Ellis Island peasants, a bored immigration officer misspelled the "McManus" family name on purpose, leaving out the second capital "M," capitalizing the "A," and turning the exalted family crest that included a bejeweled crown into a moldy spud, a rotting potato that now and forever would define an unholy family heritage. McAnus never knew the truth about his genealogy and the long trip across the water that turned County Galway pride into a fatal accident by cruel design. Either way, in a sad twist of immigrant irony, like many of his peers the mayor's great-grandfather couldn't read, write or spell anyway.

"Take a seat, gentlemen. We'll make this quick," McAnus said after checking to make sure they were behind closed doors. "Good work, O'Brien. I'm putting you in for 'The Irish Guys Medal of Honor.' At great risk to your own personal safety you got that reptile off the street before the television crews arrived. All we need is film at 11 to go viral showing our city as the home of a weenie charmer. My re-election campaign will not tolerate a Trump turncoat. I want Finnerty charged with felonious assault against a police officer, resisting arrest, and indecent assault against the congressman. Issue a press release, O'Brien."

"Roger that, Mr. Mayor," O'Brien said.

"Speaking of civil rights, Detective Duffin," McAnus said, "I'd like you to shake hands with your new partner."

Duff met O'Brien's glare. The thick Irish cop smiled, display-ing a chipped eye tooth with a tiny sliver of yellow pizza cheese at-tached to the edge.

"Okay by me, champ," O'Brien said. "The Lone Ranger had Tonto. I'll take Shaft here under my wing."

Duff figured he might as well just hit him. It's either now or later so what's the difference? If he did crack this cracker, though, sick and weak as his mother had been recently, it was hard to tell how she'd handle his firing, arrest and all the angry black man pub-licity attached to attacking a legendary "hero" cop. Duff took a slow, deep breath. The coveted gold shield attached to his belt felt like an anchor around his waist dragging him deep into a whirlpool of animosity. Don't become one of them, Duff thought.

As if on cue, the mayor's blood pressure rose, bringing a rash-like flush to already rosy cheeks.

"Goddamn you, O'Brien, you jerkoff, didn't you learn nothing in them mandatory eight hours of sensitivity training the state or-dered last year? Racialist insults and jokes even if they're funny are taboo nowadays unless it's about your own kind among your own kind. Like we can bust the Irish for being sloppy Micks and drunks but only niggers can call each other niggers."

Duff wished he was wired to get this on video and audio. Even then nobody would believe the scene was real, that grown adult professionals looked at life in such primitive, mindless terms. Turn-ing to O'Brien, McAnus went into his pocket and handed over a handful of shiny gold lapel pins. "Trump Digs Coal" spelled out in gold letters shined from the polished black metal campaign button.

"Every contribution of a hundred bucks or more at my Irish Guys campaign party at the Coal Hole after tonight's Trump rally at the arena gets one of these pins," McAnus said. "I told every cop, firefighter and member of my cabinet that I expect at least a hun-dred smackers from each of them. We'll keep fifty for the Irish Guys and put fifty in my campaign coffer. Nobody will know we're skim-ming off the top. I put the arm on the wholesaler and we got the pins for free. Top of the line made in China."

"Making America and you great again," O'Brien said.

"Thanks be to God," said the mayor.

"When Trump opens up the mines again we'll get jobs for all our kids and grandkids and everybody else we know who'll pay us for the privilege of working underground," said McAnus. "We're signing up miners for the first Trump Coal Mine grand opening in a couple weeks. Thousands of guys will pick up applications. Mr. Trump will open up a whole chain of them here in Northeastern Pennsylvania managed by Irish Guys."

"Better than more Pakistani convenience stores," O'Brien said.

Duff stood by silently, a spellbound audience of one.

"What do you think, Paddy?" said O'Brien. "Want one of these pins to wear on duty?"

Pushing the sharp pin through the cheap cloth of his blue sport coat, O'Brien adjusted the words so they resembled his life, upside down to everybody but him. Imposing his political will while on duty exemplified O'Brien's definition of public service. In Wilkes-Barre politics only the corrupt survive.

"Sorry if I offended you, Detective Duffin," O'Brien said. "I thought you was one of us. You know, just another Paddy looking for his pot of gold at the end of the rainbow."

Spitting the speck of pizza cheese onto his finger, O'Brien looked at the soft morsel not quite sure what to make of it and put it back in his mouth. He chewed and swallowed. Sliding forward on the cracked upholstery of the mayor's office couch, O'Brien leaned his face close enough that Duff smelled strong tobacco, garlic salt and stale beer.

"Relax, bro," O'Brien said. "I'm just busting you."

Duff stood.

"Anything else?" he asked McAnus, who shrugged and tossed off a weak salute.

"Oh, yeah, shit," the mayor said almost as an afterthought. "The dispatcher told me to alert you to a homicide in the American Legion parking lot. There's bingo there tonight so get the stiff tagged, bagged and towed out of there as soon as possible."

"Killing a guy is one thing. But leaving him in the Legion lot is inexcusable," O'Brien said. "That's one big fat no thank you for your service. What's wrong with people nowadays? There's no respect. No fucking decency."

"See you at the Trump rally tonight," McAnus said to O'Brien. "He's coming back to our arena because we got him elected the first time. The president didn't forget us."

"We'll have our lads from the club putting your re-election campaign pamphlets under the wipers of every car in the arena parking lot," O'Brien said. "I'm on my way right now to pick up a thousand leaflets your secretary ran off this morning on the office copy machine on city time, of course."

"Thanks a million," McAnus said. "Mr. Trump might put me up on the stage with him tonight."

"Ah, sure, he might," O'Brien said.

Looking at Duff, the mayor put on a face as serious as a pre-cancerous colonoscopy polyp photograph.

"I expect to see you in the front row at the rally," McAnus said.

Riding in silence, the two new crime-fighting partners made it to the Legion lot in about 11 minutes. O'Brien surveyed the crime scene. Duff stiffened as soon as he saw the body.

"Looks like a Mexican cartel drug killing," O'Brien said. "El Chapo."

Duff stared at the corpse in the burgundy 1990 Lincoln Town Car's open trunk. Bound and gagged with silver duct tape, the body lay hog-tied and face up. Fear had left an indelible impression on the victim's once distinguished features. The black man's blue eyes stared open and smooth as new balls on an old pool table. Duff fought to stay calm.

O'Brien sensed the tension.

"You know him?"

"Mr. Moses Garrett was my twelfth grade English teacher," Duff said. "Mr. Moses Garrett was a registered Democrat and regular voter, a loving husband. Mr. Moses Garrett sang in the Baptist church choir with my mother, loved books and could speak French. He'd been to Africa once, in the Peace Corps."

O'Brien pulled a hard, half-smoked Parodi cigar from his pants pocket and lit the tip.

"Africa, huh?" O'Brien said. "Went back where he came from, huh? Why'd didn't he stay there?"

"He came home because he loved his country, loved his city and loved teaching," Duff said.

"You ever think about going native yourself?" O'Brien said. "Bone in your nose?"

Duff felt the warm pressure of the Glock against his hip. Trying not to stare at his dead mentor, he spotted the shiny front of what looked like a metal political campaign button about as big as a half dollar. Smeared with blood, the killer had pierced the pinched skin of Moses Garrett's neck and attached the pin to the white button's metal fastener.

"Honorary Irishman," the button said in festive orange and green letters.

MAKE AMERICA GREEN AGAIN

Nothing mattered more to the Irish Guys than being Irish. Not Irish American, Irish. "Real fucking Irish," as more than one of the gutter-mouthed, trash-talking club members regularly explained to the uninitiated. "You might think you're Irish, but we're real fucking Irish."

No discussion, no explanation, no brains. These blatherskites wallowed in being what they now called "Make America Irish Again" Irish. Trump Irish. Make America white again Irish. To hear them tell it, they were authentic, 100 percent children of the Gael. Even guys who hailed from what they half-jokingly called "mixed-race" parentage, those whose mothers or fathers descended from Polish, German, Italian or other "lesser" ancestry, stretched out 24/7 on four green fields. Generational descendants of previously unswerving Irish-Catholic Democrats, they comprised frail limbs of a Gaelic family tree that defined the new 21st Century swing state "Irishman."

Of the traitorous white male Trump supporters who once took pride in pro-union, blue-collar, working-class, hard coal country, immigrant ethnic identity, only a few publicly registered as Republicans. Most remained stealth Democrats. Media accounts accuse many in this mutant demographic of voting for Barack Obama. Even though Obama won Luzerne County in 2008 and 2012, none of the Irish Guys tribe voted for him. Irish Guys, all Democrats, either sat out Election Day with a case of beer or went with former POW John McCain. Not one of them voted for Obama no matter what Rachel Maddow or other know-it-all fake news commentators claimed. They hated Obama worse than Maddow. And that's saying something.

History will forever cast shame on how they bragged about putting Trump over the top in 2016 and into the White House. More than voters in Wisconsin, Michigan or in other parts of the Commonwealth, these humps took full credit for Trump's victory. Trump emerged victorious in the Electoral College with 80,000 votes from these three states. He won Pennsylvania by 44,000 votes. In Democratic Luzerne County, population about 320,000 people, Trump clobbered Hillary. Without Luzerne County, Trump would have lost Pennsylvania. Without Pennsylvania, Trump likely would have lost the election.

Irish Guys and who knows how many countless shit-for-brains nitwits they influenced dragged Trump over the finish line. Although Protestant rednecks throughout the state joined Polacks, Germans, Italians and other ethnic rivals in hard coal country in voting their prejudices, the Irish Guys made it clear that their votes did the trick. As disorganized as they were boastful, they often took credit where credit wasn't due. Yet many national pundits and data crunchers gave Luzerne County voters credit for the win. The Irish Guys took Trump at his word, bought the bullshit, and would forever be proud of their role in making history.

Not one of their breed had visited the auld sod of Ireland and likely never would. The closest any of them got to Shannon Airport was a one-time bus trip years ago to an icy January "Celtic Woman" concert at Madison Square Garden in New York City with drastically discounted scalped tickets from a crooked Wilkes-Barre cop headed to prison and forced to liquidate his assets. But deep in their murmuring hearts, ulcerated livers, and suspended testicles, these Northeastern Pennsylvania gobshites, who banded together in boozy tribalism the way legendary chieftains once bonded in ancient provinces, shared a blockheaded origin more Irish than Paddy's pig, Paddy's Day, and all the Paddy wagons ever built to haul away future miscreant Paddy criminals put together. Their tangled roots extended so deeply into gross stupidity they never felt the stranglehold.

For example, the Irish Guys often sponsored half-price drinks to benefit the club at the Coal Hole where drink specials on "Irish Car Bombs" and "Black and Tans" prevailed. The boys didn't have a clue about the terrible historical baggage the drinks' names carried, enduring a mental famine that utterly failed to penetrate their miserably collective low IQs (Irish Quotients). Yet, blessed by fate and destiny, they shined among their own. Although most couldn't locate Galway or Dublin on a map of Ireland, these boys took great satisfaction in their annual summer showing of the 1959 Walt Disney movie, "Darby O'Gill and the Little People," on a clean white sheet hung outside the church on the grounds where the parish held the annual "lawn social," a lace-curtain Irish way of saying "picnic."

On that night once a year the Irish Guys stood for something. Ask them and they'd tell you, a different story, of course, for each man in the club. But they definitely stood for something. If nothing else, they represented a brutal innocence marked by blind loyalty that cloaked them in a special kind of stupor, a dark love of conformity that blocked the sun of change and progress from their lives and the lives of everyone they touched.

Touched?

Manhandled was more like it.

PROPERTY OF PUG

For the first time since Pug set up camp in the bunker he built by the abandoned coal breaker at the base of the coal debris mountain created by decades of anthracite waste, he thought about doing a jig just for the fun of it. Waking at noon, Pug felt famous, like one of those killers on a cable channel special. Rolling over and reaching into his backpack, Pug felt for his last can of metallic green spray paint. After Pug's big night, furious business owners across the city this morning would be calling police to report the latest homegrown terrorism against their investments and bloated impressions of themselves.

Thrilled knowing any offense against his own kind would send the inbred hierarchy over the top, Pug loved the idea of city workers scrambling to clean his obscene graffiti from walls, fences and even the water tower that stood over a once-popular and now abandoned cocktail lounge in the south side of the city. During his nighttime mission behind enemy lines, Pug hit police and fire headquarters as well as the Catholic shop, a senior citizen center, the public assistance office, a cosmetology school and a synagogue. He wondered how the mush-mouthed anchors on local television would cover his damage. A rash of "BLOW ME I'M IRISH" graffiti in bright emerald paint is tough to communicate in terms that don't offend the sensibilities of the mainstream viewing audience or local advertisers.

Stretching naked inside the warmth of his sleeping bag, Pug pondered how to spend the day. Breakfast would be pizza crusts scavenged from restaurant garbage cans. Then he'd maybe go kill something fresh. Hard choices must be made. A take-out delivery Chinaman, a Muslim college professor, a Mexican meatpacking house worker or Jew lawyer really made no difference. One was as bad as the other and all contributed to the breakdown of his city and country. Pug liked the idea of killing a Mexican, an illegal like they all are, coming here taking everybody's jobs and keeping Pug from succeeding. Make tacos out of his tonsils.

Trump would approve. The man knew who his friends were.

Media stood out as the main enemy of the people. When did the lame stream press last tell us the truth about the Roswell aliens or 9/11? What about the gooks taking all the seats in college, the coloreds grabbing the minority business jobs, and the kikes controlling everything except the hijacker ISIS ragheads who were looking for virgins and suicide belts before launching another attack? Media should interview him. Maybe he should take a rookie reporter hostage, some closet queer or pathetic egomaniac weatherman, treat him like a pet. Feed him. Burn him with lit cigarettes. Brand him with a glowing clothes hangar made to glow in the campfire so his back says "PROPERTY OF PUG."

In the world of local anarchy, Pug Mahoney ruled. He cherished the terrified looks on people's faces when they saw him coming. With pierced lips, ears and nostrils, Pug bounced when he walked in a hunched-over monkey manner that sometimes made grown men cross the street as soon as they saw his lanky frame headed their way. Sometimes, though, depressed retirees just passed him by, lost in their own sense of melancholy, too adrift to be afraid. Times were getting tougher for too many old people. Senior citizens had more than their share of problems. Trump would help them all one day. Until that happened Pug would help Trump.

On his own for the first time in his life, Pug felt good hiding out in the same area he explored since he was eight-years-old and played in the deserted coal breakers and one-time miners' work shanties that dotted the area. He knew several remaining entrances to long-ago flooded coal mines. He knew the high ground and the deep coal shelves where nobody would ever find him if he had to hide out on the run. For now his new home was a vacant brown tarpaper shack on a cinderblock base located deep in the middle of a culm dump that towered over the expressway, a massive pile of black coal waste most people in the community avoided or ignored. Most of these dirty black peaks had disappeared. Plans were underway to take the remainder down one truckload at a time, as if their removal would erase the region's vile history of corporate oppression. Like Ukrainian grandmothers who embarrassed their grandchildren by going to Mass wearing babushkas, such "eyesores" reminded many coal region natives of a past they wanted to forget. For that they shunned their sacred place in history earned by peasant ancestors who lived and died in vain, sacrificing for the reward of a better future for their families.

Pug took pride in persecution. He once checked out a library book about these miners who hauled riches from deep inside the earth to the top of the very hill where he now reclined under a speckled gray sky. Pug lived and breathed as the restless prodigy of these Irishmen, a freak who loved slag heaps and culm banks where he frolicked in the inky coal dust that took forever to wash away on his skin or on the buildings in his town. These dumping grounds reminded Pug of death camps. During the time King Coal ruled, thousands of men and boys died in its grip. Women died in childbirth or from coal-related stress. Manic depression held sway long before the economic Depression took over. Dark testament to another time, the slag hills symbolized an evil that once controlled everything and everybody in the coal region. Power and money created those environmental disasters. Free market robber barons loved every second of the toxic wastes from which they profited and gained affluence while alcoholism and black lung disease prospered among their victims.

Deep mining ended January 22, 1959, when massive pillars of coal collapsed and the Knox Mine roof caved in, sending Susquehanna River water rushing in to flood the honeycomb of mines throughout the greater Wyoming Valley. The bosses and owners had ordered coal taken from the natural walls that girded the mine ceiling and protected the men from a watery grave. "Robbing the pillars" stole twelve men who remain entombed underwater in the timbered coffin known forever as the Knox Mine Disaster.

Pug prayed to the spirits of those dead men. He wished he could die like that. At least then his fate would mean something. Picking up his cellphone and holding it at arm's length, he went live streaming on Facebook. Clutching his smart Droid with his left hand, he picked up his Mossberg Persuader eight-shot, twelve-gauge pistol-grip shotgun with his right. Coal dust covered his head, face and chest, making him look like a commando on a jungle mission. On Pug's last birthday, his father, Martin, bought two identical shotguns thinking that maybe one day he and Pug could shoot possums, rats or British soldiers together.

"Guns help you become a man," Martin said.

Pug had chewed his fingernails to the nub. Holding the gun to his lips, Pug stuck his tongue into the twenty-inch Mossberg barrel like he was French-kissing a cold, steely lover in a devil worshipper snuff film. Taking in the scene on his cellphone video camera, Pug smiled his biggest smile, minus a front tooth where his dad punched him during their recent decisive argument over a science TV show. Squaring his shoulders, Pug lowered the blue finish shotgun and spoke directly into the camera.

"Good morning. Welcome to the Pug Mahoney Show," he said. "I'm Pug Mahoney."

Pug panned up and down his demented face.

"Our guest today is the ghost of beloved Meyers High School teacher Mr. Moses Garrett, who was nice enough to give me a written reference when I applied to work at the supermarket and who will tell us how it feels to get murdered and be dead because you thought black is beautiful."

His own best audience, Pug giggled in a high frequency drone, sounding like a shock therapy machine about to launch electric bolts into his brain. As Pug moved his weight from left to right to keep his balance in the soft shifting coal residue, he tripped, stumbling and losing his balance. The Persuader went off with enough recoil that Pug fell backwards against the coal mountain. Pug gripped the pistol grip tighter and kept shooting video, streaming live on Facebook for the world to see. Looking hard at the camera, he spoke.

"Sorry, but the King of the Spooks didn't show up," he said.

Garrett's human sacrifice had gone well. White was right. Irish power forever. Why did the government allow a coon to teach him English, anyway? Pug already spoke English. Why didn't a real teacher tell him killing was easier than sex? Why couldn't Pug have been born one of Trump's sons? "Pug Trump" sounded great. Killing a black teacher should have returned him to the good graces of the neighborhood. All the Irish Guys hated spooks. Every role model Pug ever had hated spooks. People should understand he had acted as much for them as he did for himself. Didn't the Irish Guys think he was hilarious when he dressed as a Ku Klux Klan member for the eleventh grade Halloween party at the Grand Army of the Republic High School? Didn't almost every adult he knew lecture him to want to make America great again which meant decreasing the number of coloreds until the landscape looked like a winter blizzard before the crows came down from the trees?

On Election Day, Pug planned to go to the church social hall like every other Irish Guy and vote for Trump's re-election. He'd be first in line when the polls opened. Even with a murder warrant out for him, who was going to stop him? More than anything, Pug planned to get even. Just like mainstream media helped create Trump, mainstream media would tell Pug's tale, an Irish Guys story if there ever was one, a warning to America and the world that there was no turning back. New founding fathers like Pug framed the modern declaration of independence in gore. And he didn't mean Al.

Even as Wilkes-Barre labored on economic life support, no matter what the enemies of the people did to Trump or Trump did to himself, all Pug had left was Trump. Pug shivered, contorted his face, and screamed Trump words into his handheld device.

"I am your voice," he said. "I alone can fix it. I will restore law and order."

Then all shots ended: gunfire, live video and Pug's earlier smart phone selfies posted to a variety of social media accounts. Pug seemed at peace. Pulling on the desert camouflage fatigues he always wanted to wear to church, Pug scampered to his feet, picked up his weapon, and slid down the coal mountain the way he did when he was a little boy on the playground sliding board, squealing like a grade-schooler all the way to the bottom.

"Whee," he said.

BLACK POWER

S having for work, Duff froze in the middle of a downward stroke on his chin. A man he wasn't sure he knew stared from the mirror. Taking a deep breath, Duff checked out his image. For the most part he liked what he saw. Blended nicely into a balanced combination, what he assumed to be mixed-race genes created a caramel-skinned, 29-year-old light heavyweight with a straight nose and thin lips. A reddish tint showed in his hair. Several freckles dotted his neck and forehead with a few on his cheeks. Good teeth rounded out a kindly disposition.

"You're beautiful," said his dark-skinned African-American mother when he was just a few hours old.

Employment records at City Hall listed Duff as "mulatto." Thinking they were being polite, the mayor and police chief called him "colored," a term they assumed was more acceptable than tagging him a coon, spook, shine or any number of other epithets common in their overwhelmingly Caucasian city, without question one of the most racist cities in America. Familiar with the National Association for the Advancement of Colored People, city officials figured that if was good enough for those bastards it was good enough for Duff. Behind his back some cops speculated incessantly as to why his mother named him Paddy, which only registered in their minds as the prisoner transport wagon or the famous whiskey distilled in the Republic of Ireland's County Cork.

If Duff had a dollar for every time he heard, "Funny, you don't look Irish," he could build a boat big enough to send all these honkies back to Europe. But, sure enough, "Paddy" appeared on Duff's birth certificate as his formal name. Also sure enough, not one of Wilkes-Barre's finest, whose own ancestors, Paddy and otherwise, had fled oppression and came looking for freedom in the local coal mines, ever called him a friend.

Wilkes-Barre was too tough a town for its own good.

Duff scored number one on the detective's exam. Since the mayor had no choice he called a press conference that made Duff's promotion look like a memorial commemoration of the Rev. Dr. Martin Luther King Jr.'s Promised Land speech. A gold badge brought more money and a lot more responsibility for Duff, who felt ready to do the job.

To be sure, the chaos he watched unfold at the police station the other day was barbaric. Yet interfering in the confrontation was out of the question. After a few years working traffic and writing parking tickets, Duff knew all the unwritten rules that covered bad cops' behavior and guaranteed horrendous leeway for ranking officers. A lifetime of living in the city also taught Duff that the legendary detective Bop O'Brien was as rank as they come.

Cupping his hands, he scooped water from the bathroom sink and threw it on his face. Drying off, he walked into his bedroom to get ready for work. Laid out on the bed he saw the fresh, white dress shirt his mother had ironed for him.

Duff tensed, again thinking about O'Brien running around that poor fallen man like a mean little kid torturing an overturned turtle. Stone cold cruel, O'Brien's behavior constituted a brazen violation of the prisoner's civil rights no matter his alleged crime, race or ethnicity. Finnerty suffered no physical injuries and Duff would have interceded if he absolutely had to. But the thought of self-preservation kept him from giving his critics any more ammunition to add to their already loaded arsenal of foul stereotypes. Life would be tough enough working criminal cases in a town where mostly white lawbreakers as well as their white victims often shared a common dislike for African Americans who made up about ten percent of a black population that was growing slowly but surely every day.

Wilkes-Barre's citizens, isolated in a working-class ghetto that was no longer working for decent wages with health benefits or union job protection, were getting nastier each day looking for people to blame for their own deep-seated struggles. A white bigot with a job was bad enough. An unemployed white bigot was worse. Yet, while whites moved out, blacks moved in, relocating from the Bronx, Brooklyn, Philadelphia, Newark, Camden, Jersey City and other urban areas that had already disintegrated for the poor and the lost, especially people of color. Like the white ethnic immigrants who came to Wilkes-Barre before them, they, too, searched for the American Dream.

But the coal mines closed in the late 50s when river water flooded the massive underground labyrinth that never would or could reopen no matter what Trump promised. The city lost its way. Deep thinking went down for the last time. Trump assured the gullible of an impossible dream when he came to town to campaign in 2016, to reopen the mines, not resuscitate critical thinking. Countless local voters, mostly Democrats, believed this modern-day robber baron when he played them perfectly for fools.

Even Duff had to admit too many of the brothers and sisters rolling into town weren't model citizens. Ex-cons, heroin dealers and gunfire had increased in the past decade to such an extent that Duff paid to put an alarm system in his mother's house. Still, even dope fiends had a right to a new start. Duff believed none of this would be happening if Democrats truly fought Republicans on civil rights and labor issues and if Barack Obama had truly championed America's inner cities large and small populated by abandoned black residents. Obama disappointed Duff as just another rich man, a black president with a white mother who knew black but feared black. At least Obama knew his dad. Duff had no dreams from his father.

Not much remained in Wilkes-Barre for anybody except low-wage jobs, a mean-spirited working-class egotism and enough ill will toward black people to make them want to go back to Africa, as so many white people still regularly suggested. Trying to calm his own black militant tendencies, Duff often told the jitterbugs on the street to chill.

"Our day will come," he'd say. "But you got to keep the faith."

Duff's once unshakable confidence quivered. Maybe the Black Panthers and Malcolm X were right to suggest liberation by shotgun. Maybe Mexicans should start their own armed movement. Maybe Duff should line up full force with all oppressed peoples in opposition to Trump and the national malice he represented.

By any means necessary?

Maybe.

A PAIN IN THE MCANUS

Mayor McAnus' intestines constricted in a ball of seclusion, knotted deep, dark and secured so tightly in his gut he worried he'd need dynamite to get them unclogged. As the adage goes, hizzoner's bowels were in an uproar, bawling and squawling like mean alley cats zipped in a bag.

"I'm done," he said. "I'm a gone, gone gosling now."

Glum on the pot, McAnus pondered his mortality. Lately he experienced more gas than the frequent ruptures in the underground city pipes that brought natural fuel to the city. Obsessed with his regularity, McAnus compulsively compared his number twos with other fixated Irish Guys who sometimes went so far as to detail the frequency of their movements on lists in old-fashioned spiral pocket notebooks they passed around and compared whenever they ran into each other.

Regularity was an Irish Guys thing.

McAnus became so anxious he worried one day his rectum would explode and kill him, unblocking his pipes with ten times the power of shooting Power Plunger down the Coal Hole commode. Yet all that gastrointestinal distress paled in comparison to what the dirty Dems did to Trump. After the hoax impeachment and Senate trial, McAnus swore that no matter what else bad happened to Trump, he and the Irish Guys would simply refuse to accept the outcome. They hadn't accepted reality in any form so far, so the future would be easy. The lads would continue their work on his and Trump's re-election campaigns and pledge service to the national master ad infinitum even if Trump one day rotted in prison or a syphilis asylum or Melanie hired a Russian pool boy in a fur hat with flaps and matching thong to carry her off to a Siberian hot tub. Nothing mattered in the Irish Guys' love affair with the president. Not Deep State revolt in the intelligence community, assassination or burning in Hell. Shit happens. Fatal heart attacks and strokes could happen to any of them. Trump's struggle on behalf of the nation and McAnus' own little town made him and the boys feel lost and abandoned, angry, too, with that wretched Pug Mahoney on the run and trying to ruin McAnus' re-election campaign. Would life ever really improve? Could McAnus continue faking out his constituents, convincing them their best days were yet to come?

Straining until his face flushed like a swollen hemorrhoid, McAnus finished his movement, wiped and wrinkled his nose. Rising fast he slammed the lid and hit the handle.

"Drain the swamp," he said.

DOING THE JOHN-JOHN

Almost everybody in the neighborhood loved Pug when he was little.

Nobody told a joke like this kid. God knows how many stereotypic Pat and Mike Irish jokes his father, Martin, forced Pug to tell growing up. When he was five, his father taught him how to tell a few short stories he was expected to memorize and recite on demand at weddings and wakes. For years, people in their East End neighborhood, the "Irish" section, swore there was nothing cuter than little Pug telling his tales and making the crowd collapse in laughter. Pug would walk to the center of any room, barroom or living room, and begin: "The Irish Garda police arrested Pat and charged him with bank robbery and he went to trial. After a week of testimony, Mike the jury foreman announced the verdict as not guilty. 'Thanks be to God,' says Pat, 'does that mean I get to keep the money?'"

The place would go wild as Martin passed his frayed tweed cap and regularly came home with more than 50 dollars a night. OK, so maybe old man Mahoney went overboard, but everybody agreed that the end always justified the means.

Who could forget how, when Pug was six, Martin spent a weekend training him to salute like John-John Kennedy did on his third birthday after his father got assassinated just a few days before. After completing the 48-hour brainwashing cycle with time off for naps for them both, Pop Tarts and a good couple dozen cries for the lad, Martin dressed Pug in short pants and a hand-me-down blue sport coat. Between 5 p.m. and 11 p.m. on November 22, he took the kid to a half dozen VFW and American Legion hall bars where Pug "did the John-John," saluting just like the "wee one" did to famously memorialize his dear departed dad at the 1963 state funeral. Martin held a flashlight over Pug's head, highlighting his bony skull like a Hollywood spotlight at the Academy Awards. By midnight, father and son had pulled in a record haul of $245 in cash donations and got a nice write-up and photo in the Sunday Times

Leader newspaper. Martin lost the bundle the next weekend betting a professional boxing card at the Best Western Plus Genetti Hotel & Convention Center.

When Pug asked for his share of the money, Martin said no.

Pug gave his father the finger.

Martin pulled down the boy's pants and beat his soft bare buttocks with the palm of his hand so hard that the child's skin bruised after taking hits from the underside of daddy's Claddagh ring. In the tub the next night Pug tried and failed to wash off the bruises with a bar of his mother's Dove soap. Martin felt bad about the bruises, but the John-John was a sure thing. Father and son did the routine around town dozens of times over the next two years until Pug outgrew the shorts.

Any number of Irish Guys truly thought the kid possessed enough talent to become a real comedian or an actor instead of turning into a teenage basket case. Even now most people still liked Pug, a product of his environment, whatever the fuck that meant. Until his recent descent into the emerald abyss, even the Irish Guys considered him to be a nice kid.

Then there was high school English teacher Moses Garrett. Martin couldn't stand him walking around like Denzel Washington, preaching and promising equality for all. What Martin refused to acknowledge was a real teacher who saw real promise in Pug and helped get him a job as a bag boy at the Academy Supermarket. Garrett offered to write a letter of recommendation to the Luzerne County Community College. But that was before Garrett unknowingly stepped into the stagnant, bubbling gray matter of Pug's battered and unravelling psyche. On the morning of Pug's implosion, Garrett lost his life as a stunning African-American role model in an overwhelmingly mean white community.

Before he knew his son was responsible, Martin Mahoney joked that Garrett's murder marked the start of "Black History Month" because, well, the man was history. More people in his circle laughed than didn't. Wilkes-Barre business and political leaders never grew strong enough to cross the racial divide. Despite their own history as oppressed peoples, the Irish were some of the biggest offenders who felt nobody ever cared about who might discriminate against them.

"My ancestors didn't own slaves," Martin once said at a City Council meeting. "My ancestors were slaves."

For that profundity he received a standing ovation.

In search of the American Dream, hundreds of thousands of Irish greenhorns and others immigrated to what is still called the Greater Wilkes-Barre/Scranton area to mine hard anthracite coal in the late 19th and early 20th centuries. Some found great promise in the work. Some died searching. A number of the Irish went straight into a long line of justifiable larcenies, including politics at the top and, at the bottom, working dog hole bootleg mines they dug on company or private property they didn't own to remove all the coal they could steal, crack and sell in the neighborhood.

Pug's great-grandfather vanished in a deep mine explosion, leaving a wife, nine children, three geese, a fine tomato garden, and a stainless steel growler he filled with beer and carried into the mines when he was a young man. Pug's father often repeated to the Irish Guys the story of how he carried that same canteen filled with suds in the Paddy's Day parade each year. Pug inherited the old fellow's collection of pipes when he died, which old man Mahoney knew he recently used to smoke weed, crack and heroin whenever he could get his hands on local dope.

None of that mattered now.

With the Tuesday, November 3rd presidential election here before you knew it, Martin Mahoney marveled at how, despite impeachment, a rigged, Senate witch hunt and everything else Trump haters threw at the president, local supporters, including most City Council members, officially declared Wilkes-Barre as "Trump Town." Bumper stickers and flags inscribed with the right-wing battle cry already were selling out in downtown stores, neighborhood bars and at all Roman Catholic social events. "Trump Town" emblazoned items were available for purchase on a small table set up in the front lobby of City Hall with all proceeds going to the mayor's re-election committee disguised as a "crippled" children's charity.

Just like the presidency, illegal or otherwise, one way or the other "Trump Town" ruled. Nobody could stop the Trump train. His election gave local public servants permission to do as they pleased, validating their civic insanity in all its numbskull glory. Fox News sent one of their blondest female reporters in a red dress and Mayor McAnus personally invited Republican FOX god Sean Hannity to visit the city, which never happened.

Wilkes-Barre specialized in political corruption. But the Trump presidency allowed countless coal crackers to pull off a coup, an ethnic phenomenon in which they danced on societal quicksand into which one day they would sink without ever knowing what sunk them. The Irish Guys social club spawned many members of that duplicitous cult.

Now Pug was screwing up everything.

For years Wilkes-Barre exhibited hope, even called itself "The City with a Heart." Mahoney, McAnus and the rest of the guys enjoyed nothing better than marching up the middle of South Main Street, usually on the Sunday before March 17 which marked the official high holy date reserved for the blessed all-male annual dinner sponsored by the Irish Guys.

Men of Irish descent in Scranton, twenty miles north, operated in the same male chauvinist manner with their men-only "Friendly Sons" dinner. So did male posers in nearby Pittston town. As a result, Northeastern Pennsylvania hard coal country, particularly its pale, penile high priests, celebrated St. Patrick's Day for at least a week before the official dinners.

Men of Irish ancestry in the East End section of Wilkes-Barre craved the camaraderie that made the splendor of the day an event to revere. Almost every grown man and conditioned woman in the neighborhood groomed every child's total immersion in the sluggish tribal traditions that always went from bad to worse and trapped them all.

Boys would be boys.

Girls would be whatever their fathers told them to be.

Until now, Pug mostly did as he was told. For more years than there are apostles, Pug listened to the grandiose refrains of otherwise borderline decent men who nonetheless treated their wives like wet bar rags and, without the benefit of a college degree, lectured regularly and publicly about politics, religion and race with the confidence of academic scholars at some bygone pipe and porter college in Dublin. Several of these legendary neighborhood oracles died in car accidents or from cigarette and alcohol-related disease before they hit forty. Others lived well past their prime and into a crusty undeserved old age. Pickled in cheap liquor and syrupy cologne, the survivors brooded every Saturday night of their lives in the same dim bars of their youth, freshly shaved and chain smoking, sometimes falling asleep with the arms of wrinkled shirts and limited cash bills sopping from puddles on the bar. Despite piss poor temperament, their blood lines advanced.

But, if being Irish meant so much, why did Pug's father throw him, his first and only born, out of the house, shattering their sacred blood bond? Why did his mother pray so much that she wore filthy holes in the knees of her nylons? Why did Pug want to give up? Ireland might be a little taste of heaven, but Pug preferred to take a big bite out of hell. It wouldn't take long for the cops to pin the Garrett homicide on him. The same Irish Guys who once welcomed Pug now feared him. Word went viral about the awful blow-up between him and his father who told anyone who would listen how he had disowned his own flesh and blood because the kid "shit on the shamrock."

No Irish Guy in Trump Town forgives that kind of sin.

BIKERS FOR TRUMP

Danny "Junior" Duggan blasted off like the devil just hot-wired his butt. Giving the heavy hog gas and heading to the Trump rally at 90 miles an hour, nothing mattered except control of the Harley. With wind tearing at thinning hair grown to Messiah length and visions of grandeur in his head, Junior was somebody now, not just some stumbling Irish drunk in a lint-covered Guinness costume, but a two-fisted very important person, one hip VIP if you ever saw one.

Developing a reputation as the walking pint of Guinness defined him for a while but Junior's reputation peaked when his father fixed it so Junior took over as president of the Luzerne County chapter of "Bikers for Trump." Junior now saw himself on par with outlaw biker legend Sonny Barger, Marlon Brando in that leather cap, and Captain America in "Easy Rider." Junior collected famous motorcycle movies and knew he could lead a pack of wild men over a cliff with his eyes closed.

Instead of wobbling drunk into pool parties and girls-night-out gatherings as the staggering furry Guinness fool, Junior now rode a shiny bike that loomed large in his life, as big a motorcycle as Junior had ever seen let alone thought about riding. The 2016 Softail Fat Boy cost a wholesale methamphetamine dealer from Birmingham, Alabama, $17,499 before Wilkes-Barre police stopped him outside the local Outlaws motorcycle gang clubhouse when city police raided the dump and "Danny Boy" Duggan interviewed him. The dealer returned to the Confederacy and his home Outlaws chapter minus his drugs, his beloved bike, and an arrest record in Wilkes-Barre. "Danny Boy" kept the dope to sell to the coloreds who hung out under the bridge and came home with a priceless present for his goofball son.

With chopped chrome pipes and two new thick stolen black Dunlop tires that bounced as he rode so low to the ground Junior felt his balls would drag on the interstate highway, authority mattered for the first time in his life. The lower and faster he went the freer he felt. Strength, toughness, even basic leadership skills, everything he lacked as the walking pint with a perpetual yellow piss stain on his crotch, morphed into a new man. Junior might even start looking for a fresh girlfriend, an old lady, as bikers called the girls of their drunken dreams.

Cruising on the big bike his dad wheeled from the police station big ticket item evidence room cluttered with snow blowers, lawn mowers and ATVs, was better than a full-time county maintenance job. When "Danny Boy" came home with the gift that night, he rolled the machine into the living room of the house where he was born and lived all his life. Bringing home the bike was better than the Christmas when little Danny was ten and waiting for his first potato pellet gun. This time "Danny Boy" wasn't as drunk as he usually got on Christmas. Looking out for his chip-off-the-old-blockhead offspring and working to re-elect Trump was serious business. "Bikers for Trump" would make "Danny Boy" Duggan great again because "Bikers for Trump" would make Junior Duggan great again. Greatness didn't normally run in the Duggan family so they took whatever they could get.

Junior fully expected to dip into the Trump campaign contributions from Northeastern Pennsylvania bikers' fundraisers and have enough money on hand to cover his day-to-day expenses like beer, cigarettes and massages. Fringe benefits constitute a sacred piece of freedom and what America is supposed to be all about. As fringe as they come, Junior loved living the biker dream more than he once cherished the dream of driving a stock car on a dirt track. That would have suited him, too. But until the career change, he took refuge in lugging endless beer kegs into clambakes for a variety of local political snake oil salesmen, forged absentee ballots, and drove local Democratic Party bit players from one rubber chicken dinner to the next in a borrowed car for a 20 here and a 50 there, all under-the-table profit.

Supporting Trump was different, especially when America's con man lived in the White House. Maybe a job as a Trump bodyguard would materialize after the re-election or at least an entry-level security guard gig at one of the Trump hotel properties or golf courses, maybe in Florida. Junior loved Florida even though he had never been there.

Feeling pleased that the beer distributor's daughter told him to go fuck himself, Junior knew he was better than the role that shaped his world during the time he worked as a local bagman for politicians and bookies. When their relationship crashed, Junior burned the Guinness "uniform" in the Coal Hole trash can behind the bar. Now an executive "Biker for Trump," Junior took his new responsibility so seriously he wrote a letter to the editor of The Times Leader newspaper, vowing to drink one shot of Jameson whiskey on election night for every municipality in Luzerne County that went for Trump's re-election.

"You know there's 78 municipalities in the county, Mr. Duggan," an editorial page assistant said when she called to confirm the letter.

"Michael Savage will interview me on the radio," Junior said.

"We'll make sure to have a reporter there," the assistant said. "In case you die."

"I'll do my best," Junior said.

Severely impressed with himself, Junior didn't try to talk himself out of this ridiculous promise, telling himself anything was possible with Trump. If fatal alcohol poisoning was what it took as a consequence of getting Trump re-elected, then bring it on. Fame, if not fortune, appealed to Junior. CNN would likely go live for his bigly biker funeral. No fake news here. Junior would go down doing shots, a human death wish, so to speak, which got Duggan to thinking about a new nickname.

In October 2015 Trump told a campaign rally in Nashville that the 1974 Charles Bronson vigilante film "Death Wish" was his favorite movie. Trump then incited the crowd to chant the movie's name which they did.

"Death Wish" Duggan it was.

PEGGY DIDN'T FEEL A THING

If any woman could have made the cut fair and square and got elected to official Irish Guy status, Peggy Flynn could have been elected president.

Stately as legendary pirate queen Grace O'Malley, this auburn-haired natural-born beauty guzzled shots and beers with the worst of them, sucker punched women and men in bar fights, and believed in nothing sacred. At her high school prom she pulled a prophylactic over the head of her passed-out date who was lucky his football team buddies found and resuscitated him before he suffocated and died in the back seat of his father's used Buick.

Stands to reason Peggy reigned as the dead-on favorite to win the 1983 "First Annual Irish Guys Case-O-Beer Throw," an event the lads decided to make a neighborhood tradition and pass down through the ages. Empty village idiot rituals often wound up commemorated as itemized charges on hospital bills.

Mikey Hoyle took credit for the case of beer launch because his shirttail cousin Pete did the throw in Philly years ago. Cheers and shouts of "oo-rah," a battle cry some of the lads heard in Marine movies, greeted the proposal. For most of the Irish Guys, being in the service meant serving up paper plates of steamed clams at the parish picnic. In their own defense they'd tell you at least they weren't draft dodgers like Bill Clinton. They made no mention of Trump's bone spurs. With the draft ending in 1973 and an all-volunteer military in place, their justification made no sense anyway. They pledged to be available for the next one if their country called.

So the Irish Guys voted unanimously to sponsor the "case-o-beer" contest to support our troops wherever they stood guard in defense of liberty. Proceeds would finance the annual weekend trip to Notre Dame for a football game where all the guys posed drunk and hungover in front of the Touchdown Jesus.

The day of the opening toss, morning dawned bright as a tracer bullet. Peggy stood first in line to sign up. The men seemed confused and began mumbling about no girls allowed and men only and other gender-based insults they made sure she couldn't hear.

"Peggy says she's entering and that we can go fuck ourselves," Hoyle said.

Duggan grinned.

"You going to tell her she can't?"

This went back and forth for about two minutes before Hoyle slid the entry form across the bar. Peggy scratched an illegible signature and gave Hoyle a look dirtier than a Coal Hole urinal. He turned, poured half-a-glass of Jameson into a small water glass, and pushed the whiskey back across the bar. Peggy drained the double, wiped her mouth with the back of a hand streaked with cat scratches, and unbuckled the cracked, thick, black leather belt she wore across her shoulder like a machine gun bandolier.

Hoyle couldn't help himself.

"What in the name of God is that?"

"My father's police belt," she said.

The late Pat Flynn was the fattest cop in the history of the Wilkes-Barre police department. He spent the last decade of his life and career working the graveyard shift on the reception desk at police headquarters, where he regularly dozed behind the bullet-proof glass. One morning his heart just stopped. It didn't dawn on the cops until the next day's three-to-eleven shift change that he had expired. The family buried him with full honors in a custom-made steel grey coffin that looked more like a super-sized beer keg than a casket.

Fear showed in Hoyle's eyes.

Peggy explained.

"Remember when David dropped that big sack of shit Goliath with a slingshot? This is like that."

Confused, Mikey shook his head.

"So what's a sling got to do with our case-o-beer throw?"

When the contest got underway, Peggy stepped up to the curb and the lads realized her father's police belt had everything to do with the case-o-beer throw. Tilting the full case of warm Stegmaier cans forward, she slid the belt underneath the cardboard container. Lining up both ends of the cracked belt in her hands, she leaned back until the strap went taut. Then she began to spin, turning and turning and turning some more, rotating like a husky German Olympic discus thrower. In a fundamental combination of aerodynamic science and Peggy's Amazon-like agility, the case lifted off the ground. Peggy maintained control, leaning back into the turn, and picking up speed as she spun. When she finally let go of the belt the case soared airborne, clearing the stop sign and crashing through 97-year-old Mrs. Sweeney's front parlor window. Standing on her porch watching the festivities in her housecoat, dementia-ridden Mrs. Sweeney squealed and clapped her hands.

"The beer is mine," she said, rushing into the parlor and locking the door behind her. "Ha-ha, the beer is mine."

Nobody beat the throw. Nobody even came close. Contestant Cheddar O'Malley did make the edge of the far curb, exerting himself to such a great degree in the release that he soiled his golf shorts, earning the nickname "Shit-The-Pants" O'Malley until the end of time.

At the after-party, a drunken Duggan, in a fit of fascination over Peggy's victory, asked her to marry him. She slurred an acceptance and promptly passed out face-down on the pool table. The lucky couple exchanged vows without witnesses in a private ceremony the following week before the neighborhood justice of the peace.

By their first anniversary Duggan celebrated by planning Peggy's funeral. Coming home from reveling in mutual bliss at the Pizza Kings pizza parlor, an unexpected incident forced Duggan to leave the motor running while he jumped from his 1980 Ford Mustang to remove the remains of a stray Chihuahua dog he ran over while racing from the pizzeria parking lot. The dog might have lived except for when two dozen beer cans the lads tied to Duggan's rear bumper to commemorate last year's wedding got tangled around the poor mutt's throat and strangled him. While reaching to pull the carcass from the undercarriage of the Cobra, a taxi cab approached from behind doing 70 miles-per-hour and slammed into the car. Peggy died of blunt force trauma injuries at the scene. The severely inebriated cabbie crawled from the wreck wearing a shit eating grin with his hands raised over his head not in a gesture of surrender to police but in the spirit of Evel Knievel walking away from yet another death-defying stunt. Drunk and relieved to be alive, Duggan immediately passed out at the scene and collapsed into the gutter.

When Duggan picked up the baby the next day at his mother's he told her what happened.

"I hope she didn't suffer," Mrs. Duggan said.

"No way, Ma, she was more loaded than me and the driver put together," Duggan said. "Peggy didn't feel a thing."

On the day of the funeral, Duggan met with the life insurance company representative and received a check. He also asked one of the Irish Guys who happened to be an assistant district attorney to accept a distracted driving plea bargain from the cab driver whose lawyer paid Duggan in cash as part of an under-the-table settlement. Duggan used the money to buy a brand new green Cadillac with mud flaps that matched the white and orange of the Republic of Ireland tri-color. The judge, another Irish Guy, sentenced the cabbie to one year of community service that involved driving his cab without pay for the same cab company for which he worked before the accident, a business owned by the judge's brother-in-law, another longtime Irish Guy.

Tucking two-month-old Junior into his crib the night of Peggy's funeral, Duggan realized he had no idea how to change a diaper. So he wrapped the little tyke's messy butt in the front page of the Citizens' Voice newspaper like the kid was a take-out order of fish and chips and went to bed. Duggan's mother tended to the child-rearing chores over the next few years so her boy could get on with his law enforcement career. Duggan felt guilty for the rest of his life about losing Peggy because he had swerved to hit the Mexican dog on purpose.

"Bet that taco mutt doesn't have papers," he said to Peggy before steering the car over the scrawny animal.

"Goddamn illegal mongrels crossing the border to take belly rubs away from American dogs in decent God-fearing families," Peggy said.

Two mushy peas in a pod, they were.

PADDY'S DAY IN TRUMP TOWN

Love is blind in Wilkes-Barre.
Drunk, too.

SHOPPING FOR THE FUTURE

Mayor "Spuds" McAnus spotted Martin Mahoney leaning against the potato bin at the Wegman's supermarket where a family pack of white potatoes sold for $2.29.

"You can't go wrong with spuds," he said. "Spuds for everybody. That's my new campaign slogan. What do you think?"

Mahoney ignored him.

McAnus grimaced.

"Bad mood?"

"Trump's getting crazier," Mahoney said. "The president's capable of anything."

McAnus brightened noticeably.

"So are we," he said. "That's why we all get along."

Mahoney started to sweat.

"I'm worried Trump might take a stroke, push the button, resign, get shot or defect to Russia. What do we do then?"

"We go with the flow."

"What's that even mean? The flow? You're not talking about them pee pee tapes the hookers in Moscow got on him, are you?"

McAnus waved his arms around like the leader of McNamara's Band on Adderall.

"We refuse to accept whatever bad happens to Mr. Trump," McAnus said. "Even when he leaves office, if he ever leaves, we act like he's still president. We refuse to accept reality."

"We're experts at that, all right."

McAnus slapped a devilish look on his puss.

"Tweet," he said.

Mahoney looked stunned.

"Tweet tweet," McAnus said.

Mahoney got so excited he spit when he spoke.

"What is wrong with you?"

McAnus stood to full height, the way he did when he received Holy Communion at Mass.

"I'm tweeting, just like the president. C'mon, you try it."

Mahoney wanted to run.

"C'mon," McAnus said. "Your turn."

Mahoney blessed himself.

"Tweet," he said.

"Atta boy," McAnus said.

"Jesus Christ, I'm as bad as you," Mahoney said.

"Woo woo," McAnus said. "Woo woo."

Mahoney put his fist to his mouth, unconsciously biting into his forefinger so hard his front teeth left marks.

"Sweet Mother of Christ, now what are you doing?"

"That's the Trump train," McAnus said. "All aboard."

Mahoney felt faint.

"We're all in this together," McAnus said. "Either you're with us or you're against us. C'mon, lad. Toot the whistle on the Trump train. Time to get on board."

Mahoney looked left.

Mahoney looked right.

"Woo," he said. "Woo woo."

"Tweet," McAnus said.

"Tweet," Mahoney said.

McAnus raised his palm and waited for a high five that didn't come.

"Yes!" he said.

"We've lost our minds," Mahoney said.

"Beautiful," McAnus said. "We got nowhere to go but up."

COULD WE GET A KITTEN?

L ike a monster under the bed in a terrified kindergartner's bedroom, the Trump rally grew more ominous with each frenzied beat of Junior's heart.

"Death Wish" sounded as ballsy as any nickname Junior ever heard. One day he'd just drop the "Junior" handle altogether, call himself "D.W. Duggan" on formal occasions like on the guest list at the 2021 inaugural ball. "Death Wish" carried a harsh, rugged connotation.

The curdled white peasant rage he and most of the Irish Guys carried around like two-by-fours on their shoulders held new meaning, too. The power of making America great again meant targeting everybody who failed the bloodline. Lads like himself would determine national purity with a reckless abandon bordering on anarchy. Irish Guys already blamed everything wrong in America on everybody who wasn't what the tribe stood for even if they weren't sure what those attributes entailed. As die-hard, frustrated white extremists whose behavior President Trump condoned and validated, they swore to do everything in their limited power to support, encourage and enable the worst, most dangerous, most severely flawed president in the history of the American republic. Then they'd call in their chips. Quid pro quo (you blow my penny whistle, I'll blow yours) meant the same in any language.

Junior decided to formally announce his new nickname when he got his "Bikers for Trump" business cards. For now, because nobody knew him as anything other than Junior, he'd still go by Junior. Making decisions always gave him a headache. Why was life so hard? Because he was white, that's why. Junior knew he'd fare far better if he were black. Ironically, his grizzly genome characteristics matched what some people called "Black Irish," a person of dark complexion and black hair. The mix that germinated from ancient DNA infected the Irish when the Spanish Armada docked on the Irish west coast. An unknown number of flamenco-dancing gypsies jumped ship and washed ashore. Since Junior hated all people of color, it made perfect sense that he hated himself.

On this stirring March Wednesday, after rolling his bike into one of the 50 or so reserved "Bikers for Trump" spaces township police arranged for rally parking at the arena in exchange for a modest bribe, Junior immediately sensed scalding eyeballs searing the most private parts of his body.

Flat-chested with several days' worth of brownish-yellow suck marks on her neck, the young woman reminded Junior of a Jack Russell terrier. Beady shrimp-like eyes set too far apart aroused him, a perpetual bottom feeder, and juiced his primal gauge of hotness. Junior licked his lips, put on his best field sobriety test strut, and bopped toward the front door.

In line fifteen minutes later, there she was again, this thin skanky woman built like a stripper pole standing behind him breathing warm alcohol fumes down his neck. Junior turned and looked into what he could see of her eyes below the smeared white and blue mascara and red Make America Great Again (MAGA) baseball cap.

"What time is it, beautiful?" Junior asked her.

"Trump time," she said.

"You remind me of Melania," Junior said. "But there's something I need to tell you about Nancy Pelosi. You want to hear?"

"Tell me, you big throbbing knob of patriotism, you," she said.

Junior let rip his best rallying cry.

"Lock her up, lock her up, lock her up!"

Excited now by the rotgut odor of Southern Comfort and 7UP on her breath, Junior's eyes bugged out as his lithe admirer started yelling so loud in response she shot a glob of white spittle the size of a grub worm down the front of the sleeveless black leather vest Junior wore shirtless with "Bikers for Trump" emblazoned on the back in gold letters. His father ordered the vests for him and his boys as a gift, billing the expense to the police motorcycle cops' uniform account.

Writhing like a Holy Roller snake handler in the throes of evangelical ecstasy, this Trumpette strumpet simulated oral sex with jerky fist movements to her mouth as she cawed, "CNN sucks, CNN sucks!" Close to passing out from the adrenaline rush shooting into her head like a frozen slushy brain freeze at the Dairy Queen (to which she always added vodka), she spun in a semi-circle and threw double-barreled middle fingers at the media riser at the rear of the arena.

Not quite believing his good fortune, Junior stuck with his new piece of class as they pushed their way all the way to the front row. When the rally finally got under way in the vast concrete bunker where the two-bit Pittsburgh Penguins farm team hockey team played, she fired her best shot when Trump brought up his promise to keep building a big beautiful wall. Her words poured forth in a rapid-fire flurry of guttural squeals like a family of pigs being slaughtered for a Ku Klux Klan barbecue.

"WHO'S GONNA PAY FOR IT?"

Junior responded instinctively with a blast furnace howl.

"MEXICO!"

When the rally ended, they held hands, pinkie fingers entwined like rusty fish hooks linked in a bait bag.

"What's your name, hot stuff?"

"SueReen."

"Sounds like a kamikaze pilot's name," Junior said. "Like spoiled sushi food poisoning in a Chinese restaurant."

"My mother's a twin. She's the Sue part. Her identical nut sister is Laureen. She's the Reen part. One's as miserable as the other. I'm as bad as the two of them put together. Laureen's doing time in the county jail for opioid sales my mother says got her constipated. Mom testified against Aunt Laureen at the trial. Said opioid-induced blockage violated her constipational rights."

"You sound like my kind of girl," Junior said. "Call me Death Wish. Maybe we can go to Florida together when Mr. Trump wins his second term."

"OMG," SueReen said. "Florida's like where you can do everything and don't have to be smart enough to do anything."

"Yeah, settle down, drink White Russians in our underwear on days off," Junior said.

"I could sell old vinyl Lynyrd Skynyrd records at flea markets,"

SueReen said. "Or my dream job to market used Ivanka Trump shoes on eBay."

Getting teary-eyed, SueReen sniffled.

"Could we get a kitten?"

"As long as it's not one of them Siamese refugee cats," Junior said. "And you make sure my recliner massage chair's got no cat pubic hair on it and a pillow so I'm comfortable playing my "Muslim Massacre" video combat game when I come home from work."

Giddy star-crossed lovers on a national highway to hell, they jumped into each other's arms. Junior lifted SueReen with one arm by her waist. Throwing her over his shoulder, he hoisted her up and down and all around like she was riding a mechanical bull in a shit-kicker saloon. Although SueReen rhymed with serene, her glow-in-the-dark mood swings never quite let up, especially under pressure. Still, this woman who could turn on you like a tarantula in the Sam's Club banana bin fit Junior like an old shoe matched an old sock. Tight at first sight, they twined like fuzzy belly button lint. Thanks to Trump they felt humbled by the glorious prestige of being winners for the first time in their achy breaky lives.

With the rally finished, unable to control themselves in the pangs of political passion, they scrambled amid the shelter of dark shadows under the wheels of a parked 18-wheeler. Coupled like bush animals, they squirmed beneath a big rig decorated with dreadful anti-Hillary and magnificent pro-Trump slogans painted on the Mack truck's sides. After coition, what a moaning Junior breathlessly called "doing the Donald," they fell asleep nestled in each other's odious armpits. Oblivious to the gravel scarring their skin or the engine's diesel fumes when the mutant ex-con owner/operator turned over the ignition, neither noticed when the trucker laid rubber as he tore out of the illegal parking space in a cloud of black smoke.

Junior reclined naked except for his unbuttoned black leather vest. SueReen wore nothing but her red baseball cap pulled tightly over her ears. Exposed, these two blissfully spent Trump disciples finally believed in the future. Their X-rated romp marked an unmistakable beginning amid satisfied snores echoing in the empty asphalt parking lot, blaring like a Third Reich band at a Nuremberg beer festival.

The incredible seed Junior planted for tomorrow swam in SueReen's innards. Like a perfect seamless weld on a county prison cell door, their bond grew even as they slept. Grinding his teeth in a coma-like snooze, Junior dreamed of his firstborn son graduating from a new and improved Trump University built with cash donated by Americans who truly understood the art of the deal. But when Junior drooled into a pool of spit he dreamed was an oasis, falling deeper into stupefying slumber, SueReen's reverie turned chilling.

In her dream, she's chained to the bumper of a campaign tour bus. The president's talking about her with a fawning television host who laughs at the president's story. Trump's words blister SueReen's subconscious, leaving raw emotional trauma she can't shake or escape.

"I did try and fuck her," Trump says.

SueReen whimpers in her sleep.

"I moved on her like a bitch," Trump says. "But I couldn't get there...Then all of a sudden I see her, she's now got the big phony tits and everything. She's totally changed her look."

Clutching her golf ball-sized breasts, SueReen curls into a tight fetal position.

"Yeah, that's her," Trump says. "I better use some Tic Tacs just in case I start kissing her. You know, I'm automatically attracted to beautiful... I just start kissing them. It's like a magnet. Just kiss. I don't even wait. And when you're a star, they let you do it. You can do anything."

SueRreen says, "Don't do it."

"Grab 'em by the pussy," Trump says. "You can do anything."

"Please, Mr. President," SueReen says.

Trump rushes SueReen, grabbing her by the crotch, squeezing, pinching, pulling with his thick, stubby fingers. Now he's on her like a magnet, kissing, smothering her with his mouth, tearing at the fork in her blue jeans, slobbering on her chin. Pulling Trump's straw-like orange hair with both hands, SueReen can no longer breathe. Screaming in terror, buried beneath a heavily made-up face, an obese body and a mountain of white Tic Tacs, SueReen surrenders.

Straddling SueReen's body, the president exposes himself and throws a thumbs-up.

"Melania said this was OK," Trump says.

WATCH YOUR MOUTH, MISTER

Hunched over a mustard-and-onions smeared plate in Aladdin's Dogs on Public Square, Bop O'Brien swallowed the last bite of one charbroiled wiener with the works before turning his attention to sucking gooey brown chili meat topping from a hole he gnawed in the side of another bun. O'Brien always ate three hot dogs with everything, all but inhaling them the same way every time, a sloppy ritual of gluttony. Then he ordered three to go. Looking up, O'Brien noticed the hand-lettered "GOING OUT OF BUSINESS" sign made from masking tape and stuck across the front window. After staying open all night for years, owners decided to close the joint's doors for good.

O'Brien hated the customers, lowlife senior citizens on fixed incomes, working single mothers, public assistance recipients, and others whose lives he scorned. And this was just the white riffraff. The owners probably made the dogs from camel meat, anyway. Fuck 'em and the magic carpet they rode in on. That the proprietors were second generation born-in-the-USA Arab Americans made no difference to O'Brien. Mexicans, Syrians, Lebanese, Jews and the rest on his shit list were all trouble no matter what year they arrived or where they were born, including here.

Belching and tasting bitter sauce on his tongue, O'Brien turned his attention to the waitress writing up his check. With smooth calves and perfect teeth, Cookie had been his fantasy girl since he ogled her in county criminal court at her sentencing. Spotting purple fluorescent fingernail polish, O'Brien wondered if she wore the same paint on her toes. Staring at her legs and the white canvas sneakers she washed each week in Clorox, he imagined her walking on his back in bare feet. Her only flaws included a snooty attitude and three flesh colored Band-Aids she wore on the inside of her left forearm. O'Brien wondered what kind of sore wouldn't go away. Hippie bitch probably carried some kind of venereal chancre she caught watching the Woodstock movie.

O'Brien remembered running her license plate for an address

after seeing the "Hillary" bumper sticker on her car back in 2008. He sometimes parked outside her apartment for an hour or so when he was in the neighborhood and needed a place to read his porn magazines and pull at himself. Once he saw her at the window and flashed the spotlight until she pulled the curtain. Once he followed her to work, making sure she saw him. Cookie showed no fear. After all, she had gunned down an allegedly abusive husband. O'Brien judged her lucky not to be doing life or living on death row with a black dyke cellmate from West Philadelphia.

Sensing O'Brien's stare, Cookie refused to look his way when the owner yelled.

"Three up. Everything."

Holding three buns in the crook of her right arm, Cookie slathered mustard and onions before dipping the dull metal ladle into the stained metal pot containing Aladdin's secret sauce. The owners cooked up the mixture in the cellar every morning and brought it upstairs one pot at a time. More than once Cookie pulled a mystery hair or poached roach from the steaming glop and thanked God she turned vegetarian.

In many Pennsylvania towns, Greeks cornered the hot dog market. In Wilkes-Barre, Syrians controlled the dog houses, working equally hard over scorching grills that never stopped sizzling. Although you could eat off the floors in most of these wiener establishments, Aladdin's stood apart as a ptomaine palace. Cookie's prison counselor recommended the spot because his brother-in-law owned the restaurant and needed cheap help.

Cookie wanted desperately to get out of county jail after three years inside after pleading guilty to voluntary manslaughter and having the "Battered Women's Syndrome" expert testify on her behalf. A woman judge sentenced her with compassion, not much but some. Supervisory conditions would continue for some time after her parole ended. At least she got out. At least she breathed free. As much as Cookie hated to admit O'Brien scared her, one look her way gave her goose bumps. Still, the stare pissed her off. Turning to face the gross detective, she said, "Really, do you have a problem, or what?"

Pushing away from the counter, O'Brien grabbed the bag containing his take-out and walked out on his check the way he did at least once a month.

"I'll call the mayor," Cookie shouted after him although she knew her threat rang empty. Even if she ran down the street to the magistrate's office and personally filed a complaint, her boss threatened to fire her if she ever pulled such a stunt.

"I'll call your judge," O'Brien shot back.

For a moment Cookie panicked and felt light-headed.

Outside O'Brien paused to pull his boxer shorts from his crack. Then he walked to the corner to hang out for a while, pick his teeth, and daydream about retiring to Ireland. A foul man with a belly the size of a half barrel of sour beer, 58-year-old O'Brien's career was the stuff of which depravity is made. Despite more than three decades of police work under his belt, he clung to his detective's badge with the uncertainty of a high-rise window cleaner dangling from a ledge. Each day he amazed himself that he stayed on the job as long as he did.

Public service meant nothing to O'Brien. Pushing people around, stealing cash and other swag from drug dealers, and getting everything from complementary meals to free booze provided O'Brien with wondrous power and control. The most amazing part of his charmed existence was how some people actually respected him. Mostly, though, people feared him. That's why Cookie drove him crazy, standing up to him at her own risk. O'Brien despised everybody but really hated her. Each year his rancor grew worse. Feeling unappreciated became his specialty.

Scratching his testicles and lounging on the corner, O'Brien dug into the hot dog bag and tried to figure out his next move. Pulling out the dog, he tossed the waxed paper on the ground. O'Brien gobbled the rubbery tube in three loud bites. Screw Cookie and the dick she rode in on. He'd give her a wiener. Slip her the pork. But what if she was serious about calling the mayor? McAnus warned O'Brien countless times not to do anything that might call negative attention to his re-election campaign, especially since O'Brien illegally collected overtime tacking up the mayor's "Spuds For Everybody" re-election campaign posters all over town and working for the Trump re-election campaign.

One day he'd fix Cookie's buns for good. But he better watch himself. O'Brien rushed back inside the restaurant.

"Give me my check and three more to go," he said. "Make sure there's double waxed paper in between so the shit sauce doesn't get them stuck together."

"Watch your mouth, mister," Cookie said, putting her hands on her hips. "I swear to God, I'm warning you."

Bop O'Brien picked his teeth with the corner of a match pack and spit a hunk of brown onion on the clean polished counter where it clung like a question mark in an evolution debate.

"You really are disgusting," Cookie said.

O'Brien made kissing sounds, waited for his bag of dogs and stood ogling Cookie's body.

For the first time in the two years she worked at the restaurant, Cookie suddenly felt a dreadful sense of confinement that alarmed her worse than jail. Maybe she'd never escape. Like a tortured prisoner of war, despite working through the emotional wounds of her marriage and the trauma of pulling the trigger on her abusive husband, she truly had no idea how long she could last.

Life's gross uncertainty would all change when Trump lost, Cookie often told herself. But how many times had she started a conversation with the words, "When Hillary's president," only to forget Hillary lost and the world spinning out of control defined the norm?

O'Brien leered at Cookie's legs, ass and chest until she handed over the bag of dogs. Intimidated and feeling violated, the stand-off made Cookie wonder if she should just quit. Smart as she was, she didn't know if her agent would allow her to move when her parole was up. Maybe she wasn't strong enough to go anywhere else. Or smart enough. Maybe she wasn't meant to go anywhere else. Maybe she should just struggle to make the best of where and what she was.

Wilkes-Barre defined her. Home wasn't jail, although living in her hometown often felt like solitary. Prison time once made her think of suicide. But she fought the urge. Cookie knew surviving yourself presented strength. Maybe she could pull it off.

Reaching under the counter she pulled a pair of thin disposable gloves from a blue cardboard box. Putting them on while wearing her best kiss-my-ass smile she snatched O'Brien's money from his hand.

"Can't be too careful," she said. "A woman's liable to catch all sorts of diseases these days."

O'Brien took his change, walked outside and immediately stopped three Catholic high school girls wearing saddle shoes and pleated green-and-black plaid skirts. Flashing his badge he grilled them while finishing off two dogs, dripping sauce on the cheap brown loafers his wife Agnes bought him at a two-for-one Shoe Carnival sale.

"You carrying protection for the prevention of disease only without a license? Want me to strip search your purses? Bet you got rubbers hid in your panties."

O'Brien slowly rubbed his crotch three times in a circle like he expected a genie to jump out of his pants. His voice took on a huskiness that made him sound like a phone sex caller.

"You girls Irish?"

Cowering, the dark-skinned Indian-American teenagers held each other before they started to cry.

SMASHED POTATOES

P ug loved living the new life of a vegetarian. He could help save the world just by not eating meat. Pity the poor cannibals in Africa, but they'd probably feel better if they switched to corn on the cob instead of eating their enemies. Our government would save money on the inner city welfare fast food burgers all the boogs ate, as well. Saving the planet meant something to Pug he could never admit to anyone except maybe Binkie.

With winter temperature rising and falling abruptly, Pug built a bonfire at his camp most nights. Dancing naked in a circle around the flames he waved the hand-carved shillelagh he made from an ash branch and stared into the shimmering flames with the fervent focus of a Druid priest offering human sacrifice at an ancient pagan ritual. Ash trees dotted the woods near the culm mountain for more than 100 years. One night Pug hung from a low-hanging branch for ten minutes, bouncing and tugging with all his weight like a delinquent orangutan until the bark cracked and he could tear the new four-foot weapon he called a "nigger knocker" from a main branch of the tree. Using his blood-stained killing blade, he carved and shaped the wood below a baseball-sized knot into an almost smooth stock. Pug only put the club aside when his stomach growled and he needed to eat.

For years dinnertime with his family shaped the center of his life. Quickly grabbing a chair at the table and tucking a paper towel into the frayed collar of his shirt even when his father got drunk and his mother cried into the gravy, Pug always dug in first. Mashed potatoes made him feel better whenever he dropped half a stick of butter into the hole he created by pounding the center of the pile with his soup spoon. Adding a dozen shakes of salt, enough pepper to cover the mess with black specks, more salt and sometimes the other half-stick of butter, he attacked the pile, gorging himself on the thick milky lump with the zeal of a death row diner digging into his last meal.

Cooking for himself now, what he called "smashed potatoes"

made up his favorite meal. He read once that the Irish lived on potatoes until the crop rotted and the dirty English tried to starve them to death by shipping all other food sources to markets elsewhere. The least Pug could do to respect his heritage was eat as many potatoes as his stomach could handle. Making smashed potatoes always turned into a spud bath. Lining up a dozen tubers in their dirty jackets on a large flat rock he used as an altar, Pug went down the line with his shillelagh, crushing one after another after another, eventually collecting the pulverized remains in his hands and dropping them into the big pot he stole from the GAR High School cafeteria during a midnight break-in. Talking incessantly to himself, he'd put another tater on the flat rock cutting board and hammer away, jabbering all the while. Over and over he'd repeat himself. Laughing and babbling gibberish he imagined was Gaelic, he talked himself into a trance of short-fuse agitation before going silent and sitting down to eat. Stewing and depressed, he'd raise his shillelagh above his head, bringing it down with all his might on the remains of his meal.

The sound of Pug's voice would have petrified any civilized person who heard its shrill impact. But he hunkered down too far inside the woods near the culm dump for anyone to hear. When his stomach growled, Pug growled back.

Growing up, ham always shaped the main course at Sunday dinner at home. No more. Pug refused to eat what he called swine and thought about stealing himself a pig somewhere, training the little porker to attack like a Doberman pit bull mix guard dog. That'd be nice, a nasty-assed snarling pig pet he could dress up in children's clothes and call a friend.

Pug loved animals because people caused problems.

Pug lived like an animal because Pug renounced humanity.

SAVE THE BABIES

After a long day in seclusion backed up by hefty three-a-day belts of Thorazine, the doctors moved Franny Finnerty into a dingy private room with a view of the mountains and the river.

"My, my, aren't we looking fit today, Francis," said a social worker with white hair and a blue-and-green ribbon attached with a safety pin to the pocket of her jacket.

"What's with the bow?" Franny asked, pointing with a bony but steady finger.

"Save the babies," the social worker said. "Abortion is murder."

"Save the babies for what? So the boys can grow up to become Irish Guys? Or the girls can run for president of the ILFS?"

"What's the ILFS?"

"The Irish Ladies Flatulence Society."

Finnerty lifted his leg and let one fly.

Another poor evaluation from the social worker and an increase in dosage worked quicker to quell insurrection in Franny's soul than the Good Friday Agreement did to pacify northeastern Ireland. Yet, even with enough medication in his system to drop a coal mine mule, Franny remained true to his convictions. Although he told no one, his heritage meant everything to him. History mattered more than sanity. Rebellion embodied his one true love. Fighting against all odds, perseverance and resistance defined liberty. None of that silly Irish Guys blarney came close to the depths of his regard for his ancestry.

Irish Guys leaned heavily on predictability, caricature and shallow symbolism. They defined their Irishness with Notre Dame football, leprechauns, watching "The Quiet Man" movie over and over and over again, wildly laughing, crying and cheering each time like it was the first. Franny got that. But when it came time to vote on whether to let Franny into the club when he got back from Atlantic City all those years ago, after being released from mental health treatment the first time, they voted him down, unanimously blackballing him and calling him a "weirdo."

Franny knew they rigged the vote, that people he hoped might welcome him home to the fold sabotaged his bid for acceptance, just like powerful Democratic Party insiders did to Hillary Clinton in 2008. Then they dragged their feet in 2016 when she won the nomination, helping Trump gain support through their laziness in places like Wilkes-Barre. The Irish Guys did more to secure Trump's victory than anybody and raved about how they put him over the top. This pack of louts flaunted more deplorable traits than informers. Informers exemplified the worst. Irish Guys embodied worse than the worst.

Even today the idea of a woman president clouded many Wilkes-Barre minds, including "their" women's minds. Wilkes-Barre didn't even have a woman firefighter. Neither did Scranton. Too many closed minds throughout Luzerne and Lackawanna counties remained sealed. At least Hillary won Lackawanna County and Scranton by a slim margin. The Irish Guys killed her in the adjacent southern county, charging the Coal Hole after the returns came in like Confederate rebels at Chancellorsville yelling how they finally rose again.

Franny nervously called himself a feminist. If more people voted for a female presidential candidate, the better the odds America would move toward equality. That meant better mental health treatment, too. Until then, Franny planned to battle reality as long as he could and fight his demons alone. Trump seemed to be a far more dangerous man.

In his darkest moments of psychiatric ward isolation, he thought of Ireland, his Ireland, a nation once again, his adopted homeland. One day he'd visit, go for refuge, maybe live out the rest of his life. One day he'd walk the land of his ancestors, a free man with a free mind.

Upon release from the hospital, Franny returned to his cramped room in a decrepit building on South Main Street. Feeling weak, he abandoned his Irish aspirations. Who was he kidding? As he often did with bouts of loneliness and sorrow, he kept his beloved Irish cause to himself. Sometimes, though, sitting alone in his third-floor quarters, his excitement returned, boiling over the edges of his mind like the big pots of fresh bubbling oatmeal he used to cook on his hot plate and eat with piles of white sugar and milk he kept cool on the window sill. During his most recent absence somebody snuck into his room and stole his cherished two-burner hot plate. Nowadays, Franny took his fiber from little packets of hot cereal he stirred into cups of hot water drawn from the common bathroom sink in the hallway. Instead of freshly brewed tea in a pot he now reused the same soggy tea bag three times before throwing it away. Most mornings, sitting with his thin instant oatmeal and lukewarm weak tea, he wore the striped flannel Irish grandfather's shirt his sister had brought back for him decades ago from one of her trips to County Galway. Sometimes he'd wear his Irish hat and read Irish novels in his underwear.

On his second day home a security guard and creative writing graduate student at Wilkes University who lived across the hall punched Franny in the face and knocked him down for making disparaging comments about the president when the guard asked him to buy a Trump armband.

"Traitor," the security guard said. "Retard."

Franny looked up from the floor.

The guard kicked Franny in his left ear with a scuffed German paratrooper boot and went off to work second shift at the college where he wrote dystopian porn for his master's thesis during his lunch break. Franny curled up like a bug on the grimy hallway floor. Shaking in a terrible daze, barely able to whisper, Franny knew his life meant nothing.

"All I ever wanted to be was Irish," Franny said.

FLIPPING GOD THE BIRD

Most Irish Catholics played by the rules.

Breaking them was half the fun of redemption.

The Irish Guys gathered in executive session in one unruly brooding mass, assembled as uncomfortably in the Coal Hole backroom as a reunion of former gonorrhea patients. With little more than a week to go until blessed St. Patrick's Day, which everybody in the city called Paddy's Day, the Church tossed a wrench into the whole shebang.

This would be the first year parade officials accepted a private sponsor for the event, choosing the Irish Guys' low bid over several other groups that offered more money to sponsor the parade, mostly Protestant Masons who Mayor McAnus considered devil worshippers. Total bribe cost for these practicing Catholics who needed all the practice they could get was $5,000 in small bills stuffed into a brown paper bag delivered to St. Al's Monsignor Moody who headed the parade committee and held great sway with the majority that made the selection. As a simple gesture of thanks, Monsignor Moody would pump a nice infusion of laundered campaign money he skimmed from the Bishop's Annual Appeal into McAnus' re-election campaign war chest. All it took for the monsignor to cinch the deal for the Irish Guys were some Olive Garden discount coupons and a couple of the worst seats in the arena tickets for the upcoming Elton John concert slid to the majority of parade committee members.

In return, the Irish Guys hit the jackpot, hitting up each float sponsor and group that wanted to march. That, coupled with the proceeds from illegal sweepstakes tickets, lotteries, chances and punch boards, as well as kickbacks from service organization fixers and longtime crooked business executives in return for the best marching position, prime street corners for vendors, etc., the Irish Guys figured to make a killing, ten, twenty times their initial $5,000 investment.

Bribes paid off when you pulled them off.

The law of a lawless land is pure genius.

Yet, a problem had arisen.

"We'll make complete arses of ourselves if we march as a unit," said Irish Guys President "Bop" O'Brien. "Leave it to a woman to ruin everything."

Club Vice-President Martin Mahoney threw up his hands in frustration.

"Don't expect me to march neither with that gal as grand marshal," he said. "Didn't we vote for Congressman Flood to march in absentia as the grand marshal?"

"Where's in absentia," begged an almost incoherent member groggy with drink. "I thought we were marching in Wilkes-Barre. I can't take more time off work to go out of town."

O'Brien screamed for order.

"In absentia is where your brain lives, you idiot. It means dear Dan Flood is dead and won't be here with us," O'Brien said. "In absentia means it's symbolic that the dearly departed congressman's soul will lead us symbolically. Like a guardian angel."

Mahoney pouted.

"So who changed the rules on us? Who changed the way we do things? Do we still call our own shots here or no? Who nominated this girl to lead the parade, anyway?"

O'Brien spoke through clenched teeth.

"Look, Monsignor Moody wants his sister to lead the parade as grand marshal. He made a $500 contribution to our Notre Dame Club fund he stole from the abuse settlement fund and wants to spotlight her because she's thinking about running for county council next year and nobody ever heard of her before because she never did nothing but go to Mass and confession and receive communion for the past umpteen years. The parade will be great exposure for her. Get her out of the house. But rules is rules, especially our rules. No bitches. That goes for the monsignor and his sister."

Blushing and flushing from drink, the club chaplain spoke in a whisper.

"Now, now, gentlemen, please," Father Iggy O'Toole said.

O'Toole sported a sensitive ruddy complexion and drank martinis until his face bled.

"You'd all be singing a different tune if Mary herself asked to lead the parade, now, wouldn't ye?"

"Mary who?" O'Brien said.

"Blessed Mary, Mother of God," the priest said.

O'Brien sneered.

"She related to Monsignor Moody, too?"

Although the joke wasn't that funny, the intensity of the Irish Guys' guffaws rivaled the roar you would hear if famous Irish comedian Hal Roach came back to life and put on a benefit at the Coal Hole. Typically the Irish Guys treated the lamest gag as if it was the most hilarious quip they ever heard. Loyal camaraderie justified existence and validated the inane lifestyle the lads lived. When they weren't cracking up at each other's jokes they were brooding, crying, borrowing money from each other or making excuses why they couldn't pay it back.

No matter how smart they thought they were, though, no matter what they said or did, they were shit-out-of -luck as far as the St. Patrick's Day parade went. Nobody ever expected the monsignor to push his sister to the front of the parade. Monsignor Moody hated women. Everybody knew that.

Mahoney stood and raised his arms.

"Listen up," he said. "I know this is a dreary time to bring it up, but I'd like permission to address the floor," Mahoney said.

"Permission granted," said O'Brien.

Mahoney cleared his throat.

"I've done me best over the years," he said, affecting the bogus brogue that Irish Guys used regularly for effect. "Sweet Jesus, I've tried. But this does it for me. I won't follow no grand marshal with tits. I'm tired of having to change. This dispute is a sign, an omen like in the 'Exorcist' movie. That's why I move we disband the club and cancel our part in the parade. We have more important matters at hand."

The first beer mugs came in high from the back of the room.

Two or three chairs slammed against the wall and overturned when irate Irish Guys leaped from their seats. One Irish Guy tripped and went down. Curses flew. Friends held back friends from rushing Mahoney.

Father O'Toole sputtered and wailed.

"Cancel the parade? Why don't you go shit in your hat?"

O'Brien was on his feet and stalking his vice president. Closing the distance, he said, "OK, that's it, Mahoney. I move we move you ass over elbows out of the meeting room."

"Please, Bop," Mahoney said, his voice dripping with despondency. "Everything we ever stood for is under attack. We're not doing anything to stop it. We're drunk all the time, telling the same stories day in and day out, slapping each other on the back. Planning the parade like it's the most important event in our lives."

That confused a number of Irish Guys to whom the parade always was and always would be the most important event in their lives, including their weddings and the births of their children.

"That's what's wrong with us," Mahoney said.

A younger guy in the back threw a plastic pitcher and yelled, "Hey douchebag, you ever think maybe you're what's wrong with us?"

The Irish Guys roared their approval.

Mahoney soldiered on.

"We better regroup or we're history. The bosses at work abuse us like always. The government and the companies are partners. The unions sold us out a long time ago. The labor councils are crooked. The monsignor even turned on us. We're losing all that's holy. The powerbrokers are leaving us to choke on the fish bones while they're eating the fillets."

After overreacting to Mahoney's initial blasphemy, some of the Irish Guys settled down and went back to swigging beers. But they started to pay attention. This was getting good.

"I see this evil destruction in my own kid. Pug's on the loose with every cop in the state looking for him," Mahoney said. "Before he went unhinged he was talking to himself and laughing when there's nothing funny. Telling his mother he was thinking about putting an earring through the head of his dick. Think about that for a moment, lads. When you attend a Confirmation for your nephew or son and the guest of honor shows up telling the bishop he's wearing an earring in his dick. The church is in on it, too, with the monsignor supporting women's liberation in our parade. For all I know he's wearing an earring in his dick."

"Just wait one fucking minute," interrupted Father O'Toole, who immediately slapped both hands across his mouth. "You are out of control here."

Mahoney dropped to his knees, as if in prayer.

"Please now, Father, bear with me. We've got no order in this neighborhood anymore. That's why our kids are using the drugs, waiting for these New York monkeys getting off the buses with their bags of heroin. Those blacks in blue Yankees caps are not Mickey Mantle. We got Jamaicans here, too. I never seen a Jamaican in my whole goddamn life except that little shit on the Hawaiian Punch television commercial and never thought I would. Now they're using their accents on your daughters coming home from school. Our girls could be dating Snoop Dog before the week is out. Smoking who knows what, talking this hip hop shit that makes no sense. I don't mean the Easter Bunny hip hopping down the bunny trail, either. Not listening to their mothers. Not listening to you. Flipping God the bird."

Mahoney held up his middle finger, moving it in a slow arc across one side of the room and then back again to the other.

"Flipping God the bird."

You could have heard a swizzle stick drop. A few men blessed themselves. Mahoney was getting through. Even Father O'Toole sat googly-eyed paying attention.

"That's why I brought this," Mahoney said, reaching into his camouflage fatigue jacket and pulling out a bundle of dynamite. Waving the explosive sticks he shouted, "Gentlemen, start your engines."

A few Irish Guys hit the deck. Others pushed their way to the door. O'Brien slid his hand under his sport coat, fingering the handle of his .38.

"Mister Mahoney, that'll be enough. Blow up this room and

you're a dead man."

"Listen to me," Mahoney said. "It's time to take back what our ancestors fought for. Most of the men in George Washington's army were Irish. Real fucking Irish."

"Like us," a drunk in the corner screamed.

A few of the nastier, unemployed and laid-off drunken men who recognized the instant appeal in gratuitous violence and blowing shit up seemed impressed and interested but not quite sure how to proceed.

"That's why we need the Green Hand," Mahoney said. "The Irish version of what them Italians had in the old Black Hand days. We'll be modern day Molly Maguires, only better. The system won't hang us by the neck until dead because we're politically connected this time around. Trump will understand. He hates these fuckers, too."

Teary-eyed, Mahoney continued speaking about true life Irish-American insurrection in the coal fields with the ease of the late great Irish actor Richard Harris in the 1969 Molly movie. Hollywood executives actually filmed just south of Wilkes-Barre, in and around Hazleton, going so far as to build a fake company town and coal breaker in Eckley, an official state historic site which nowadays is empty almost all the time.

"I hereby declare the Green Hand open for membership."

Bop slammed his gavel on the table and the meeting immediately adjourned as members moved quickly to the bar. Frustrated at nobody taking up his invitation to join the new flying column, Mahoney soon grabbed his beret and trench coat and left without another word. O'Brien wasn't sure how to handle Mahoney's lamebrain attempt to organize an armed white paramilitary sons of the Mollies group. Christ, even the Irish Republican Army decommissioned their arms and ammunition as well as explosives years ago. You could always count on Trump Town Paddies to manufacture a crisis.

The evening ended calmly enough with half-price green Jell-O shots and O'Brien auctioning off a framed portrait of Jesus purchased by mail from an Irish website affiliated with the Knock

Shrine in County Mayo. One of the less lucid drunks paid $100 for the $20 optical illusion savior whose eyes opened and closed when you walked past the Lord's face. Garbled singing of the Irish National Anthem, "The Soldier's Song," followed last call (at which time most patrons ordered three and four drinks at once) topped off with a nice professional boxing bout on the big-screen TV between two white heavyweights, both of whom were nicknamed Irish this or Irish that or the Irish something or other. At closing time, head bartender Mikey Hoyle locked the doors to keep everybody in until the last customers left at five in the morning.

Nobody uttered another word about Mahoney or the Green Hand.

The next morning O'Brien called Monsignor Moody and told him the Irish Guys agreed they'd march behind his sister, or any woman for that matter, just as soon as Moody resigned and recommended a woman to take his job. Sensing lethality in O'Brien's voice, the monsignor agreed the club should keep his donation. He immediately notified his sister she'd have to hold tight for a spot on the council but arranged for her to be appointed to a do-nothing position on the municipal authority that oversaw the arena where the second-rate Pittsburgh Penguins "Baby Pens" hockey team played. Within a month, a bruiser of a Bosnian puck chaser accused her of stalking him, calling her an obsessed groupie and demanding a restraining order.

"He was asking for it," she told the Luzerne County judge who ordered ICE to contest the player's immigration status after Monsignor Moody appeared as a character witness for his sister and called all Bosnians communist threats to the free world.

In an emergency Irish Guys' meeting the following day, club members unanimously voted in Father O'Toole as parade grand marshal and voted out Mahoney, not for his threats of potential mayhem and death, but for suggesting the organization be disbanded. Nobody enlisted in the Green Hand. Rather, Father O'Toole introduced a motion stating that nothing was more crucial to living the good life of a good Catholic than rooting for Notre Dame, being an Irish Guy in good standing, and offering fealty to the edicts of the holy Roman Catholic Church. When the motion sailed to acceptance, the Irish Guys gave themselves a standing ovation and retired to the bar to celebrate.

That night Mahoney decided he couldn't beat them. He refused to join them. So he had to dismiss them. By midnight he went completely rogue, founding the "Mar-a-Lago Militia," an army of one that represented the best ideals of his commander-in-chief who won the White House on a promise to blow up Washington beltway business as usual. Trump alone inspired Mahoney. All Mahoney needed to do now was figure out what to blow up to prove his allegiance to his hero.

Rising from the kitchen table, Mahoney threw a straight-armed salute into the air.

"America first," he said.

SHIT ON THE SHAMROCK

Bop thought he peed the bed.

Waking beneath the cool, wet pile of blankets, he struggled to kick off the sheet and quilts that smothered his bloated body. Sweating profusely, Bop needed a drink. The dream had never been this bad. He had only been asleep in the guest room he claimed years ago for about twenty minutes after sneaking home from the "round-the-clock" homicide investigation he had worked for about forty minutes, including time for the two meatloaf sandwiches his wife, Agnes, made for him before he left for work. Sitting up with an audible gasp, Bop believed he was having a heart attack, an event which could come any day, according to the police department physician and brother-in-law to the mayor.

Sweat dropped down his spine and pooled in his underwear shorts beneath the fleshy small of his back. Wide awake and staring across the room, Bop locked eyes with the empty plaster stare of the Infant of Prague statue. The religious icon sparkled like a museum piece because Agnes dusted the little bastard dozens of times a day. A wedding gift from her late mother a quarter of a century ago, Agnes refused to put the little shit in the closet as Bop had ordered her to do the night he threatened to shoot the crown from its head like he was Elvis watching Robert Goulet on the TV.

For the past two years, as Agnes' manic depression got cloudier, she had taken to cuddling the pudgy idol of the holy child, cooing and baby-talking like the thing was her own flesh and blood. O'Brien regularly considered taking a baseball bat to the figure but worried Agnes would stick a butcher knife in his head while he slept like in that Clancy Brothers' song about the "babby" he played on the Coal Hole jukebox until the record wore out. Rather that she talk to the figure than talk to him. Let her find comfort in Vatican fantasy. Wasn't that the role of the Church in the first place? If Jesus was her anchor, who was he to rock the boat? Let Agnes steal silly solace from a life already haunted by her disturbingly spooky nature. In the process she was getting worse.

"Agnes, cut the shit, would you?" Bop said one hot afternoon when he stopped by the house for an on-duty nap in the air conditioning.

Agnes smiled, went to the toilet, and returned twenty minutes later with a little pile of poop she had scooped from the commode, cut into nugget-sized pieces and brought to her hubby on one of their best department store dinner plates. Groggy after just falling into a deep sleep, Bop shook her so hard by the shoulders of her flower-print duster she passed out. Hauling her bodily to the bed, he restrained her by tying her arms and legs to the posts with her pantyhose. Then he called some of the Irish Guys who sent their wives to the house to sprinkle holy water around her pillow and light votive candles. Agnes pulled out a day or so later. Thank God sweet son Michael was away at college and the neighbors kept their yaps shut. People in the neighborhood knew how to close quarters around their own. After the breakdown, other than making sure Agnes was always heavily medicated with pills Bop mooched from an alcoholic pharmacist he knew from the betting window at the harness racing track, Bop pretty much left his wife do as she pleased.

After delivering Michael into the world twenty-one years earlier, Agnes' future loomed as barren as her husband's conscience. Since death almost claimed her on the operating table, this loving, righteous God-fearing woman reached out to her faith as never before. Instead of granting Bop the huge ham-and-cabbage-sucking brood he desired and expected, she pledged to do God's work in exchange for Him saving her life and rewarding her with one-and-only sweet baby Michael.

Accepting a life of hard labor, each day Agnes visited the Blessed Mother grotto on North Street to pray, arrange and re-arrange hundreds of bouquets of donated flowers busy undertakers unloaded in a city loaded with elderly customers. Inhaling the clear light of salvation that refreshed her every breath, Agnes' unreserved passion smacked of purity.

Embarrassed as a teenager by his mother's public devotion, Michael eventually came to deeply appreciate his mother's simple goodness. He thought of her strength whenever he felt hatred for his father. Michael often thought of his mother's goodness. A quiet child, shy and handsome with striking black hair, Michael led naturally, excelled in athletics, and did well in his school work. Chosen once to serve requiem High Mass with a visiting cardinal, he never missed a tinkling of the bell. The packed house actually applauded when the celebrant accidentally dumped the chalice full of hosts and football all-star altar boy Michael snagged them intact before the hardware hit the ground.

Since hands like that only grow on the blessed, when Notre Dame called, Michael answered. But fate fumbled a happy ending. A Chicano defensive back from Los Angeles took Michael's legs from under him after a picturesque catch, perfectly legal and expected at that level, during freshman practice. Michael's left knee never completely healed.

Smelling a set-up and a wiretap, the bartender at the South Bend Fraternal Order of Police told Bop to go fuck himself the day Bop called to seek revenge.

"How much will it cost me to get one of your cops to plant drugs in that beaner's locker?" Bop asked.

Thinking about missing all those "Fighting Irish" bus trips fired Bop's emotions with the blinding glow of a short-circuiting electric beer sign. Discovering Michael's secret, though, blew all the circuits and felt like dying. Bop had nowhere to go but down. That wonderful baby boy Bop dangled on his knee at the christening party had come out to his mother as gay. Fathering an admitted homosexual is not something that helps you win man of the year honors at the Irish Guys' Paddy's Day dinner. All Bop thought about for months was who in his family tree infected him with that one queer sperm that came squirting out of him and grew up to ruin his family.

Agnes protected the mystery for years, nuzzling the secret close to her chest the way a mother deer licks a wounded fawn. Only once did she think of mentioning the situation to her husband.

"Brendan," she said one night shortly before Michael started college, after bringing her husband a nice thick boiled ham and raw Bermuda onion sandwich with extra salt and a pilsner glass of Lionshead Lager while he watched a Kojak re-run. "Maybe we'll talk about something when your show's over."

"The show's not over," he said.

"Brendan, it's about our Michael. We should talk about it. Husbands and wives talk. Men and women can talk. I watched Oprah when she did a show on marriage."

"Shhhhh," Bop said, hissing wildly as his police show resumed. "If this bastard Theo wasn't one of them goat-fucking Greeks I'd like the show a lot better. Why can't he be an Irish cop?"

"The police aren't all Irish, Brendan," she said.

"They should be."

"Can we talk about Michael?"

"Tell it to the statue."

Hurt again, Agnes cried herself to sleep in front of the television. When she awoke, Bop had already left for the Coal Hole. Bearing her burden alone, she recalled how she always pampered Michael, raising her lovely boy with reassurance and love. Whatever made him the perfect son was good enough for her.

"I'm proud of you, of what you are," Agnes told Michael a few nights later, as they drank hot cocoa at the kitchen table. "Even though I don't understand."

"Me neither, Mom," Michael said. "I probably understand least of all."

"God made you and Jesus loves you just the way you are," Agnes said.

Eavesdropping from the other side of the door with a warm six-pack under one arm and a brown bag full of greasy crab cakes and greasier limp fries under the other, Bop heard every word. Rushing into the room, he threw the beer bag at his son, who caught it with one hand, the deep fried lumps at his wife and a lumbering left hook at the wall. Plaster flew, the knuckle on his ring finger broke, and his identity shattered like a commemorative glass detective shield slammed on a concrete floor.

"Just the way you are? What way is that, faggo? What way are you?"

Pivoting to face Agnes, he bellowed.

"It's your side of the family. You got some rotten eggs growing inside you, up in you somewhere. There's never been anything but real men in my family. All my brothers and uncles and cousins are alike. Nobody's different from nobody else."

"That's your problem," Agnes said calmly, surprisingly regaining her composure and exhibiting a remarkable strength. "You're all more alike than you want to know."

When Bop jumped to reach for her throat Michael jumped faster.

"No," he said, standing between his father and mother.

Nothing short of a hand grenade could deter Bop O'Brien in mid-tirade. But he stopped. Nothing short of a broken heart could make him deny his son. But disavow he did.

"You shit on the shamrock," Bop said. "That's what you did. You shit on the shamrock."

After Michael graduated from Notre Dame with his degree in Irish Literature and his mother in the audience, he tried to get a teaching job in Wilkes-Barre to no avail. A convicted SEAL war criminal would have had a better shot teaching at one of the city high schools. Thank you for your service. Closeted Michael moved out of the house and took a job tending bar at one of the city's fairly invisible gay bars where he rented a small room upstairs.

Bop slept in his unmarked police car the night he found out. Snuggled against the butt of his Glock 22, he snored and once again dreamed the dream. When he awoke screaming and sitting up, he clawed into his shirt pocket, pulled out a cracked Pall Mall and lit the tip. Burning his finger on the match he let the butt drop to the floor as his mind clung to the dream that always made him sweat. The dream brought back a different time that created what some people might call a problem. Real men don't talk about problems. Real men are problems, proud to have the guts to do as they please. But the dream refused to go away. Bop kept dreaming the dream, watching the wrath of his own imagination show up behind his eyes like an old-fashioned home movie screen, a relentless black and white vision of his youth, a sordid sleep terror that never got better. The dream reminded him of the man he once embraced, a man despite mistakes and excesses who blazed a path for the future.

That future was now.

Bop reigned as a meat-eater king of the jungle where he ruled by one rule and one rule only: It's better to be pissed off than pissed on.

STOP SINNING

Father O'Toole slowly slid open the St. Pat's confessional screen and pushed his nose against the mesh. Pug smelled garlic from the pasta the priest's housekeeper made him for lunch. Bushmills whiskey fumes shot through the screen like cyanide hissing into the gas chamber. Penance time.

"Bless me, Father, for I have sinned. This is your last confession."

Distracted by his own thoughts of self-absorbed gluttony, O'Toole responded automatically.

"Yes, my son," O'Toole said. "Go on."

"No, you go on."

The priest looked up into darkness.

"I'm sorry?"

"Now we're getting somewhere, amigo."

O'Toole recognized the voice.

"Is that you, Pug Mahoney?"

"Yeah, just the two of us, Father, or should I call you Iggy, short for Ignatius, short for wetback?"

O'Toole stifled a laugh.

"I'm 100 percent Irish, you crazy boy," the priest said.

"Ignatius is a Mexican name, isn't it, Father? Ignatio? Short for Nacho? Like nacho chips? As in illegal? You ought to be ashamed of yourself, impersonating an Irish Guy for all these years. You fooled them thick bastards in the Coal Hole, but you can't fool me."

O'Toole fought to stay calm.

"Are you confessing your sins or not? What do you want to tell God?"

"I don't want to tell God nothing. I want you to tell him, to confess your sins, tell him what you did, what you know, what you covered up. Tell God about the children your silence hurt. Time to practice what you preach, Nacho, so make a good Act of Contrition before you enter the barbecue grill of Hell."

"Get out of here right now, Mr. Mahoney. You need help greater than that I can give."

"Time to stop sinning. Time to meet your maker."

Father O'Toole got ready to bolt. Smelling fear rise above the Royal Copenhagen cologne splash O'Toole favored and bought in bulk at Walmart on the parish credit card, Pug raised the thick, homemade shillelagh. The stick still smelled of fresh ash. Screeching, he thrust the sharpened tip through the center of the confessional screen. The point caught the priest in the middle of his white collar-covered throat, tearing starched fabric, skin and cartilage, bursting through the soft base of his balding skull and sending red raw flesh to blend with dyed black hair.

Pug whooped with glee. Tearing his shillelagh from the dying parish priest's throat, he fell from the booth and ran from the church singing a song he learned in the old days when he truly believed every day was Paddy's Day and all the drinks were free.

"Tread on the tail of me coat, ha ha. Tread on the tail of me co-oat. You're in for a row and a ruction, if you tread on the tail of me coat."

ON THE JOB

Decades before Trump's re-election campaign, Wilkes-Barre probationary police officer Brendan "Bop" O'Brien snapped his blue clip-on necktie into place, adjusted his cap at the proper jaunty angle, slammed closed the cylinder of his shiny new .38 caliber pistol, and slid into the passenger seat of a marked Wilkes-Barre police squad car to begin his career.

"Welcome aboard, lad," said Officer Daniel "Danny Boy" Duggan.

Senior traffic training officer Duggan then struck a pose which years before turned him into a major local celebrity, a certified character who knew no bounds. Holding his fists one curled in front of the other, he scrunched up his nose. The posture added an abrupt tilt to the slant of his head. Tucking his chin, he held this posture for a silent ten-second count.

O'Brien immediately recognized Duggan as the living spitting image of the Notre Dame Fighting Irish Leprechaun, a world-famous brand that turned an abundance of deep Irish culture into a cheap and derogatory cartoon. Neither man had any idea how British propagandists invented similar mocking caricatures as the powerful portrayal of a species the lords and ladies considered on par with monkeys jumping from trees. Chimpanzee-faced creatures with high foreheads, clay pipes and all the appeal of your friendly neighborhood caveman, the Irish played into the twisted Brit notion of simple-minded primitives racing around the island interfering with the British ascendency. The same bullish sentiment motivated business titans who wielded coal company power in Northeastern Pennsylvania for well over 100 years, using and abusing countless Irishmen and their families, often maiming and killing them in the process with the ease of seasoned big game hunters.

Only a handful of Irish Americans had any idea that every leprechaun image ridiculed their humanity. Despite the precision of this racial attack, most Irish Americans wallowed in the derogatory imitation of their ancestry, unknowingly spreading unconscious humiliation with the zeal of scarlet fever germs that swept the coal fields in the 1920s.

With fists raised in his pug-nosed pose, Duggan refused to move until he received a response to this one act he could do better than anybody, this single move he had down pat and could do so very well. The stance posed a problem for O'Brien. Reacting in just the right way meant everything for his future. His career depended on it. Not one to kiss anybody's ass, O'Brien also was nobody's fool. Erupting with laughter that began in the deepest reaches of his bile ducts and traveled through every part of his body before lodging in his throat, O'Brien shrieked louder than a chorus of chained ghosts pining for freedom from the hull of a coffin ship carrying Irish greenhorns from the Famine. Uncontrollable laughter sparkled in O'Brien's eyes like flashes of Waterford crystal gifts stacked side-by-side at a church social hall wedding reception. O'Brien pounded the dashboard with both hands. Thick veins strained against tight skin on both sides of his head. Rocking back and forth in his seat, O'Brien laughed and laughed and laughed until phlegm caught in his throat with the force of a police academy chokehold and sent him into a coughing fit, a spasm that would have propelled an older cop into cardiac arrest. Almost hysterical, O'Brien kept the act going nonstop for two long minutes.

Tickled by the reception his impression received, Duggan beamed like a sacristy wine salesman who succeeded in persuading the priest to upgrade the altar gargle. It was almost as good as the day he held the pose for five whole minutes at Notre Dame Stadium in South Bend during halftime and thousands of fans wildly applauded and snapped his picture. Duggan later confessed to a local priest that the pose taken on that sacred ground required every ounce of control he had to keep from "bawling my eyes out like a little girl."

In the East End Irish section of Wilkes-Barre where both Duggan and O'Brien were raised, old men and women pointed to the famous city cop and similarly raised their fists in that flattering salute. Whenever people saw Duggan driving through their part of town, even children imitated the one-and-only most well-known cop in the city. Duggan once told a high school graduating class the adulation helped him remember where he came from.

"If I can fucking do it, you can fucking do it," he said to awkward giggles from the senior class members and their stunned parents.

Now Duggan turned to face his new partner with that twinkle in his eye you hear so much about in Paddy's Day greeting cards. In reality it meant that Duggan's first two shots of on-duty Paddy's whiskey had kicked in and he was ready for anything.

"All right, bud," O'Brien said. "Now I've got something for you."

Undoing his belt buckle, O'Brien unzipped his pants. Duggan's eyes widened with panic. Blood drained from his face. Sensing Duggan's dread, O'Brien smirked.

"Bear with me now, officer," he said in his own local yokel brogue. "Work with me on this one. After all, Danny me boy, we're partners, right? We got to trust our partners, right?"

"We are and we do," Duggan said, appearing confused but willing to give the kid the benefit of the doubt. After all, O'Brien's mother's brother, an Irish Guy in good standing who sold knock-off Rolex watches to city workers with a ten dollar finder's fee going to Duggan for every customer he delivered, recommended O'Brien for the job.

Pulling down his pants, O'Brien looked out the window to make sure nobody was watching the shift change too closely. Other officers walked to their cars bullshitting in typical cop fashion, not paying much attention to anything. Turning the other cheek so to speak, O'Brien pulled down the right side of his shorts and there on his butt a stunning tattoo of the "Fighting Irish" leprechaun the size of a softball revealed his ethnic pride in full living color. With tiny upturned fists and a swarthy beard of red, the ham-faced little bugger was nothing short of a masterpiece.

Duggan collapsed in laughter.

O'Brien joined in the chorus.

With a few millenniums worth of once-pure Brehon Law and innate Celtic intellect gone awry, Duggan bellowed overwhelming approval for this tribal rite. To him this was what being Irish was all about. True happiness sprung from gleeful ties to total foolishness. Forget the complex nature of friendship found in Irish literature. Say goodbye to the deep sense of justice, music, magic, poetry and decency that characterized the essence of this great race.

"We're going to be quite the team, we are," Duggan said with tears in his eyes, emotion bubbling forth like manufactured soap suds in an Irish Spring commercial.

"You and me, pal," O'Brien said.

Reaching across the seat to pull the young officer's face so close to his own that O'Brien smelled bad teeth beneath the booze, Duggan spoke in a hushed tone that came as close to expressing love as he'd ever get.

"When we get off duty in the morning, I want you to come with me to the Coal Hole. I have a key. It's a place of our own. We'll have a few drinks and you can pick up an Irish Guys application. I'll sponsor you. With us, every day is Paddy's Day. We hold a huge men-only dinner once a year and everything. Plus we all march in the parade together. Like a real family, a real Irish family."

Most of the guys already had real families at home. But, to them, the club family loomed with far more significance in their lives than their blood and marriage families, a profoundly bewildering inclination that made no sense to anybody but them.

Duggan trembled on the verge of tears.

After knowing many of these Irish Guys for years, this one was worse than O'Brien ever imagined. He had done his best to avoid them but this time found no escape.

"Us East Enders got to stick together," Duggan said. "We're drawn from the shepherd's flock in the toughest part of the toughest town with the toughest of the toughest people ever put on the face of the earth."

"What about Scranton? I hear the Minooka Section Irish are tough, too."

"If washing your feet in the same water you use to cook your soup makes you tough, then, yeah, I guess they are tough," Duggan said. "They don't even take the dishes out of the sink before they piss in it."

O'Brien howled.

Actually, residents of both cities, twenty miles apart along Interstate 81, maintained edges hard as calluses on a beat cop's feet. Various insular groups in both towns operated much like medieval warlords. Rivalries and a wide assortment of ethnic and political hatreds simmered, sometimes erupted, and would forever keep the coal region from solid progress. Most people liked it that way. Most Irish also stayed in their own respective city. In years gone by, it was not uncommon for people from one town to never set foot in the other. Fate at birth immediately sentenced most coal crackers to a perpetual state of exile, isolation and xenophobia.

Hailing from Wilkes-Barre in Luzerne County meant going through life with a perpetual mental tic, a convulsion of provincial insanity from which damn near everybody suffered to one extent or another and refused to accept treatment. In the past most people kept their tiny minds to themselves. Few people wanted to wear ignorance like a badge of courage. With Trump's rise, though, more and more people began to take bold pride in stupidity, not only adopting their candidate's severe character flaws and personality disorders, but publicly calling them their own.

Bop O'Brien loved their gullible menace, the madness brimming among hundreds of thousands of townspeople who embraced each other's asininity as if simplemindedness equaled stature. In many ways they were just like him. Only he was smarter. O'Brien considered his brains a match for his brawn. Both characteristics set him up for disaster. The battle between deep personal weakness and selfish aspiration always ended in a draw.

Now Duggan began to blubber, unleashing tears the way they flowed whenever he heard what he called his "theme song" that now started playing in his head. The song came out of nowhere, as if his mind were working by itself, for better or for worse. Originality wasn't Duggan's strong suit.

Whenever he heard the lyrics, "Oh, Danny boy, the pipes, the pipes are caaa-aaa-ling," the words sent him without fail reeling into predictable spasms of sloppy sentiment. Duggan could be shopping at the drug store for pile paste to smooth his intermittent rectal eruptions, hear the instrumental version of the tune filtering barely audible through cracked ceiling speakers, and immediately stop and break down in tears. For whatever the reason, that song stood the test of time, pricking primal senses of millions of Irish Americans, reducing them to emotional wrecks the moment the first note crept into their consciousness. Guys who couldn't carry a tune in a golf bag would receive amazing encouragement if they broke into an off-key rendition of the goddamn song. The neighborhood Micks always took the gesture to be sincere. No level of inebriation could sway the gratitude expressed by those who heard the ditty warbled in a bar, at a family event, or in the back of a police car after being apprehended for falling asleep drunk during the changing of a traffic light.

The only time Duggan turned down a rendition was when the girl he was seeing a few years ago bought him the 1962 album "Connie Francis Sings Irish Favorites" for Christmas one year and Duggan went ballistic.

"She's the one who let the boon in her room and then yelled rape," he said. "I won't have that record in the house."

"Sweetie, please, she was wonderful to her mother. A black man broke into her motel room. I believe Connie," the girlfriend said

Duggan backhanded the then love-of-his-life lightly across the right eyebrow, just hard enough to open up a small gash with his Meyers High School ring. The cut didn't bleed much. Duggan torched the album in a rusted trash barrel he kept in the garden in which he burned garbage by his beloved cabbage and turnip patch. He never asked the girl out again. She never told.

Reaching out gently, Duggan touched Bop's shoulder in as caring a gesture you'd ever get from a Wilkes-Barre cop short of petting a senile police dog about to be put down.

"Sing with me, partner," Duggan said. "It's important."

No further encouragement was necessary. Throwing back his head, O'Brien fired away, assaulting octave after octave and mumbling unintelligibly whenever he forgot the words. Barking with more than enough enthusiasm to match Duggan's feverish shrieking, O'Brien crooned like the "The Irish Tenors" performing on RTE with severely sprained groin muscles.

If nothing else, O'Brien knew teamwork, however tiresome, equaled survival. Anything could happen and usually did in immigrant hard coal country.

"Ah, you'll make a grand Irish Guy, Bop," Duggan said when they finished the number.

Turning over the engine, the men cruised slowly from the lot. Pulling a full Paddy's bottle from the glove compartment, Duggan twisted off the cap and took a healthy swig. Tugging at himself, he adjusted his nuts and bolt into the proper position of penile pliability necessary for a comfortable overnight patrol.

"I want you to listen to me closely," Duggan said.

O'Brien waited for the punch line. Again ready to cry, this time Duggan launched into a soliloquy that outdid Shakespearean length if not quality. The gospel according to Duggan was off and running.

"Irish Guys share a cause and a purpose," Duggan said. "We get together, see, and tell each other what it means to be Irish, to know where we come from even if we don't know where we come from exactly in Ireland. We all come from Ireland. That's all that matters."

O'Brien tried not to laugh.

"Things happen to us, right," Duggan said. "Good things that don't happen to nobody else. Like you getting the job because you have an Irish Guy connection. You'll see. Promotions happen to us even when we don't deserve them. We got police and fire department Irish Guys, garbage men Irish Guys. Some city and even county jobs require a college degree. The best jobs require an Irish Guy. Summer jobs for our sons and daughters, too. Hoyle got his cousin a lifeguard job two summers ago. The city doesn't have a swimming pool and the kid can't swim. Hoyle's other cousin was the animal control officer and the only animals he had to watch were himself and his mother."

At this, yelling and punching each other in uproarious laughter, Duggan and O'Brien dried their eyes with their sleeves and the backs of their hands. Immersion in this kind of lunacy happened every day to card-carrying club members. Yucking it up among friends gave them something to look forward to.

"We get moral support, too," Duggan said. "Like you never seen in your life. Last year I tried to stop smoking because the doctor said my heart was slow and I couldn't do it all by myself so one night me and the guys got together to figure out a plan. We're always figuring something out, us Irish Guys. So we meet at the Coal Hole and talk it over about how maybe I can quit the smokes. One or two of them had done it, but I needed heavy support like maybe the way the drunks do when they take the pledge at church and get together with the priest for coffee at the rectory every morning instead of waiting outside for the state liquor store to open. So the guys come up with this brilliant idea that nobody but Irish Guys could come up with. Whenever I wanted a smoke, and that was all the time, I had to kiss the feet of the Blessed Mother. When I wasn't home where I keep a statue in the closet, I carried a little plastic Mary in my pocket all day and went to the grotto by the courthouse to the big statue whenever I could swing by. At night when I'd get up from the sack too nervous to sleep or when I had to pee, I'd open the closet door and kiss the Holy Mother's feet where she was standing back behind my two spare uniform shirts. I kissed that statue's feet so many times, sixty times a day, I eventually pulled her out and put her in the bed with me so all I had to do was roll over and give her a peck. I kissed the fucking Blessed Mother's feet so many times each day I had to carry around a jar of Vicks Vaseline petroleum jelly in my pocket for the chapped lips."

Duggan took a breath, sighed deeply and started up again with all the urgency of an air raid siren.

"The skin on me kisser looked like plaster peeling off a Puerto Rican's apartment wall. Each kiss, I threw away a cigarette. I'm a three-pack-a-day man. That's sixty smokes a day. Sixty smootches. Sixty times a day. But you know what? Deep down I always loved the Blessed Mother. Kissing her was easy. Sometimes I'd start thinking I was kissing her for real, thinking back to when I was a kid and liked thinking about her when after Mass I'd touch her lightly on her plaster parts. But I felt guilty now. I'm an adult and felt like I was trying to use her to cheat on Joseph and he'd get pissed if he found out and maybe slap her. I was going to pray to St. Joe, you know, tell him about me and Mary, but figured that would just start shit between him and me."

O'Brien sat dumbstruck in the middle of this blasphemous blarney. He was Irish from Wilkes-Barre, too, and knew how deep the dogmatic dysfunction ran, but a hot-to-trot Mary turning on this basket case while he's trying to kick the chain smoking made the Dead Sea Scrolls look like Hustler magazine.

Duggan continued.

"The point is the Irish Guys stuck by me all the way, even Father O'Toole when I confessed to him about the impure thoughts I had with the Blessed Mother. And you know what happened?"

"O'Toole admitted he had them, too?"

"Yeah, yeah, yeah," Duggan said, laughing so hard O'Brien thought he'd take a stroke. "He said he liked Mary better than Ann Margaret in the Elvis movies."

"And you're still off the cigarettes," O'Brien said.

Reaching into his pocket, Duggan pulled out a little yellowed plastic Mary.

"Go on, O'Brien, give her a little peck on the cheek. "

O'Brien did as he was told, kissing the mini-Mary statue on the mouth.

"Bless you," O'Brien said. "And bless the Irish Guys."

Now O'Brien turned in his seat and pulled down his pants to show his indelible imprint of all things Irish. Duggan threw up his hands and struck his "Fighting Irish" pose, holding it for only ten seconds before doubling over in a fit of snorting giggles. With the moon hanging in the sky white and pure as a communion host, Duggan turned over the ignition and pulled from the police department parking lot. He cruised slowly down the avenue and pulled into an alley behind the senior citizen high rise. Turning off the key he reached under the seat and pulled out a fresh bottle of Paddy's. Within an hour, both men snored with the pent-up power of ticking time bombs.

Thus began the first of countless tours of duty for two new buddies, partners in time and crime, two pals sworn to protect and serve and grab whatever they could wrap their mitts around without getting caught.

WHEN TEARS TOUCHED

Each time Pug cut himself with his knife he screamed her name. Slowly, methodically pulling the blade across his wrists, his belly and his chest, he lost blood. Not a lot since he got lucky avoiding a vein or artery. Pug wasn't ready to die just yet. Getting weaker he wailed.

"Binkeeeee."

Pug wanted so much to hold the skanky little dumpster girl. Pulsing memories of their first and only date pounded in his mind. She smelled of cold French Fries and soggy Big Macs on a fast food stained mattress where they flopped to do it, their hormones mixing with the sour scent of tart pickles and spicy apple pie. Binkee wore mustard in her hair. A special mayonnaise sauce dotted her boobies.

"I love you, Puggy," Binkee told him after they humped like gray squirrels in the McDonald's garbage. Snuggling against his chest she whispered that their intercourse was beautiful. Lewd as he was, even Pug knew getting boned in a trash container was pretty gross, but he let it pass. Binkee made him happy.

"Will you be my friend?" she called to him when he first heard a noise inside the huge metal trough where she was scavenging for supper. Dumbstruck, Pug eyeballed the squeaky beggar with robot eyes. Worried she might be an alien with a radioactive laser tongue, he kept walking.

"That's okay," she said. "I don't talk much, either. I need a buddy. Bet you do, too. I'm lonesome. Want to cuddle?"

Reaching into a multi-colored shoulder bag, she pulled out a double cheeseburger with two small bites taken from the crusty edge.

"Here," she said. "Almost like new."

Pug reversed course, snatched and gobbled the burger.

"How about these babies," Binkee said, this time offering a folded napkin containing six gummy chicken nuggets.

When they finished their meal, they grabbed at each other with the urgency of an emergency room doctor cutting away a shooting victim's clothes and joined forces against the world. With her clinging to his neck and him hammering her frail body, Pug drove home his point as if a whole species lacking love depended on them for survival. Living on fast food scraps, the teenybopper runaway with a soft face could have broken the hardest heart when Pug finished and she whispered, "You're really cool."

Pug mocked her.

"You got the brains of a shamrock shake," he said.

Binkee covered her mouth with both hands to keep the giggles in.

"This shit ain't funny. I'm not cool," he said.

Binkee bounced through a field of greasy colored wrappers and shredded lettuce to throw her skinny arms around Pug's pimpled neck.

"You're nice even if you don't know it," she said, nudging her face deep into his sparse chest hair. "That's what I meant. Honest. It's OK if you're using drugs. We can try to quit together."

When their tears touched, he pulled away ashamed. Simple emotional blending had saved her life even if she had seen him cry. If Pug had followed the increasingly uncontrollable killer orders from deep within his psyche, he would have squeezed every last drip of affection from her nasty little ass and left her to rot among the rest of the decaying food scrapings. But he balked, erring on the side of humanity.

"I saw a documentary on the National Geographic channel once about how beautiful lotus flowers are rooted in mud, how they bloom and survive to re-germinate for thousands of years," Pug said. "You live like a lotus flower. I respect that. I'll save you from the monsters. You registered to vote?"

"I'm only 15," Binkee said.

"Jailbait," Pug said.

After picking her up like a wounded puppy, when Binkee expected a hug, Pug heaved her over the side of the dumpster. Tossing her Doc Martins, black tights and torn "Luzerne County Community College DUI Team" hooded sweatshirt after her, he leaped from the garbage, his back wet from rolling in limp day-old bacon strips.

"I smell STDs," he said.

Binkee picked herself up from the fall, not injured physically other than a few scrapes. Walking away, her tears came so fast and so hard that Pug thought he could hear them hit the street, splattering like soft wax from the flickering red votive candles he stole for fun at the Polish and Italian cemeteries and smashed against headstones of the dearly departed.

"Don't go away mad, just go away," he said.

Now Pug didn't know how he could live without her. Cutting thin lines into his nose, blood ran down his face and into his mouth. Licking his lips, Pug got a rush knowing he tasted his own hemoglobin. Such plasma rites would fuel all vampire fighters in this new millennium. Bet Binkee would cut herself if he showed her how. Maybe she already knew. They could cut each other and bleed together. If that wasn't love, what was?

Training was everything. Being prepared was a commandment of survival. Who knew when Dracula would rise or Satanic UFOs would land? When Trump would call and ask him to head up the Space Force rangers? Binkee probably didn't want to fight, but he'd train her anyway. Pug could tell she was peaceful because she had pinned a peace sign button on her shoulder bag that Pug spotted when they were linked like two runaway coal cars and he was ramming and jamming her so hard he thought her legs might snap like extra crispy chicken wings. Maybe she'd compromise. They could just drink blood on holidays and special occasions like the roundheads his old man worked with at the security guard company, losers who still made blood soup from geese every Christmas like their great-grandmothers did back in Poland. Binkee would make a good vampire. She probably had AIDS already, so Pug made a mental note to find and drink some HIV blood one day soon. Nothing could infect him but revenge.

WHY NOT A BLACK NAME?

Parking with two passenger-side wheels on the sidewalk the way coal crackers have done ever since they started driving mule-drawn carts in the coal fields, Duff cut the ignition, opened the squad car door with a little kick, and stepped onto time-worn slabs of gray slate that led to the shrine.

Atheist to the bone, Duff had to admit the "Our Lady of Fatima Grotto" up the hill from the county courthouse was gorgeous. Stretching, Duff raised his arms. Rolling his head then his shoulders like a fighter warming up for ring introductions, he threw small jabs and uppercuts as he walked slowly up the path toward the marble pedestal on which Mary the Mother of God stood with downcast eyes and a ceramic halo many people believed radiated beatitude straight to heaven's door.

With Garrett's murder and a tsunami of gross vandalism popping up all over the city, Duff needed to clear his head. An already tense populace shuddered on high alert. The mayor personally instructed Duff to immediately check the grotto to make sure nobody had tampered with the statue.

"Make sure nobody's fucking with our girl," the mayor said.

"Beautifully put, your honor," Duff said.

Reporters from all over the country lit up City Hall phone lines ever since Pug Mahoney posted his first unhinged rant on Facebook. Every teenage nut and white nationalist in America was rooting for him to continue the blitzkrieg on minority invaders. On his last live stream, Pug wore a Trump t-shirt speckled with blood splatter and waved a brick-sized American flag while screaming "Thank you for your service" to nobody in particular. Anti-social media lunatics pushed his posts around the globe. Pug's disease went viral.

Junior Duggan, on behalf of "Bikers for Trump," issued a rambling press statement asking Trump to pardon Pug no matter what his crime or how many murders he might commit. "George Washington and the founding fathers killed people," Junior Duggan said in the statement. "This young man is just another victim of affirmative action driven crazy by reverse discrimination."

In response, scads of international online white supremacists goose-stepped into action. Waving swastikas in their own live Facebook feeds, they marched, saluted and threatened to come to Wilkes-Barre for a pro-Pug rally and cross-burning. A far-right contingent from Bavaria offered to visit and burn down a West Side Jewish deli. A Serbian commune of heavy metal goths promised to come to town for a nude blood wrestling orgy and defense fund rally.

The only goodness in this sordid mosh pit of revulsion came from a few courageous black, white, Latino and Asian kids at the high school multicultural club who contacted Duff saying Pug hated Garrett and had unjustly accused the best teacher they ever had of looking at him with bad intentions, the false result of a warped mind sinking fast.

Standing in this holy place dedicated to the most famous mother of all time, Duff thought about his own mother. Among lit candles and flamboyant floral displays, Duff took a seat on a cool concrete bench and wondered if he could convince his mother to leave this dirty old town and move with him to Florida. She was all about religion and goodness, healing and helping. Strong, Christian and packing what she called "a method to my madness," she lived life loaded with the Holy Spirit that filled her soul. Some years ago, a few days after he graduated with an Administration of Justice degree from Penn State Wilkes-Barre, when he grew brave enough to bring up the name he bore and despised, Duff asked his mother the big question.

"So what was the method to your madness when you named me Paddy?"

"Hush," Delores said.

"Why not a black name?"

Calling him Paddy was wrong, happening fast when the nurse stepped into her room that night and abruptly asked, "Miss Duffin, have you chosen a name for your baby so we can write up his birth certificate?"

A name for this child was far from her mind. Still medicated, she didn't remember what exactly she told the nurse when she accepted the small blue bundle. No matter what, this baby lived and breathed as her flesh and blood. In a moment of defiant freedom, Delores claimed full ownership of this wondrous consolation prize, deflecting white society's two-fisted control over black women who men of all colors treated like castaways. She refused to allow creation's circumstances to define her or her child. One day dear Paddy would learn the merciless origin of his life. One day he would hopefully forgive her for branding him the way masters branded slaves.

Duff's questions kept coming as he tried to dig up his roots.

"My father's first name was Paddy, wasn't it? Paddy's Irish, right? Like Patrick? Pat? He's white, isn't he?"

Delores stood silent. Smart as he was, he didn't know the meaning of the word. Few people used the archaic Paddy smear anymore. Parade day remained one of the few times you'd hear the word once used against the Irish when they came to America's shores a long time ago. Too bad black and white folks alike couldn't stop using another slur and calling her people "nigger" the way the father of her child cursed her that night nine months before Duff's birth after stopping her on the dark walk home from work at the all-night convenience store when her shift ended at 11.

"You want a ride?"

"No thank you," she said.

"Get in the car," he said.

What was she to do?

Noticing the crossed Irish-American flags on his lapel pin, she tried to make small talk.

"Are you Irish?"

"Full-blooded Paddy," he said, "and proud of it."

The first punch caught Delores in the eye with knuckles big as ham hocks, a balled fist that tore her retina beyond repair and would eventually require a glass eye. She tried to forget the beating. She tried to forget the trauma that followed. She tried to forget and failed.

"Hush," Delores said to Duff. "Let it go, baby."

The only other time Duff brought up his origin was the day he graduated from the police academy. Delores stood with him after the ceremony, holding her plastic purse, breathing heavily on a sweltering day and perspiring through her best bargain-basement dress. Duff seethed.

"All the other new cops are laughing at me and my name," he said.

"You're a grown man, Mr. Paddy 'Duff' Duffin," Delores said. "A brand new Wilkes-Barre police officer. Some things a person shouldn't know until a person needs to know. Some things a person never needs to know."

Delores dreaded telling him the truth.

Reacting with jagged defensive anger, Duff worried he disrespected his mother by pushing too hard on a day she should celebrate, searching for a live wire connection to the past she, for some reason, put to rest. This remarkable woman who gave him life and so much to live for deserved better.

"I'm sorry," Duff said.

Delores took his hand and kissed him on the cheek. Duff tried not to cry. No wonder Duff had given up on Christianity as easily as he had. Where was God when he needed him? Delores prayed daily over his harsh rejection of the body and blood of Christ. Not sure what he believed, he knew what he didn't believe. Like a Zen monk, Duff grooved on being alive and knowing it. Jaded as he was, the immaculate Catholic grotto touched him with its simple grace. A beacon of serenity for those who accepted its inspiration, the shrine provided peace to those willing to believe. Everybody needed to believe in something.

Duff wished his mother would retire. For too many years to remember, she worked cleaning houses for professional white people who lived on South and West River streets. Once this gaggle of pampered white ladies knew she worked hard and followed orders, they sometimes asked the same rude question like they owned her and could demand anything from her servitude.

"How did you lose your eye, dear?"

"Mad dog took it out when I was a child," Delores said in practiced chilly response.

"Oh, my," came the usual retort, answered in a typically appalled manner by which the snobs cloaked discomfort whenever unsightly matters of any kind came their way. Mystery and mirage played a major role in Delores' life. Secrets also ruled the obedient son who wondered about his mother's eye but stayed silent because he loved her too much to ask.

Duff wondered how people could hold true to faith when their prayers always went unanswered. Maybe that's why too many Christians seemed so mean. Duff wanted love. He wanted people to get along. But life usually got worse instead of better. When he mentioned moving, his mother said she was weak, getting old and didn't want to start over anywhere. Duff should leave, she said, step into the future with dignity. She'd give him her blessing. Burning out, Duff needed a new beginning. Rubbing his eyes, he sensed goodness in the Blessed Mother's backstory and knew his mother loved him more than she loved anything or anybody, the same way Mary loved Jesus in the Bible stories he knew by heart from childhood. When he thought about his invisible father he wondered if the man ever thought about him. Not once did Duff think his father might not know he existed.

Or want to kill him if he did.

EVOLUTION SOLUTION

Feeling the urge to hunt, Pug left his bunker, hiked into town, and climbed the crumbling metal steps of the abandoned structure adjacent to the former Stegmaier brewery. The building now served as bustling federal offices for a United States senator, the Social Security Administration and other elite white bureaucrats. Wilkes-Barre public officials are always white.

Sitting by himself in the bowels of the rusted metal shell that never got remodeled, he looked forward to drinking beer, popping pills, eating shoplifted cupcakes, searching the sky for favorite stars, and planning his getaway. The vacated property served for years as his home away from home, a fort where he and his former buddies smoked dope, joked, beat off and busted each other's balls.

Curious about the interior of the federal building, Pug went looking for a way to get in. Within a few minutes one dopey security guard smoking a cigar by an open door rushed around the side of the building in pursuit of a flaming feral cat. Pug torched the animal after dousing the critter with lighter fluid he used to start campfires and kept in his backpack. Up the stairs like a shadow, Pug soon balanced on the edge of an uneven roof that overlooked the brash lights of his town. Taking off his clothes, the anemic flesh of Pug's bare skin stood out against the moonlight. The smudged shamrock tattoo at the base of his skull radiated where his brain stem pulsed. After only six months, the cheap green ink had begun to fade. Pug's grasp on reality faded much faster.

Barefoot, his bony toes curled into talons as he struggled to keep from falling. A green plastic St. Patrick's Day derby he found in the garbage behind the Coal Hole perched precariously on the mutant teenager's head. Filthy fingers clutched the neck of a bottle of Lionshead pilsner, Pug's sixth beer of the evening. Tavern break-ins were easier than he thought. Living on the run juiced him more than laughing at his mother when she got drunk and sang along to the songs she loved listening to on the oldies radio station before she started her final retreat into her own head.

At 11:45 p.m. the time and temperature clock at the bank showed 40 degrees. Pug enjoyed the night air. Cold appealed to him. Blowing kisses at the sky, he taunted Mother Nature, imagining her naked and looking like Tiffany Trump, the dumb daughter everybody mocked, or the porn stars daddy Trump used to jump. Pug liked looking at porn online, fantasizing about making a video of Ivanka tied up with those long red neckties her father liked and almost tripped over when he got off Air Force One.

Pug howled his banshee howl.

When Binkee pushed her way into his thoughts he felt ashamed thinking about Ivanka. Grabbing at himself, Pug's pecker climbed in his pants like a snake in the Garden of Eden searching for a warm place in paradise. Lured by his own sickness he swallowed blood from the cut on his head that re-opened and started to ooze. Pain with purpose could be pleasant, especially for the victor. Pug finally won, picking up a girlfriend in the process. Murder turned him into a conqueror speeding through barriers of discomfort that always stunted his achievement. No longer would he succumb to misery. Pug welcomed torment as a gift.

Taking Garrett as a human trophy felt a hundred times better than killing small animals. God only knew the number of dogs, cats, hamsters and pet birds Pug poisoned, baked, buried alive, blew apart with fireworks, or tied to the bumpers of stolen cars and dragged down Brown Street in the Heights at four in the morning. Pug once stole a beer truck and drove to a farm in rural Sweet Valley where he struggled hacking a cow to death with a machete. He eventually wrestled the poor bovine to the ground and cut its throat.

Killing a black man felt better than all his previous bloodshed put together.

Now he loved animals. All God's beastly creatures found a place in his heart except for humans that made life miserable for people like him. Humans must pay for their transgressions. Pug thought about Noah saving the animals. Then he thought about God, the father. Pug would never forgive humans for they knew exactly what they did.

Maybe he'd get himself a bunny.

Binkee would love a bunny.

A thin grin stretched from one teacup-handled ear to the other. Frigid wind bit into his cheeks front and back, turning bare flesh the color of contraband cherry bombs ready to explode. Thrilled with death's kinship, Pug wallowed in its embrace. Homicide healed. Pug decided to lynch the next one, a necktie party with an extra-long Trump tie left over from his Ivanka bondage party. Trump might even pay his legal fees. Extermination is the greatest equalizer.

Scarlet flashes of mayhem surged against the walls of his head, making his eyeballs feel as if they might burst from the sockets. Pug briefly pondered his fate and what he had done, questioning what he had become.

Slamming his bony heels together, he stood rigidly at attention. Grabbing for his phone he fumbled to connect with Facebook Live, streaming and holding the camera at arm's length while he kicked into his now signature Irish dance drawn from the drunken jigs he watched his grandfather perform in the living room as the family clapped in unison so very long ago. Dancing with both arms held tight to his sides, the streaming view offered a bizarre window into heightened psychosis. Pug lost his breath in 30 seconds as the camera documented his shaky Irish-American lunacy in full meltdown mode.

As in all great causes, derangement frequently decides destiny. The American empire of the lost had crowned a new prince. Pug took a long swig of beer then danced again as countless Facebookers watched Wilkes-Barre's latest demon develop a following that rivaled the most popular death metal band. Mostly angst-ridden teenagers danced along to Pug's videos, loners snorting meth, drinking beer, vaping, binging anti-depressants, and screaming insults at a planet spinning out of control as they posted all night online about their new savior. Facebook comments captured countless young teens vowing to grow up to be just like Pug Mahoney.

"Our Jesus," wrote one frenzied fan on a page dedicated to Pug.

"White Powered by Trump," wrote another.

Adjusting his plastic derby Pug pranced in small pixie circles. Reversing direction his face registered determination as he lifted one knee and kicked his leg toward the horizon. Surprisingly agile for a maniacal addict, Pug kicked his other leg, sending his foot waist high. Dancing as fast as he could finally tripped him up, sending him sprawling on his back where he stretched out breathing in the staggered gasps of a frantic man.

Pug shut down the phone.

"Show's over," he said.

With wide eyes scanning outer space, he saw his father's face amid blurred constellations. Last month's super argument started so simply. All Pug wanted was to watch a shark special on the Discovery Channel. Martin Mahoney wanted to watch "The Molly Maguires," his favorite movie starring Richard Harris and Sean Connery that he had seen dozens of times.

"C'mon, Dad, you can watch the Mollies anytime." Pug said, trying to be nice and feel part of a normal family. "My show is a real documentary about how humans might have come from sharks or other kind of fish. Like we swam around for millions of years, then crawled out on the sand and climbed trees and came down when it was safe and started walking around looking for something to eat. It's not that simple, I know. But that's why I want to watch the show to learn, OK, Dad?"

Momentarily numb, Mahoney gawked and frowned at his only begotten son. Pug sat at the dining room table smiling above a soup bowl loaded with multi-grain Cheerios he was eating for supper. Pug so much wanted to show his father he wasn't as dumb as he looked that he blushed.

"Don't talk that blasphemous shit in my house," Mahoney said.

Seriously puzzled, Pug looked up.

"What?" he asked sincerely.

Mahoney placed his Guinness can on the TV tray, pushed off the worn recliner, and walked to the big book shelf where he displayed his collection of a half dozen round metal beer trays waitresses used to serve beer in bowling alleys during the 50s and 60s. Choosing a Gibbons tray, Mahoney walked to Pug's side and without warning slammed the flat side of the tray against the side of his son's head. The shot connected so hard Pug spit a mouth full of little Os and sugared milk all the way across the plastic tablecloth. When Pug's face slammed against the table, a broken front tooth dangled from loose skin behind his upper lip. Mahoney roared like a wounded bull elephant.

"God made man. After all I've done to set a good example, a moral fucking example, my own flesh and blood is telling me I'm descended from a fish sandwich? We're Roman Catholics here. Evolution does not exist in this house. You got that? God lives here. God rules here, goddammit."

The assault sent Pug closer to the edge than ever, rattling chemicals and battered passions that were unstable to begin with. Boiling with rage, he spotted his father's long retired aluminum softball bat leaning against the wall in the corner. Resisting the urge to slam his father so hard in the kidneys the old man pissed blood for a week, Pug kicked his chair from the table and stood hyperventilating with clenched fists.

Dropping the National Enquirer story she was reading about a woman who gave birth to triplets who all looked like former Vice President Joe Biden, including the girl, Bridget gasped. She blessed herself and covered her face with her hands. Mahoney stared at his son, recognizing apocalypse in his offspring's eyes.

"Out, out, out of my house," Mahoney said.

Life as Pug knew it ended. Momentarily feeling like bursting into tears and running to his mother's side, he placed both hands firmly under the edge of the table top. Facing Bridget with a tame look that only further alarmed her when she peeked, Pug turned over the heavy antique table and ran for the door.

That night led to this night.

Struggling to his feet, Pug reeled and raced to the edge of the building where he balanced on one foot and then the other. Closing his eyes he wondered how it must feel to soar as an avenging angel, swooping on those who deserved to die. Maybe he could convince the Discovery Channel to make a documentary about him. Stepping back from the brink, his stomach growled.

"I sure could eat a fish sandwich," he said.

Dressing, he left the building and headed to the McDonald's

dumpster looking for Binkee and a couple of day-old filets.

A LITTLE SECRET

Alone at the kitchen table, O'Brien drank a wee Kilbeggan whiskey from a water glass. Zoned out after another day on the job, he allowed his mind to wander like an abandoned soul trying to escape purgatory. O'Brien hated being a cop. He hated the Irish Guys. But one thought about Irish America stuck in his head more than any other.

What's with the Blarney Stone?

Real Irish people in Ireland must express great awe at the Irish-American obsession with kissing the Blarney Stone. Men, women and children tourists getting their pictures taken upside down with their lips attached to the cold moss-infested stone at Blarney Castle in 2020 must amaze even the most skeptical native.

"Let me tell you a little Irish secret, O'Brien," said a senior member of the Irish police force An Garda Siochana one year in Philadelphia at a "Defending Police Brutality" international law enforcement conference. "Each night when the pubs close, local hooligans converge on the castle staircase, climb to the top, and piss on the stone like their kidneys had no tomorrow. Fresh piss aged for a few hours to greet the fine tastes of visitors who anticipate the gift of gab after a grand taste of the liquid excrement."

Together the brother officers roared with laughter, sharing the ancient secrets of the Gael that no CIE tour bus driver would ever tell the mobs of Irish-American sightseers who flock to the castle each year. No, these terrible truths would only be shared with those who deserve to know. But when O'Brien got home, none of the "Irish Guys" believed the Garda's story.

"You're making that up," Mikey Hoyle said.

The few who did take him at his word held the truth against him.

"Why would you tell me something like that? My mother kissed the Blarney Stone," Mayor McAnus said.

Fewer people would have hated O'Brien had he admitted breeding with an Irish Setter. Some might have been more forgiving of that act of animal husbandry. After all, a setter's a good-looking dog. But screwing with the Blarney Stone? In Trump Town, some things are sacred whether they warrant that status or not.

For now, though, like it or not, the Irish Guys was all O'Brien had left. If he was honest, and he avoided that quandary at all cost, he had to admit living life as a full-time Irish Guy at the Coal Hole made life worth living. Wearing the official bar t-shirt even felt good. Printed in bold green letters across the front, the shirt said: "Coal Hole Tavern." Across the back in bigger print the shirt said: "Where every day is Paddy's Day and all the drinks are free."

The motto was bullshit, of course. A lump of coal is not a black diamond. But in the mind of any truly committed Irish Guy, even O'Brien, every day was Paddy's Day. So what if all the drinks weren't free. The obedient loved their identity. All the guys felt more at home in the beer garden than they did at home, a refuge where they accepted limitations the way wounded soldiers accepted Purple Hearts at a time of war. Aligned against forces of darkness beyond their control (primarily people of color abetted by an increasing number of white women who threatened to think for themselves but rarely followed through), Irish Guys fought tirelessly each day in an Irish-American class struggle, a war against liberals who disrespected everything in which the Irish Guys believed.

One accepted academic premise defines politics as the way people live. Everything is political. Anybody who tells you otherwise, especially a politician, is either stupid or lying. Either way, the Irish Guys fought constantly for their right to dwell to the very end in impenetrable foggy dew.

An act as simple as playing the juke box created a soundtrack for their personality-disordered driven world. Most Irish Guys still valued old-time Bing Crosby, John McCormack or Dennis Day singing Irish tunes from the past. The same songs played in the neighborhood forever. Mixed drinks like a highball (ginger ale and Four Roses whiskey) cost $1.50 in a small glass. And, as much fun as the tavern could be on a good night, it was mostly just another depressing escape with a dented out-of-order condom machine in the men's toilet and framed pictures of the Pope and John. F. Kennedy hanging behind the bar from bent nails pounded into the wall with a wooden pickax handle the bartender used to break up disputes.

Pennsylvania drinking age is twenty-one, of course, but the Coal Hole served some sixteen-year-olds as long as their Irish Guys fathers approved. Until recently, on-the-run maniac Pug Mahoney even occasionally stopped by the bar with his father, Martin. When Pug turned fifteen, the Irish Guys lowered their own already low bar and agreed he was old enough to drink draft beer and bet the ball games with the house bookie.

"Now you're like us," his father said, "old enough to lose."

Friday night was Texas line dance lesson night with a teacher who owned the polka school that went out of business. Saturday was karaoke. O'Brien once brought down the house and won first prize by showing up in blackface to sing "Sexual Healing" by Marvin Gaye. And, on the third Tuesday of each month, the Irish Guys met to brainstorm about their Paddy's Day parade float for the upcoming year. Planning the float took all year with the result inevitably taking shape as a variation on the float from the previous year.

Numbskull conversations occurred nightly at the bar. No topic including religion, politics or sports was immune to a barrage of misstatement, error and blatant lies the Irish Guys swore were true. Only their gall matched their drunken know-it-all lunacy. In the old days, when people acknowledged shame in themselves, very few held stupidity in high esteem. You knew better than to get into an argument or conversation that was clearly over your head. Now these dumb bastards wore their ignorance on both sleeves and, in winter, the flap of their long underwear.

For example, O'Brien knew Trump was a blockhead. But these guys, his brothers in the struggle, were Trump voters all their lives, way before Trump came along. Trump just showed up one day and told the idiots they were finally free to go, to roam the land like bog zombies and eventually vote him into office as president. The time had finally come to wallow in brainlessness. Back-up was always on the way and they never walked alone. In some ways they were the most dangerous men in America.

If this year's Nobel Prize winner in physics walked into the

Coal Hole and brought up nuclear fission, the first Irish Guy to challenge established scientific knowledge would quickly be joined by one, two and three more Irish Guys offering their own opinionated reinforcement, ganging up on intellect like hyenas attacking a baby calf. Without a college degree between them they would easily handle topics of thermonuclear matter and the intricacies of climate change denial. When the Nobel winner left in disbelief at what he had just experienced, the Irish Guys would buy each other drinks until closing time, telling the tale until the end of time about how they showed that know-it-all egghead who was boss in his ivory tower.

To an Irish Guy student of hard knocks, going to the Coal Hole on any given night was more impressive than going to King's College for five or six years to graduate with a criminal justice bachelor's degree.

And the Irish Guys got better jobs.

O'Brien poured another whiskey, bigger this time.

"Love it or leave it," he said. "Count me out."

WHEN WE'RE AT OUR WORST

P ug pondered what kicked off his one-man race war.
Like most of what went wrong with America, blame the niggers.

"So, Mr. Sean Mahoney, how would you like me to write you a letter of reference so you can enroll at the community college?" Moses Garrett asked Pug when he found him lurking near the high school gym doors. "I wrote you one for the part-time supermarket job. How about college?"

"Call me Pug. I hate my Christian name. I quit the supermarket job. I'm quitting school. Fuck the community college," Pug said.

Garrett tried to get through. A vibrant brain lived beneath this young man's rebellion. Garrett wanted to help. Creativity dies unless the muse is nurtured.

"We can hook you up if we work at it," Garrett said. "After two years, if you apply yourself, maybe Penn State. You're a born English major, man. These poems of yours show serious promise. Authentic moodiness burns in your work. That's where the magic starts, sometimes, in the darkest fog on the loneliest nights."

Snatching the notebook Garrett held out, Pug snapped.

"Where'd you get my stuff?"

Garrett stayed cool.

"You left them in the restroom. Your name's on the notebook."

Pug saw the soft-spoken teacher as nothing more than a pretty boy coming on to him, using college as a means to get close. Pug failed to see any other reason why the man would take an interest in his private thoughts, a black man, no less, more likely interested in his private parts.

Garrett truly believed he could help. The kid had a shot at college, Garrett explained to his wife that night as they sat on the couch watching the news on MSNBC. The next day he called Pug's father to try to enlist him in the cause of higher education for his son.

"I know a mind is a terrible thing to waste, Garrett," Mahoney said. "So how about concentrating on your own kind? With all the trouble you people get yourselves into, I'm not sure what advice you can offer my son."

You people.

Garrett knew real brains lurked behind problems that one day would eat this boy alive unless he got the help and encouragement he needed. But Garrett backed off, sensing how his concerns might backfire and create more turmoil at home than a teenager could resolve.

Juanita Garrett knew Mahoney hurt her husband's feelings. The softest man she ever met of any race, all Moses wanted was to share his intellectual gifts with people who understood how art in all its forms held the power to pacify the most unbridled beast. Recognizing a similar raw artistic expression he once discovered in himself, Moses Garrett felt a hunger for words thunder from each rugged line in the dozen or so verses he found in a lavatory stall. Pug called his poems, "Read This and Die," and signed his name in blood red letters, willing to take full credit or blame for the work. Struggling for years to write his own poems, Garrett dug deep inside himself for honest, positive images. When he finally located beauty in his feelings, hidden beneath the hatred and fear of life growing up in a housing project in South Wilkes-Barre, in a city he tagged "a gladiator pit for people like me," Garrett felt like he discovered buried treasure.

Maybe this young man would strike gold, too. But despite their smooth rhythm, a deeply sinister meter riddled the boy's poetic expression with stark tales of lightning strikes that killed a Brownie pack, a hit-and-run car accident that mangled five teenagers eating ice cream at a picnic table, a fatal alcohol poisoning at a first-grade dance, and bras that came alive and strangled feminists who refused to wear them. Suicide, gunfire and drug overdoses also appeared as major themes in Pug's work.

What scared Garrett most was the rich reality of the teenager's words. A poetry reading at a poetry slam downtown could have been an awesome outlet. But the boy was probably too far gone. Poetry is supposed to light a spark in people, not burn them alive.

Still, Garrett believed everybody is worth the effort. A few minutes of support might help suppress the violence in the images the boy described. Maybe he could help head off a piece of that temper that left unchecked one day would slay hope.

"Our words might be best when we're at our worst," he told his creative writing class students.

With work this kid might get it, channel chaos into something beneficial to him and others. Rhyme sometimes creates reason. Maybe Garrett would stand one day with Pug at a school assembly and read some of his own inept lines, just to show the students how to neutralize fear, turn anxiety into an advantage. Garrett wanted desperately to lead this invisible army of frazzled young teens struggling and lost in the city. He wanted to show them how to tap into identity. Public speaking of any kind always unnerved the introverted English teacher, but he kept working at bravery. Garrett really thought he could pull it off.

But when Garrett tried to talk with the poet, Pug grabbed his poems, gave Garrett a killer glare, and split.

Days later at the mini-mart they met again, Garrett buying two packs of sugarless gum and Pug creeping through the aisles. Decked out in cranberry suede loafers, a matching turtleneck, designer jeans and a black, double-breasted blazer with brass buttons, Garrett's fashionable appearance worried Pug that the teacher would flirt with him. The spook would want Binkee, too. Black sex fiends like Garrett swung both ways. Nobody fucked with Binkee and him. By now, Pug believed Garrett would try to get them snared in an international trafficking ring. Gorilla pimps and monster hookers would kill him and Binkee.

"Read any good poetry lately?" Pug asked in a voice smooth as chocolate pudding. Stepping from behind the potato chip rack carrying a handful of Slim Jims and a body loaded with adrenaline, Pug forced himself to smile.

Garrett stiffened.

"You still writing?" the teacher asked, nervous but committed to helping if and whenever he could, especially impressed when a youngster showed enough courage to step beyond his own hard luck to initiate a conversation .

Pug felt his brain prepping to explode.

"Yeah, a lot about how bad everything is," Pug said. "I'm reflecting on disorder and trying to make society better. I want to be a social justice poet, Mr. Garrett. Help people fight injustice with my words. Touch their thoughts with my thoughts. Connect, you know?"

Stunned, Garrett asked, "You serious, dude?"

"Serious as pulling the pin on a hand grenade," Pug said.

Garrett laughed out loud.

"My man," he said,

Pug grabbed a family-sized bag of barbecue chips and poured himself a black coffee from the pot on the counter. Then he shoved the chips back on the shelf when he went into his pocket for change and knew he was short. The Buck knife felt smooth against his fingers as they grazed the handle. The urge to pull the weapon and flip open the blade in one smooth practiced motion was almost too much to bear. Pug saw himself sliding the blade into Garrett's belly sharp side up, plunging the cold steel all the way to the hilt, twisting clockwise then counter-clockwise before withdrawing and maybe stabbing again, this time to Garrett's neck. Ninja style, he called the attack, although that description really made no sense. Pug just liked the way the words sounded.

"I'll take care of that," Garrett said.

He paid for Pug's chips, coffee and his own purchases. When they got outside, Pug stopped walking. He looked at the ground. Garrett grew concerned.

"Mr. Garrett, would you read my new poems sometime? Help me learn how I can get better at writing?"

"Of course I will."

"I buried my poems up the high school. I'm worried people will destroy them or make fun of me if they find them. Is it OK if we go get them?"

"A journey of discovery is always a worthwhile adventure," Garrett said.

Pulling onto South Wilkes-Barre Boulevard, Garrett took a

right on Hill, passing the church where he and his wife sang in the choir. Pug said he buried his poems "up the high school." As they drove, Garrett thought about how even college graduates in this part of the state constantly dropped the words "to" and "at" from basic simple sentence construction. Locals continually made fun of each other for the way they spoke even when they spoke that way themselves. Going "up the mall" became a running joke and just another way people perpetuated their negative self-image. Any number of people still ended sentences that asked questions with the construct "heyna," as in, "Nice day, heyna?" The term meant "isn't it so" as in "ain't" or "aynot" that Garrett believed might be drawn from early German or Pennsylvania Dutch. Garrett wasn't sure about the linguistic history of "heyna" but believed the sloppy usage originated with early immigrants from somewhere learning English language structure. "Heyna or no?" became another piercing example of self-deprecation and derision among people who used those words themselves.

Mockery molded Northeastern Pennsylvania.

Garrett thought too much and too deeply about the people who shared his small city. He had to know their background to help them dig out of the holes in which they lived. Both whites and blacks needed survival training. Latinos now moving into NEPA shaped a whole new force in the community. Other immigrants shaped a prismatic dynamic that could nurture or smother the future. Women of color particularly needed support in their increasing resistance to "the man." Still, white people felt most threatened by the cultural pecking order. As always, they presented the biggest impediment to improvement.

As a teacher and a black man, Garrett knew Trump made sense to Wilkes-Barre white people. They could see Trump, maybe even touch Trump. Trump cared. Trump understood. Trump would gladly die for their sins. Trump stood as one of them even though he had nothing in common with any of them. Yet, the people of this shattered city worshipped him. Trump appealed to them more than Jesus.

"Where exactly did you hide your poems?"

"Right there under the bleachers by the football field," Pug said.

The muscles in Pug's neck twitched as he fought to keep himself together for just a few more minutes. Garrett pulled behind the school building. Pushing the gearshift into park, he looked at Pug with tears in his eyes. Being nice paid off. As corny as it sounded, Jesse Jackson's words "keep hope alive" and Obama's slogan, "yes we can," rang like melodies in his mind when the bell tolled.

Abrupt pain and sharp pressure ripped into Garrett's right side. For a split second he had no idea he was being carved. He looked down and saw blood gush from the excavation Pug tore into his torso. Withdrawing the knife, Pug's second gash caught Garrett in the right side of his neck, below the external carotid artery, slicing through the external jugular vein in his neck. Reaching across Garrett's contorted face Pug slammed home a third blow with such power the thrust opened the internal carotid artery on the other side of Garrett's neck. Blood soaked the now dripping fabric of Garrett's cashmere turtleneck. Pug's prey never resisted. Garrett did not fight back. A victim of the times, the preacher said during the eulogy, Moses Garrett, a man of peace, practiced non-violence until the end.

Driving Garrett's car to the American Legion, Pug tuned the radio to the local news talk station and listened to another sorry host defend a Republican senator who wanted to dump poor people from their health care plans. Pug loved the host, because her unfeeling attitude toward minorities reminded him of a nurse at a Nazi death camp listening to violin music while pointing the way to the showers.

Popping the trunk after pulling into the deserted lot, Pug bound Garrett's hands and feet, leaving him exposed with the motor running, the four-ways flashing, and the doors open to draw attention to his work. That's when the idea of tagging the body like a big buck at hunting camp came to him. Reaching into his leather jacket pocket, he pulled out a metal campaign-type button he tore from a drunken college kid's sweatshirt last Paddy's Day. Pug pinched Garrett's skin between his thumb and forefinger. He stuck the sharp metal pin into his teacher's neck.

"You'll never be one of us," Pug said to the corpse. "But I'll make you an honorary Irishman just this once."

Race cleansing helped empower primacy. Killing Garrett purified Pug's soul. Destroying black success erased Irish failure. Kill old. Replace with new. Pug longed for a white American time the way Trump said society used to be, even if Pug had no idea what that was.

Stepping unseen into the shadows, Pug hiked five miles back to his coal mountain hideout, built a fire in the safety of the miners' shack, and cooked four boiled potatoes he stole at the supermarket. Eating them scalding hot in their jackets burned the roof of his mouth. Roughing it was fun. Yeah, fuck the community college. Loser lib professors would probably make him take an African-American studies course. He'd rather apply for a scholarship to work full-time as a Trump youth summer camp counselor.

Teach the new breed to hate.

Target the enemies of the people.

Make Trump king forever.

ROOM 69

When Martin Mahoney rushed into the Wilkes-Barre General Hospital that night 18 years ago, a well-meaning nurse asked if he wanted to help out in the delivery room. "Maybe I should marry my dog, too," he said.

Thirty minutes earlier the father-to-be was busy getting dressed to go to an Irish Guys sponsored boxing match where he was scheduled to be the ring announcer when he got the call from Bridget's bingo partner at the American Legion. The baby was on the way. Showing up at the hospital with beer on his breath in his rented tuxedo, Martin laughed and talked so loud that several nurses demanded he be quiet. Martin waited in the lounge with a half-dozen drunken buddies who started showing up after he called the Coal Hole to announce the event, telling anybody who would listen that accompanying his wife into the operating room and seeing her displayed in such a wide-open condition violated his religion. Any father who would film the event should get locked up on child pornography charges. Modest mother-to-be Bridget told the medical team she understood her husband's reluctance.

The next day Bridget carried baby Sean, soon-to-be called Pug, home to Anthracite Street. Her girlfriends on the narrow block where she and Martin lived hung bright orange, white and green crepe paper bows on the iron mesh gate that opened onto a cracked slate sidewalk. The men on the block constructed a cardboard sign from beer boxes they cut and taped together and displayed in the bay window of the modest stucco home. The sign said in green crayon, "Our Irish Eyes Are Smilin'. "

More broken gray slate slabs led to the front door of the Mahoney family's working-class dream, a plain house just like the other decrepit boxes built in the 1920s that predator real estate agents sold up and down block after block on street after street in traditional Wilkes-Barre neighborhoods. Life was a handyman's special made of stucco or wood covered in brown tarpaper supposed to resemble real bricks.

On the day of the wee one's homecoming, one Martin Timothy Mahoney, a very different man than the out-of-shape maniac who slugged his kid in the chops seventeen years later, oozed strength, pride and potential. Easily hoisting the 100-pound chunk of hard coal he kept in the basement for sentimental reasons for a few years, Mahoney lugged the block up the wooden steps and out into the middle of the bald front patch of yard without having to stop to catch his breath. Working for hours with a railroad spike and a ballpeen hammer, Mahoney carved the words "Erin go bragh," which he knew meant "Ireland Forever," across the face of the big black piece of coal. The inscription looked like a primordial cave drawing no scholar could decipher. But Martin knew what it said and loved his creation. He loved the chip off the old block as well. After chugging three cold beers one after the other, Martin dug a hole with his grandfather's antique pick from the mines and planted the huge piece of coal where he believed it would remain forever. The birth of his new son meant as much to him as the flag-raising on Iwo Jima meant to a grateful nation near the end of World War II.

That night when the christening party spilled out the front and back doors and off the porch into the street, celebrating with his buddies in the open air swathed Martin in pure joy. Eating dozens of spicy chicken wings, tossing the bones in the yard, and throwing his arms around Irish Guys' shoulders made him feel more in tune with the neighborhood and his heritage than ever. Listening in on the ladies' giggling and doing the dishes in the kitchen made him happy to be a family man. The phrase "family man" sounded just right, too, bouncing around his brain like a puppy running into walls on Christmas morning. Sniffling to hold back the tears, he knew the promise of the American Dream had finally come true for him, and that everything his grandparents worked for to raise their kids and their kids had done to raise theirs had paid off.

Standing alone in the front yard at 3 a.m., swaying in the cold wind, this brand new daddy thrilled to be a Mahoney living in Wilkes-Barre fell flat on his puss. Snoring as soon as his face hit the stray cinders he threw down on the driveway to get traction in the snow, he crawled a few inches and snuggled up beside the beautiful coal monument to his paternal prowess.

Dreaming of Ireland, Mahoney listened to the soft bleating of sheep, passed tiny thatched cottages on a bicycle, and called out to the old fellows stinking of bitter stout and rain-soaked tweed as they tipped their caps. Martin wept in his sleep from happiness and tipped his dream cap until he could tip no more. He awoke to the sound of car horns and the normal morning stretch of his block coming alive as it did every day, most days the same, without severe surprise, as they were meant to be lived among your own. Children laughed and cried, dogs barked and a sense of awe engulfed most of the men and women who settled there. Ah, sure, wasn't life grand? And wasn't his Bridget the grandest girl of them all?

When his dear wife wasn't able to wake him about 5 to come inside, she tossed his favorite itchy tan Army blanket across his body and placed beneath his head a faded pillow she took from a bent lawn chair. The Irish Guys had asked if Bridget wanted them to carry Martin upstairs to bed but she demurred, afraid her husband might get a panic attack if he awakened abruptly and thought he died and the pall bearers were already on the job. Bridget even wondered if Martin really wanted to sleep outside, engaged in some obsolete pre-Christian custom to be performed by a father on the night of his first son's birth. What did she know of such behavior? She was only a woman. Filling the barbecue grill with coal from the cellar, she lit a railroad flare, one from a boxful an Irish Guy city cop left for Martin to light the coal hopper when it went out. Sticking the lit flare into the pile of coal, Bridget built a nice fire near Martin's head so he would get some heat during the night.

"Bridget loves big baby Marty and little baby Sean," she whispered in his ear before going inside to rock her new bundle of bliss. Every hour or so, Bridget checked on her husband to make sure he seemed all right and hadn't stopped breathing because he rolled over and inhaled dirt from the yard. Running out and running back carrying Sean because she knew better than to leave a baby alone, she couldn't believe she could feel so happy. She laughed out loud at the thought of her big baby asleep in the yard. All that bubbly emotion made her feel fresh. Bridget knew the feeling couldn't last. At least she was married and now a mother. Happiness belonged to her no matter how long the spell endured. Some women wanted more. She wanted nothing. Satisfaction would keep her from sticking her head in the oven, turning on the gas burners, and lighting a match because she felt unfulfilled. A woman in Wilkes-Barre had to believe in herself or she was doomed. Bridget mostly believed in Martin and Sean. A baby and a husband was all she needed. A few rough years would likely come in the beginning, but they would pass.

Strong-willed and relatively smart, working full-time at the hat factory, Martin believed he and Bridget were on their way. But Martin wanted more, expected more. After all, he was a man, a real fucking Irishman just counting the days until he could buy a new television set and take a week's vacation at the New Jersey shore. Carrying his new bride over the threshold of the house where he was born and raised had given him immense pleasure. The home originally belonged to Martin's grandfather who left it to Martin's parents. One day Martin's father just stopped breathing from all the coal dust he inhaled into his lungs during his years working in the mines. Martin's mother died a few years later, fatally injured in a dress factory accident when an experimental sewing machine meant to cut back on labor costs exploded and sent a dozen needles into her face causing her to expire from shock and puncture wounds.

Mom left the house to Martin. At the time, he and Bridget had been going together for years after having first met at a church bazaar when they were 14 and playing the diocese-sponsored cash gambling games. A small wedding sufficed, performed by a beloved local priest with waxy lips, a hairpiece and a phony brogue. Martin's best man got so drunk at the social hall reception he threw up in the macaroni salad. All the Irish Guys laughed.

The honeymoon in the Poconos wasn't much fun, either. Martin's biggest accomplishment during the weekend was to keep from smacking Bridget when she told him to slow down on the beer at breakfast. The punch held until her birthday a few weeks later. Domestic violence on holidays was nothing new, but Martin promised himself he'd work on his self-control now that they were married. Still, Bridget had a knack for making him hit her.

Bridget spent a long and lonely afternoon horseback riding because Martin refused to go. Returning to the dark motel freaked her out when all of a sudden she feared Martin for the first time. He sat waiting for her with all the curtains drawn in a hot room swirling with blue-gray cigarette smoke. Still wearing the rented tuxedo jacket from the day before, the groom sat barefoot in front of the television, watching Barney Miller re-runs and wearing boxer shorts, farting and burping and telling Bridget that before she got too comfortable she might want to run across the road and pick up a couple more six packs and some jumbo hard-boiled eggs the hillbillies sold from an uncovered bowl on the bar. He remembered the bar from when he drove up there one year with one of the Irish Guys for a union meeting about the strike they never had at the hat factory. Trying not to cry as she backed out the door, Bridget almost got hit by a tow truck as she stumbled rushing across the two-lane highway. Inside the bar, ruined men in faded flannel shirts leered as she waited to order the beer. A woman with a Mohawk haircut asked Bridget if she wanted to dance to an Aerosmith song playing on the juke box. Biker chicks at the bar mocked and imitated her when she got confused by the beer brands. Somewhere a dog cried. Petrified she'd get run down by an 18-wheeler, Bridget closed her eyes when she raced back across the macadam, falling on the double yellow line and tearing skin from her knee.

"It's good the eggs are hard boiled," Martin said as she burst into the room looking for a hug. He popped another Budweiser, cracked an egg shell on his forehead, and turned up the volume on a Phillies spring training game from Clearwater, Florida.

"I put all our wedding cash on the game," he said.

"The baby's college fund money?" Bridget said.

Surprising herself by speaking up, she headed into the bathroom where she got sick to her stomach on the smell of cheap knotty pine toilet cleaner. Martin got so drunk he couldn't follow the bouncing baseball or hold onto the five hard-boiled eggs that rolled from his lap when he passed out.

Room "69," the honeymoon suite at the "Dear Lodge," came with a pink heart-shaped toilet but no champagne glass-shaped hot tub like the more expensive resorts cut deep in the mountains that found the love business on hard times at the turn of a new century. This love nest boasted a vibrating bed for a quarter and plastic cups and wire hangers in a closet that lacked a door or curtain. Nothing distinguished the place as a honeymoon spot other than a well-thumbed copy of a nudist magazine Bridget found in the bureau drawer beside the Bible.

When the dry heaves stopped, Bridget sat on the bed and read brochures from some of the nicer tourist places. She imagined herself in a turquoise one-piece bathing suit, lounging poolside at one of the places where they hadn't registered. Letting her mind wander for a few seconds, she fantasized sitting naked in a champagne glass with John Travolta, but immediately bowed her head in shame and launched into a litany of Hail Holy Queens for a half hour to overcome her mental sin of the flesh.

> Hail, Holy Queen, Mother of mercy,
> our life, our sweetness and our hope.
> To thee do we cry, poor banished children of Eve:
> to thee do we send up our sighs,
> mourning and weeping in this valley of tears.
> Turn then, most gracious Advocate,
> thine eyes of mercy toward us,
> and after this our exile,
> show unto us the blessed fruit of thy womb, Jesus.
> O clement, O loving, O sweet Virgin Mary! Amen.

Of course, Bridget had no idea what clement meant. Taking her wedding vows seriously, she tried her best to love Martin. Once pregnant, she wept with joy, convinced the baby would be the turning point. She almost couldn't talk through the tears when she broke the news to Martin who pumped his fists in the air and ran around in little circles.

"Yes, yes, yes," he said.

A beaming Bridget closed her eyes for a kiss. Finally life would go her way. Evading her outstretched arms, Martin grabbed his cap and blackthorn stick and high-tailed it out the door, skipping down the street to the Coal Hole where he found the bar loaded with laughing Irish deadbeats enjoying their Saturday afternoon.

"Drinks for the house," Martin said.

Boasting of his manhood and enough muscle in his genes for his soon-to-be born "great white hope" seed to one day win the heavyweight boxing championship of the world, Martin blew the grocery money and the electric bill while Bridget hugged the porcelain bowl in the tiny bathroom upstairs.

After fifteen years of rather unspectacular predictability passed in their marriage, Chinese investors based in New York bought the hat factory and let Martin go. Qualifying for unemployment, he collected for the next year. Not once did he think about the damage he did by pilfering the small savings Bridget collected from her part-time cosmetics sales and stashed in a tea pot in the cupboard. Security guard jobs came and went, one at the dog food factory and another at an automotive warehouse where he slept off his hangovers on piles of truck tires.

One night out of sheer frustration, Bridget smashed the ceramic soft-boiled egg holder decorated with tiny shamrocks she bought Martin one Father's Day. Scrambled devastation pointed to the signs of more breakage to come. Unraveling came easy to any man with a ball of green twine for a brain. After landing yet another low wage security guard job, this time at a hospital where, until he lost the job, Martin wore a blue sport coat from Sears and a paisley polyester necktie and called himself a professional, he focused on becoming more and more disjointed from everything he despised about his life. That meant pretty much everything except the Irish Guys.

Now, though, he was getting the shits of them, as well, and decided the time had come for a makeover. First the goatee, then the Irish rebel music blasting at all hours of the day and night, followed by an arsenal of guns and ammunition. Booze and fantasy took center stage in Martin's mind. He strongly hinted around town that he had joined an active service unit of the Irish Republican Army even though the blessed IRA had many years earlier decommissioned their weapons and stopped operations to work political magic through the Sinn Fein political party. The IRA never operated in the United States, anyway, but none of the Irish Guys knew that. Zooming in with all the expectations of a Derry dissident group's surface-to-air missile plan to take out Buckingham Palace, the Green Hand took root in his mind.

His own Irish Guys should have jumped at the chance to join up and get even with the corporations that screwed them not to mention the niggers, Jews, illegals, refugees, Syrians, Mexicans, anchor babies, feminists, the press and every other freak who made life miserable for good God-fearing Irish Americans like himself.

The Irish Guys passed on the chance to organize and get even.

Mahoney would fight this war alone.

THERE'S A CHILD IN HERE

Loving Pug forged an awesome dilemma for Binkee.

A relationship with him was like waking up after a blackout drunk with rats in your bed. But love Pug she did. Calling herself a hopeless romantic, she once stood on Public Square in a snowstorm holding a homemade cardboard sign that said "Hugs for the Homeless."

In a wrinkled olive-colored Army raincoat and her favorite t-shirt from the secondhand shop (a Woodstock knock off with a dove perched on the neck of a guitar), Binkee stunk of harsh body odor. Holes in the knees of her jeans signaled wear and tear, not fashion. In ripped black Converse high-top sneakers without socks, she sat on a rock under the Market Street Bridge by the river gripping her knees tightly to her chest. The thin coat with faded sergeant's stripes sewn on the sleeve wasn't nearly heavy enough to cut the chill and keep her warm.

She called the rock her lucky rock, where she sat in the summer dangling her pale bare feet in the oily Susquehanna, trying to think happy thoughts. Now her thoughts turned mournful. The breeze brought a shiver and goosebumps on her arms. Feeling low and ugly, she sometimes heard homeless alcoholics fighting in their tent camps by the bridge, cursing their losses to anyone who might help beat their misery. When anxiety hit, muscles in her throat constricted involuntarily. Sweat dripped from her forehead. Taking deep breaths to calm herself like she read about in the yoga magazines she shoplifted at Wegman's supermarket, she fought to keep from suffocating. Worried she might die from the CIA poisoning the sunshine and killing all the flowers, Binkee struggled to keep from passing out.

Cookie at the hot dog shop seemed to understand. Lately, though, she seemed barely able to handle her own tough life. Cookie offered Binkee lunch for free whenever she stopped by. Worried Cookie might pity her, Binkee always turned her down. So she stopped for a glass of water every few days and ate one hot dog bun with ketchup and no hot dog. Cookie pitied her more than ever.

The boss ordered Cookie to cover up the tattoo she wore on her ankle, a very cool peace sign about the size of a beer bottle bottom she showed Binkee one day. All psychedelic purple, blue, green, yellow and red, the tattoo started a conversation about love. Despite their age difference, each believed in love. No generation gap could come between their common goal of peace and love.

The day Binkee first saw Cookie's tattoo, she said, "I can't wait to get my own mark. Like maybe a rising sun on my shoulder or a butterfly or a piece of French toast with a square of melted butter. I love French toast. I want to pierce my nipples. Shave my head. Go to Nepal. Make a baby with a lama. Have a pet baby llama. They're two different kinds, you know."

Cookie reached across the counter and gently took hold of the teenager's shoulders.

"Whoa, whoa, whoa," she said. "Your future should be simple, easier."

Cookie wasn't sure she could save her.

"A monk's baby? Really? All three of you running around the monastery with shaved heads? Riding llamas? The ink can wait. Trust me. You're groovy and pretty already."

Together they laughed. For a few seconds Binkee and Cookie felt light, like they could fly. Then Binkee heard the boss' harsh voice from the back of the restaurant that slammed into their hippie head trips. When Cookie jumped Binkee smelled fear.

"Hey, Little Miss Ex-Convict, quit bullshitting with the juvenile delinquent and make a fresh pot of coffee," the boss said. He walked to the front of the shop. "Unbutton another button on your blouse while you're at it. Boobies make for better business."

Embarrassed for Binkee and herself, Cookie reddened.

"There's a child in here," she said.

The boss walked back to his office where his work involved sucking cigars and cheating on his state sales taxes as well as his wife. Binkee felt terrible for Cookie. She felt sorry for herself.

"Bye, Cookie," she said. "Sorry."

Back under the bridge that night, a skinny drunk kicking up

embers running through a campfire screamed about feeling better in Iraq. His trauma propelled Binkee's thoughts deep into the moment. Pushing up the tattered sleeve of her coat, she looked at her right wrist. A jagged, blood-crusted line had finally stopped bleeding. Binkee made the cut by dragging the sharp end of a nail across the weak thinness of her arm. Even if she mustered the guts to finish the do-it-yourself tattoo attempt, Binkee doubted all the letters of Pug's name would fit. Feeling even more like a loser, Binkee knew she wasn't brave enough to kill herself. So she cried some more, wondering how long it would take for the scar in the shape of a capital letter "P" to disappear forever the way she was sure Pug had disappeared forever from her life.

The next day Cookie looked out the dirty restaurant window and spotted Duff headed for the front door. Every time she saw him walking her way she worried she was going back to jail. Stress and anxiety stalked her. Working and living in Wilkes-Barre had become too much of a burden. Her parents long ago divorced and she saw her mother occasionally. An alcoholic who worked part-time at a pet washing business, she, too, had become a terrible burden. Not that her mother was ever any help. And, when the judge sentenced Cookie for killing her husband, her mother showed up intoxicated in court. Cookie asked her to stay home in the future. So she did, pretty much for good.

As much as Cookie hated to admit it, she hated living in Wilkes-Barre and hated herself for feeling that way, for turning her back on her hometown. Falling short of her basic expectations, any decent future might have already passed. Ashamed, no matter how hard she tried, Cookie felt worthless. Used. No matter what she did, she believed she'd never feel smart enough or whole enough to let Duff know how much she cared for him. A good man to be sure, a role model and inspiration, Duff always treated her with respect.

In the eyes of her neighbors, she could throw herself in front of the Pope to take an assassin's bullet and her sacrifice wouldn't be good enough to make up for her past. Not that she would save the Pope even if she could, with all his raving encyclicals targeting and hurting women for using birth control, getting abortions, and wanting to be priests. Still, after what had happened to her, after what she did, she would never be worthy of a man like Duff. What good man would want her? Who would trust her? Who wouldn't be afraid? Look what happened to the last man who took her in?

Timmy Joyce worked as a county prison guard and hit her about twice a week for two years. Once he threw boiling water on her because she overslept and didn't get up to wish him luck when he left early on an Irish Guys casino trip to Atlantic City. After the 11 o'clock news on the night of their fifth anniversary, Cookie shot him once in the back of the head with his deer rifle as he slept drunk on the couch with blood on his knuckles from her face. On the bad advice of a cocaine-addicted lawyer, Cookie went for a guilty plea to involuntary manslaughter. A jury might have acquitted her, but probably not. Cookie served every day of her sentence in the county jail where her late husband once worked. The judge ordered her to report to a parole officer when she was released.

Wilkes-Barre was a town where people believed women asked for it whatever "it" happened to be, that women asked for whatever they got that was bad. Either they drank too much, dressed too little, or tried to think too hard for themselves. How many times did Cookie hear, "Why didn't you just leave?"

Born and raised in a typically myopic Irish-Catholic family, she married Timmy because he was Timmy and she was Cookie, actually Eileen Brennan, who picked up the nickname when she won a Thin Mint eating contest at Girl Scout camp. They went to the senior prom together. She put off college. They broke up and got back together. He joined the Army and went AWOL. She worked various bartending jobs and lived alone. Eventually they married, separated, got back together again. Timmy fought other drunks in bars and lifted weights with other prison guards who were mostly sons of Irish Guys and eventually Irish Guys themselves. Timmy once took her by the hair and shoved a gun in her mouth. Pregnancy followed his tearful apology. Blessed be Planned Parenthood. A smart, sensitive woman counselor directed Cookie to a clinic where she terminated the condition she never would have carried to full term even if her life depended on it, which it probably did.

Now Cookie worried about Binkee, who had more heart and brains than most men twice her age. Guess she was asking for it, too. Bound for juvie detention, a variety of adolescent behavioral units, or the morgue, Binkee probably wouldn't make it. She kept running from foster home after foster home, getting tougher and harder along the way. Maybe she'd survive only to grow up chained to an unhappy marriage, abused and beaten into submission for the rest of her life. Maybe she'd gun down her husband, too. Cookie didn't know how to save herself let alone a teenager she loved who broke her heart every time she saw her on the street.

Just knowing Duff helped her survive. He knew her husband and accepted what had happened when she pulled the trigger. Duff stuck by her from the beginning. Visiting her in jail, he believed she acted exactly the way the battered woman syndrome expert testified in court battered women act when fighting for their lives and defending themselves. Killing Timmy involved pure self-defense. Duff definitely got that but didn't want Cookie to think he liked her as a charity case. Duff respected her, thought he might love her. Cookie worried Duff had legitimate doubts. Everybody had doubts about Cookie. Why should he be different?

"Good afternoon, officer," she said when Duff opened the door. "You got a warrant?"

SALMON WISDOM

Martin Mahoney lived as the best Irish role model he could be. A middle-aged loser with a bad back that kept him from real work, Martin grudgingly accepted part-time employment at the Coal Hole, doing odd jobs under the table for the club and making enough money to pull together a meager weekly paycheck. The back was bad, all right, but not bad enough to keep him from changing kegs at the bar and rolling a quarter barrel of lager through the front door of his house each Friday morning that would last him a week. From a barren little outpost against the world, he carved out his paramilitary operation. Comparing his resistance to authority to the Boston Tea Party, Mahoney advocated open defiance to the system that ate away real rights from most Irish Americans, white people with no privilege, people like him whose ancestors civilized the nation. Through talk radio Mahoney publicly espoused dying for his country the way the great patriots of Ireland died for theirs. Weak-kneed radio hosts loved him. One crackpot invited him into the studio for an hour-long interview.

Yet Martin still encountered difficulty trying to grasp his heritage. Unlike most of his scatterbrained bar buddies, Mahoney had not given up trying to sense deeper meaning in being Irish. Attending plays, lectures and concerts usually at the colleges loaded with Irish stuffed shirts and conniving priests, he paid attention but often didn't get the point. Reading books and relevant newspaper articles only added to his bewilderment. As much as he wanted to comprehend the roots from which he and his family grew, Mahoney felt lost. The man was in way over his head.

Although Martin still frequented second-rate Irish cabarets that came to the performing arts center downtown, he concentrated mostly on drinking and hanging out with other balls of confusion, guys he'd known since childhood. Not much changed over the years. Bravado masked cowardice. Volume replaced victory. The Irish Guys agreed they were better off loud and noticed than silent and ignored, words to live by that made them their own best audience and their own worst enemies.

Boisterous pals who shared varying degrees of superficial pride in their Celtic hoariness, they couldn't understand why Martin now seemed aloof, no longer interested in the tribe. He paid his monthly club dues, bought hundreds of tickets to the sports betting pools, and helped organize the yearly clambake. He attended most meetings. Actually his contribution was more than adequate. Irish Guys generally asked for very little and usually got less.

Mostly, despite his increasing bitterness, Martin enjoyed the Irish movies. "The Quiet Man" was his favorite, a wondrously hackneyed film that validated everything Irish Guys believed about being Irish. A classic movie starring John Wayne and Maureen O'Hara, Martin and the boys loved the part where the Duke manhandles his woman, imposing his will, and dragging her up and down the soft hills of County Mayo by her left arm with a handful of red hair and jacket collar as she bites the dust and goes face-forward into the dirt. Our man pushes and pulls and kicks her square in the behind.

"That'll show her who's boss," Martin said every time the scene played.

Without fail, that part in the movie caused the Irish Guys to cheer during the once-a-month showing in the Coal Hole backroom where they relived all the preconceived notions it took to regenerate the Quiet Man myth and mission. To them, more truth flowed from that one scene than all the salmon wisdom that ever leaped from where the river Shannon flows.

Despite the hoopla, though, living the Paddy dream was losing its luster. Even the high holy parade march was starting to wear thin, the procession in which Martin and Pug participated every year since Pug was born. When the kid was just a baby Martin dressed him like a potato and carried him on his shoulder or stuffed him in the carriage the Irish Guys made from empty beer boxes. The crowd went silly with glee when the baby waved.

Ah, what a time they had. A front page photo of father and son appeared in the Times Leader newspaper on eight separate occasions. "The Littlest Shamrock" read the cutline beneath the first picture taken when Pug was three months old and his old man in a burst of drunken exuberance accidently used latex house paint to brush a shamrock on the top of Pug's smooth bald baby head. It took Bridget a month to completely scrub the child's dome clean, waiting, of course, for the skin rash to disappear and heal. After much wailing and threatening to leave, Bridget reluctantly agreed not to call child welfare authorities or invite the new young parish priest over to the house and show him how St. Pat's glorious symbolic representation of the Father, Son and Holy Ghost (plus an extra leaf due to Martin's sheer drunken stupidity that often caused him to lose focus and turned the plant into a four-leaf clover) was being used by dim bulbs who never seemed quite able to shine or discern divine civilization from the consequences of unholy libation.

Martin carried that newspaper picture with him in his wallet everywhere he went. Pug carried it, too. Among the Irish, pride is a strange commodity. So is patriotism. Put them together somebody might die.

As far as Mahoney was concerned he had done more than his share to preserve the past. Now he worried about salvaging the present. With disrespect in full sway, Mahoney believed his country and his city were on the ropes. Blaming the usual suspects, during talk radio calls he recommended rounding up blacks, Jews, Muslims, feminists, even midgets and anybody else who disagreed with his paranoia. Lackey hosts sometimes tried unsuccessfully to wrestle him back to views of limp moderation but feared losing their jobs when rinky-dink white-bread advertisers called their bosses to complain. Mahoney knew exactly what was best for him and his kind. What was best for him and his kind was him and his kind. Birthright meant everything. Ritual ruled.

Ever since Pug turned 14, in addition to marching in the Paddy's Day parade, he and his father shared a tradition of guzzling green beer from a shallow garbage pail of nostalgia. After the parade, Pug would accompany his dad to the church social hall ham and cabbage dinner to surreptitiously sip from a foamy pitcher, slurping from the trough like Paddy's pig on an old country family farm. Pug drank because his father said he could. Wearing his green plastic derby, Pug sipped and sipped. Nobody called out Martin for pumping his severely underage kid with brew as long as they were discreet, didn't get sick or break anything, including bones. Underage drinking created few problems within the circled wagons of their closed culture. Outsiders need not apply. Convinced that such special occasions, illegal or otherwise, reinforced much needed white male supremacy, Martin considered these turning point events to be legitimate child rearing practices to which a higher power had granted immunity from man-made law. Most men and some women throughout hard coal country agreed. They knew more about raising their kids than teachers, judges or social workers.

Nicknaming the kid "Pug" seemed like a brilliant idea at the time. In the sweet language of the Gael, what sounds like "puga mahone" means "kiss my ass." As the only real Irish language expression Martin knew, he long ago made the phrase his family motto. It only made sense to play off the family surname and give his first born son a calling card people would remember. As you would expect, all the Irish Guys loved the nickname. With their worship of prizefighting, especially white ex-fighters like Jerry Quarry and Gerry Cooney, the boy's new handle automatically became "Pug" as in "pugilist" and amazingly close to "pog" in Irish. The similarity to "mo thoin" that sounded like "mahone" and fit the kid's legitimate surname exuded wisdom as well. Pug Mahoney would rule as a coal-fired prince of Ireland's greatest brood.

As expected, the Irish Guys argued for weeks about who first came up with the original idea to curse this child for life with such an inane brand. Thankfully, verbal disagreements usually turned to laughter at simpleton times such as these when the men turned yet another story into yet another legend. By midnight Mahoney could always be counted on to place his forehead in beer puddled on the bar while laughing and rolling his thick skull left and then right like his fat face was a fleshy thumb getting fingerprinted at police headquarters. Not a single Irish Guy at the bar would ever trade the overwhelming sense of belonging to this pack for any other world, class or distinction.

Upper class lace curtain Irish and other pseudo-cultured souls could argue that such irrationality was in itself a crime against civility. But the lace curtain crowd was bigoted, too. The only busing they endorsed involved Irish Guys' bus trips to East Coast Irish festivals with a tapped half keg on the bus and all the Galway cheddar and fatty baked ham sandwiches you could eat.

Martin clearly remembered how during the first ten years of Pug's life, the boy had been as much a club mascot as Balor, the Irish Wolfhound that slept by the Coal Hole door and tried his best to mind his own business. The poor dog, named after the legendary Irish giant armed with an evil eye he only opened to slay his enemies, hated the Irish Guys, but they fed him. As old as he felt, life was too far gone to change. Martin was tolerable when he filled Balor's bowl with Guinness and offered spicy beef jerky treats.

Martin provided Pug with his own little empty shot glass which the bartender filled with real beer. By the time Pug turned eleven he was tossing down several shots of beer a day. When he returned to the bar from the parade when he was 14, the Irish Guys presented him with his own seven-ounce beer glass. Pug achieved full-blown alcoholic status by 16. Although the club's bad behavior rubbed off, members agreed they'd rather Pug turn out to be a mean drunk than a sissy. Enough clannish little tough guys raised properly would once again allow their kind of Irish to rule the neighborhood, the state and the nation.

Irish Guys past, present and future felt entitled to an uneven playing field. Sports betting, sloppy bar fights, punishing tiny male heirs with belts and wooden paddles to instill discipline, low stakes dice games, the rare hooker in a moment of bachelor party weakness or spousal pregnancy, and the occasional light tap for the mouthy wife or girlfriend all helped uphold survival of the fittest, according to their unexpurgated code. Guys, Irish and otherwise, needed to stick together as society tried to shift them into an effeminate state. Muddled rules oppressed them more and more as Irish Guys fought the odds and steadfastly refused to become politically correct. They would say and do whatever they pleased.

Fuck everybody else.

Donald Trump understood their code better than anybody.

HEAVY LIFTING

As soon as Trump's re-election campaign got underway, not only did the Irish Guys get worse, their everyday dysfunction became dutiful. Every Irish Guy including Martin Mahoney felt obligated to work for Trump's second term in office, to pump every ounce of bold disgrace that flowed through their veins into Trump's aggressive push for more power. Endorsing him a second time meant endorsing themselves all over again. Trump's re-election would certify their defects as good conduct and increase their individual value as good citizens.

They loved Trump. They believed Trump loved them. Lies became truth and veracity loomed as too big a word to even try to use let alone understand. Even if Trump kicked the foreign owners out of the hat factory and brought back manufacturing tenfold, none of the Irish Guys or their descendants wanted those goddamn jobs anyway. They deserved better. They wanted city, county and state jobs. Mostly, they wanted no-show jobs that acknowledged their political clout to get paid but not work in the first place. Believing in Trump felt better than believing in God. One Irish Guy even named his newborn daughter Maga, as in "Make America Great Again." If Trump threatened to nuke Wilkes-Barre, the Irish Guys would volunteer to push the button.

Despite lacking organization, as second and third-generation registered Democrats they showed up every Election Day and did as they were told, usually handing out small slate cards printed with candidates' names. Sometimes, as in 2016, they secretly plotted and voted Republican, with judges or district attorney candidates being their favorites. But to expect them to think deeply about government or study public policy was too great an expectation. Listening to Rush rant on the radio and Mayor McAnus hold court at the bar for an hour or two was as highbrow as their political discourse got. Always up for arguing about the leftist sickness they were now convinced defined America, club members argued for the sake of arguing. Union members argued against unions. Minimum wage earners argued against increasing the minimum wage. Those lacking medical insurance argued against affordable or even free medical insurance.

So for Martin to propose the Green Hand militia was only natural, just too late. Had he made his pitch pre-Trump, he would have hit pay dirt. By now, though, Trump had stolen his thunder, siphoning off popular luster and recruitment appeal. Trump's local campaign run by second-rate party hacks easily upstaged Martin who knew his time had come and gone.

Pre-Trump, the Irish Guys might have fallen over each other in the rush to pick up a gun or a bomb or a stick of dynamite to blow up a bank, a competing barroom, or a state representative's office. They knew well the travesty of their ancestors' travails and history's impact on their own lives. Having ancestors come over on the coffin ships packed like smoked clams in a tin, current descendants paid tribute to a staunch work ethic by losing a job or two or three, getting lazy and/or drunk, and giving up the cultural donnybrook to blame their conditions on everybody but themselves.

Most of these ill-bred scions had long ago lost the desire and will to persevere, open fire and defend their birthright through force of arms. That's why it came as no surprise to anybody who paid attention that wholesale prejudice became the dull rhinestone at the center of Irish-American Wilkes-Barre's tin tribal crown. In the spirit of fairness, this gang really did hate themselves. Hostility came easy in this grim land of mystical fable and broken romance, where spectral memories of a once vibrant town dissipated like long-ago shipwreck survivors in life boats destined to crash into the rocks and die. All that remained for Martin and most of his neighbors were recollections of better times that really weren't all that good.

Let Trump do the heavy lifting. The lads were only along for the ride. Like Martin didn't have his own problems. His kid was on the run, a murderer rebelling for all the wrong reasons. Tattoos and pierced titties were not what Martin's grandfather had in mind when he came to this new land searching for freedom. All the lines of reason blurred. One or two of the younger Irish Guys even sported earrings and outlooks on life beyond any benefit of counseling. Trump was the answer even though Martin and his ilk had long ago forgotten the question.

Martin Mahoney vowed his newly-established Mar-a-Lago Militia would be better than the Green Hand and the Black Hand the guineas founded put together. His one-man show would stand for America, for the Irish, for Wilkes-Barre and Martin's family. Pug would get acquitted, get better, stronger, and start going by Sean again. He'd grow up to be like Eric or Donald Trump Jr. In the process Martin and his boy could once again join forces and maybe blow up the downtown YMCA where the board of directors presented an annual leadership award named after a Protestant ex-convict millionaire who built the Y's swimming pool. Bridget could get a facelift like Melania and a boob job, let her hair grow, and stretch out on a bearskin rug in her birthday suit. They'd have another baby, a girl this time, and name her Tiffany. The Trump family would come to the baptism, maybe even hold the family gala at the White House. Trump would award Martin Mahoney, the pride of Wilkes-Barre, the Presidential Medal of Freedom for his patriotic behind-the-lines work for promises made and promises kept. Martin would write a book. Life would look good again. He and Bridget might even have another child.

And if that next kid popped out a boy, he'd name him Doonbeg after the mighty Irish chieftain Mahoney heard Mikey Hoyle talking about one night at the Coal Hole. Doonbeg, the great Irish legend who once ruled all Ireland, offered a wondrous name to define the Mahoney fighting spirit. So what if Mahoney didn't know Doonbeg never led as much as a tinker's testicle across the boggy battlefields of the old sod because Mikey Hoyle made him up as part of another bullshit story. So what if Doonbeg is the peewee west coast town that's home to the failing Trump International Golf Links in Ireland.

Half the fun of being an Irish Guy came down to believing what you wanted to believe.

RUNNING FREE

Pangs of loneliness roared through Balor's bulky body. With tufts of grey hair falling out in handfuls and raw, pink splotches marking his skin, the massive dog the size of a Connemara pony was in a dismal state of wretchedness. Years of minimal exercise and sleeping on the Coal Hole's cold concrete floor had weakened his back legs. Waking habitually hung over to lap fitfully at the bowl of lukewarm beer one or another inebriated bar patron kept pouring had continuously clouded his mind.

The Irish Guys were killing him. So one night he fled, rushing headlong in a last ditch burst of defiance that sent him crashing through the screen door. Figuring the dog had only experienced a nightmare everybody at the bar bawled with laughter and promptly forgot about the errant Wolfhound. Little did they know Balor escaped searching for that spark in his bloodline that made him sometimes dream of fighting wolves and lions in the Colosseum. Holding his own still meant something to Balor who feared the unknown and really didn't want to fight. Brawl he would, but only as a last resort if he had to protect himself or somebody who needed help.

Roaming strange streets, Balor dreaded getting lost, stumbling or not finding enough to eat. Turning around more than once, he began the trek back to the East End where he knew they'd cheer when he came through the tattered screen door and welcome him like the friendly dopey giant of a mutt he was. But something turned him around again and kept him roving, following a peculiar Celtic hunger for freedom that put a spring in the huge paws that slapped the ground with each bounding step.

During several weeks on the run, Balor put on a few pounds and once outran an overweight cop who recognized the creature and tried to capture him by the bus station. Balor picked up speed and stamina. The fresh air tasted wondrous. On this night he drank rainwater from a puddle before making his way back to the bed of clean blankets he found by accident as he prowled the alley behind the crater of an empty lot that once housed the majestic Sterling Hotel. Labor crews took down the huge crumbling flop of a testament to yesteryear where Balor found solace in the shadows of too many other ruined buildings that would soon go the way of the wrecking ball as well.

Whoever put out the blankets also put out food. Each night Balor found more goodies to devour, including meatloaf with bacon and beef stew with potatoes and carrots that Balor gobbled in three gulps. The mystery mush helped stop his hair loss and rebuild strength in his legs. After eating his fill, he'd sleep. Craving company, he'd whimper. Even an Irish Guy would do. Heartache had overtaken the poor dog who wished only for a scratch behind the ear every now and then.

One night a tender hand reached out. For several nights Balor's benefactor had watched the great dog lope aimlessly through the darkness, free, yet restless and without direction. For several nights the old man considered approaching the dog. This night he waited for Balor to slow his gallop, eat and plop into his damp corner to collapse in a heap. Extending his hand, he opened his fingers. Opening his eyes in response, Balor licked the warm skin. Sensing kindness in the fingers that stroked him while the gentle man spoke in a reassuring whisper, the dog hungrily accepted a nightcap chocolate éclair his new friend pulled from a pillow case slung over his shoulder. Breathing easy now, Balor curled on his side and remembered being slammed in the backside each night at the bar whenever some loaded Irish Guy threw open the door on his way in or out of the saloon as Balor slowly wasted away. These lugs slid enough bowls of beer under his nose to float St. Brendan's boat. Parading on Paddy's Day had all but ruined his kidneys in the forced march during which he had to hold his water until he thought he'd bust. One year he tried to pee by rushing between two parked cars to save himself and his handlers from embarrassment, but that bastard O'Brien had pulled so hard on his leash he thought his neck would break. The ancient ones, the great dogs of Balor's lineage, had fought the best and won. Balor, too, would make it, especially now that he had a real friend.

The night he broke out, he stood on wobbly legs peering at the outside world for a few moments that felt like years He couldn't believe he just lowered his head and went over the wall, so to speak, leaving in his wake a shredded mass of meshed wire and rusty hinges swinging on loose screws torn from the frame. Dogging it down the avenue, he gulped fresh air that pushed from his lungs the acrid taint of beer fumes, cigarette and cigar smoke, urinal deodorizer and industrial mold. Other than the parade, Balor rarely walked further than the distance to the back garden to relieve himself where some Irish Guys grew cabbages in the summertime. Balor awkwardly crouched by the ash pile and dreamed of his puppy years running free near the lake called Lough Corrib on the beautiful west coast of Ireland.

Puppyhood innocence didn't last long. A loudmouthed Scranton lawyer related through marriage to a couple of Irish Guys in Wilkes-Barre spotted the pooch and bought him from a traveler at a cattle fair at Maam Cross, locking the fearful hound in the trunk of his rental car. After shipping the cute cur home in a cage, he gave the beast to relatives to settle an unpaid gambling debt. The Irish Guys raffled off the pup as grand prize in one of the many illegal lotteries they ran at the Coal Hole in the course of a year. The novelty wore off soon enough and the winner returned Balor to the bar, where he remained for the duration of his relatively young life of five years and counting. Within months Balor was pouty and puffy, a paltry example of his powerful breed. Lazy and temperamental, just like a typical Irish Guy, he took on the sullen air of his masters. By the time his hair and teeth started to go, he had actually come to resemble several of the ranking club members as much as their own homely children did.

Then the gods released him from his chains.

In his new friend, Balor sensed a closeness he hadn't experienced since he was born in the wet straw where Cornamona village cows huddled when it rained, a sweet sanctity that sensitive farmers and other decent rural people knew and loved so well.

After all these empty years, Balor had a pal.

For Franny Finnerty, the mutual feeling brought nothing but joy.

REGRESSION IS A PITY

So what if Bop O'Brien hated the Blessed Mother?

Drinking beer in the bathtub, he washed his feet with a bleach-stained wash cloth and wondered out loud what all the fuss was about. The same went for Mary's mother, St. Ann. She could fuck off, too. Don't ask why, but ever since he started embezzling his paper route money when he was 13, he couldn't stand either one of them. Who did they think they were?

Of course, in public he raved about them both. So what if Mary got Duggan off the cigarettes? That's what she's supposed to do. That's her job, right? Everybody fawned over Mary and her mother, pushing them down your throat.

"Isn't Mary stunning? Isn't St. Ann dear? Pray to St. Ann. Pray to the Blessed Mother. Pray to my arse, why don't you," O'Brien said, talking to himself in the pious tone of the faithful. "If St. Ann's so smart, how's her daughter getting away with this immaculate contraception virgin birth bullshit that nobody in their right mind would believe? Any mother smart enough to make saint would have held her daughter's head in the toilet bowl until she confessed and ratted out whoever knocked her up. I mean, who's shitting who, here?"

O'Brien took immense satisfaction in living three doors down from the upstairs mothball-scented bedroom where he was born on Scott Street. The street served as home sweet home to an assortment of mostly average people who bought into mainstream society. Nowadays some of them even played golf. Playing golf and sending your kids to college is what doomed the working class, O'Brien explained on more than one occasion. But nobody listened. That's why people get what they deserve, according to O'Brien.

Cops, firefighters, nurses, high school teachers, local government clerks and the occasional elected official from the East End comprised the cream of the city crop. Almost everybody claimed a political connection to McAnus who lived on a street parallel to O'Brien's. The neighbors felt indebted to the mayor who represented their self-absorbed greed and offered them simple privilege and access to limited power. McAnus plowed their streets when nobody else could get theirs done in a blizzard and blacktopped their roads when everybody else lost wheels to potholes. In exchange, the neighborhood residents stuck with him when re-election came along and would have remained loyal had he been indicted and convicted. Most would have written letters to the judge on his behalf. Like Trump's boast, McAnus could have killed somebody on the street and not lost a vote among his base.

Any public official the feds did indict in and around Wilkes-Barre always counted on the same litany of praise to rise like a misguided phoenix from the ashes of fiery guilt despite his (in Luzerne County the white-collar defendant is almost always a man) disgrace.

"He's a great guy" provided the modern day equivalent of "Doesn't he look like himself" at the joyous Irish wakes of old.

A chorus of spineless jokers cheered whenever some old whore of a politician got acquitted by a jury of his so-called peers despite the defendant admitting to most of what the prosecutors charged with a defense that relied heavily on ignorance of the law.

"Yeah I took the Penn State football tickets and the cash but thought it was because the lobbyist liked me and my family. I wanted to go to Penn State, but my mother got sick and I had to work to support my family when I was eighteen. I never finished high school, or elementary school, for that matter. I'm a self-made man. I'm doing it for the children."

Street smart and once willing to take calculated risks, the neighborhood apologists allowed their edges to dull. Refusing to grow, change or buy into any progress around them, they swore by the power of native delusion that clouded their thinking. The Irish Guys liked life to remain predictable. O'Brien craved the comfort of fantasy as well. Deception tasted best self-induced. Didn't Trump advisor Kellyanne Conway call his outright lies "alternative facts?" If falsehood was good enough for her, falsehood was good enough for them.

Despite social afflictions, the neighborhood masses acted like one big sappy family. Taking delight in personal limitations can be a blessing. Stupidity makes living easier. O'Brien's associates' unwavering refusal to abandon loyalty for the lure of the intellect impressed him. Their faith knew no boundaries. They played by old-school rules in an institution that remained an asylum to generation after generation of close-minded and sometimes stark, raving mad kinfolk.

Sick of the never-ending, never-changing same old, same old malarkey, O'Brien knew Mahoney was right. Admitting as much was another story. Mahoney could plan his desertion by himself. O'Brien had his own foolproof personal scheme. All he needed to do was count the days until he bolted. Meanwhile, bearing witness to deepening social regression genuinely bummed him out.

More and more aimless teenage boys hung out on the corner by the Coal Hole, biding their time before getting old enough to charge inside and waste the rest of their lives drinking and laughing like loons with a new generation of entitled Irish Guys. More and more beer cans littered the once spotless gutters where the remaining biddies still swept their sidewalks every morning with old-fashioned brooms. More fistfights broke out in the musty taprooms that dotted city cross streets like inflamed pimples on a novice pole dancer's buttocks.

Unemployed white male roofers, disgruntled electricians, irate brick layers, house painters and laborers barked too loudly too often, almost instinctively refusing to pay child support after their wives mustered the courage to leave. A small army of young and middle-aged louts took bizarre pride in being publicly labeled deadbeat dads, calling their irresponsibility men's liberation. More and more sirens broke the once quiet definition of family that used to mean a good night's sleep and now too often meant a visit to the emergency room to identify the body of a loved one lost to an opioid drug overdose or a fatal DUI car accident.

Everybody had a hard-on for everybody else.

And they all loved Trump.

O'Brien knew he needed more than a vacation. O'Brien needed rebirth. Killing his wife and fruitcake kid was out of the question, just too much trouble. Agnes would probably welcome the permanent respite from breathing. O'Brien refused to give her the satisfaction of dying. No divorce and no death certificate meant he still controlled her existence. Ireland, the getaway for which he'd been plotting and planning and saving for years shimmered in the distance as an oasis that would solve all his problems. Agnes and her little fairy prince of a son could go plumb to hell. Ireland would save O'Brien's soul.

How many nights did he lay in bed envisioning his grand entrance? After landing at Shannon he'd rent a green Mercedes, so big it would have trouble fitting on the narrow country roads. He'd find a nice room in a quaint bed and breakfast. Eat corn flakes and a soft boiled egg with Irish butter so thick on his brown bread he could write his name in it, then some oatmeal and white blood pudding, then another pot of hot tea with six sugars and orange marmalade on his toast with rashers. That's what the Irish call bacon, he told the Irish Guys one night as they listened in awe to how much O'Brien knew about Ireland. Maybe he'd have another egg. Whiskey, too. He'd be drinking the Paddy whiskey with his breakfast. God help the help who balked at his demands. He'd tell them he was with the police on special assignment and he better get all the eggs the old bird running the kitchen could lay.

Charming, that's the word O'Brien was looking for. Like Irish-American tourists say when they fawn about old Ireland, he would become charming, so fucking charming it hurt his head just thinking about it. Envisioning a lot of time spent at Irish racetracks, O'Brien expected to do some gambling, too. The horses run on the grass he told the boys one night as they marveled at his brilliance. He'd drink in pubs until they closed. Sing a song like "McSorley's Two Twins," who smother to death at the end of the tune. Tell the lads in the pub what a great detective he was in the States and how coons like Obama and feminists and media ruined everything. Offer to do assassinations for "the cause." Find a black-haired 25-year-old country girl from Clonbur, clean her up, and turn her into a perpetually smiling domestic servant to care for his every need. Drag her around the meadow like John Wayne did in the movie. Toss her aside when he got tired of her and put an ad in the weekly paper like the old farmers do to get himself another. Through it all, he'd laugh and laugh and laugh whether anybody laughed with him or not. "As happy as Larry," as the Irish Garda put it at the convention. Whatever that meant sounded good. O'Brien would win in Ireland, until he tired of winning, just like that degenerate Trump promised. The idiots he left at home would one day experience a rude awakening with Trump's lies and O'Brien's bait and switch.

Real winners take all.

From where he lounged in the bubble bath O'Brien made by pouring pink liquid dish washing detergent into the hot water, he looked through the bathroom window at a mountain in the distance that always reminded him of pictures he had seen of Connemara. He could see smoke from an underground coal mine fire, one of numerous accidental toxic infernos that burned for years, sometimes decades, underground in Northeastern Pennsylvania as hydrocarbons and sulphurous gas drifted into the atmosphere and poisoned the air. Chugging his beer and dropping the empty Harp can into the filmy water he recalled how it wasn't that many years ago when belching crevices in the ground spit fire as well as smoke.

One night long ago, reeling and standing at the Coal Hole men's room toilet bowl, O'Brien gazed out the tiny window facing the same mountain. Orange and blue flames danced across coal vein scars stitched against the ground like catgut sewn into a prizefighter's eyebrow to close meaty open flesh. Striking O'Brien at the time as one of the most beautiful sights in the world, he knew for as long as he'd live, he'd carry that heartfelt image of home in his mind and heart. Until he made it to Ireland, that mountain was as close as he'd come to heaven. For whatever reason, the hard times made him proud to be from Pennsylvania hard coal country. Back then he didn't want to be from anyplace else in the world. The universe revolved around being a cop from Wilkes-Barre. Everything he needed bloomed within city limits.

O'Brien knew he couldn't just up and leave, at least not empty-handed. He needed a score, a real score to add to his nest egg. One big caper would put him over the top. One last hurrah bonanza and he could ditch Agnes and her pledge of allegiance to the fag. He decided to leave during the Paddy's Day parade. Drive to the airport, dump the car and catch the flight to Newark. Down half a dozen pints of Guinness and take the overnight to Shannon. He'd stagger beneath the weight of the carry on loaded with cash he cleaned out of the Irish Guys' bank account. Nobody'd dare suspect him. These misfits never saw anything coming. Besides, O'Brien always had the authority to write checks from the special account and make deposits and withdrawals to balance the books. Why did survival have to come to this? He'd always held up his end of the bargain. Why couldn't ex-son Michael have just grown up to become a normal Irish Guy like his old man?

Getting out of the tub, O'Brien dried off, shaved, combed his hair, splashed on some Ice Blue Aqua Velva aftershave, dressed and headed to the Coal Hole for a couple of pops. He didn't go to work until later so he could drink for a few hours. Throwing bartender Mikey Hoyle a big thumbs-up, he walked to the jukebox, slid a five dollar bill into the slot, punched in the numbers for the shamrock ditties, and listened to the first strains of "The Unicorn" come into his head. Feeling better already, he wished he had more cash to take with him to Ireland, to carry "home" as he started to call his destination when he was talking to himself about the getaway.

Turning to Hoyle, he said, "You know what dawned on me while I was taking a bath?"

"Tell me."

"Loving the Irish means hating the Irish. Hating the Irish means loving the Irish."

"You're a poet and don't know it, Bop," Hoyle said.

"Where's the king of beasts?" O'Brien asked, pointing to the empty corner where Balor used to sleep.

"Broke out," Hoyle said. "Ran away."

"That's gratitude for you," O'Brien said. "After all we done for that mangy cur."

STRONGER TOGETHER

"Nice to see you, Mrs. Duffin," Cookie said.

Even when all the restaurant booths sat empty, the distinguished black woman in her house cleaning clothes (a dark blue uniform pants suit with thick soft-soled shoes that made her look like a housekeeper in a nice hotel) always sat at the counter. Placing her two shopping bags on the floor she inhaled and exhaled in short bursts, clearly having trouble catching her breath.

"You all right?"

"Fine, child," Mrs. Duffin said. "A little winded carrying my supplies."

Looking in the bag, Cookie saw an assortment of cleaning rags, a can of Bon Ami bathroom disinfectant and two large bottles of Windex. Mrs. Duffin seemed preoccupied.

"Something on your mind?"

"I'm thinking about the next president," Mrs. Duffin said.

"Aren't we all."

"I voted for Hillary every chance I had. In 2008 and in 2016," Mrs. Duffin said. "Remember the 2008 primary? Hillary won Pennsylvania, remember?"

"I voted for her," Cookie said. "Does Duff know about 2008? As crazy as he was about Barack."

"I told him right up front," Mrs. Duffin said. "Told him nobody knows black is beautiful more than I do but women need to rise. Hillary earned my vote then. And the next time. But, look what we got."

Mrs. Duffin sighed.

"I liked Elizabeth this time," she said.

"Me, too," Cookie said.

"Voters hate women presidential candidates," Mrs. Duffin said. "Most women voters hate women. White women hate themselves most. But the men? Lord. I worked cleaning bathrooms at the Westmoreland Club today. All those starched white shirt bankers and know-it-all lawyers. Republicans and Democrats married to rich men's daughters act like they own the world. Now they're plotting to re-elect Trump. Just like before. Not just working class white folks going for Trump but rich white men going for that chump, too."

Mrs. Duffin never had a bad word to say about anybody.

Cookie leaned in and whispered her only recollection about the Westmoreland Club.

"Remember the black bartender who worked at the club?"

"Hugh McGhee. He was 93 when he got murdered," Mrs. Duffin said. "The cops messed up that case something awful. That's one reason Duff wanted to become a police officer. A black man and a white woman walked. A black man's doing life. Police weren't going to arrest that white girl with them. Then they charged a wrong black man and had to let him go."

"I remember," Cookie said. "I heard the detective tell my boss that he knew all along he was the wrong man but they needed another...."

Cookie stopped talking.

"They needed another nigger? Is that what he said?"

"I'm sorry," Cookie said.

Delores Duffin carried herself as the finest, most straight-forward woman Cookie ever met. Honest and confident, always chugging along like a freight train loaded with truth, Mrs. Duffin practiced what she preached.

"You are something else, Mrs. Duffin," Cookie said. "How's Duff holding up with everything going on?"

Mrs. Duffin frowned.

"Working too hard on poor Mr. Garrett's death for one thing. He's tired all the time but won't let on the case is getting him down. After all those years of dreaming about being a detective, now he is one and doesn't like it. This murder is hurting him too much. And talk about this virus is getting worse."

Cookie didn't want to pry.

"You want a hot dog?"

"I wouldn't eat one of those foul dogs if you paid me," Mrs. Duffin said. "A glass of water and some French Fries with hot sauce would be nice."

Cookie went for the fries thinking about police brutality. At least the crooked white cop who arrested an innocent black man and made the racist slur went to federal prison years later on an unrelated charge. He served a couple of months and then got out.

Cookie felt like she was still doing time.

POT OF GOLD

St. Pat's sparkled after the renovation.

Hallowed ground built 150 years ago now resembled a 70s disco far more than a sanctuary for lost souls in a dead coal country town. Religious old-timers said prayers for younger parishioners who wore shorts, sneakers and flip flops to Mass. A new breed took over, a gang led by immigrants' grandsons who had become wealthy lawyers, insurance men, local elected officials, financial advisors, real estate agents and other businessmen. Most of these types meant well. They prevailed in real decision-making about the church renovation because they waved fatter checkbooks. Loyal senior citizen pensioners and widowed lonely hearts living on fixed incomes couldn't afford to repair their crumbling homes scattered throughout the one-time vibrant Irish immigrant neighborhood let alone remodel their church.

Brazen in their burst of progress, the powerful parish men even voted to auction off bricks contractors uncovered behind the white-washed church walls. These once sturdy symbols of peasant faith would eventually adorn halls of personal privilege. Some of the crusty bricks would decorate dens in lavish homes that a number of miners' offspring built in a swanky development up the hill from a ski lodge moguls constructed a few years back. The giant slalom looms high above worn headstones that mark a somber ethnic graveyard of yesteryear. Commemorative bricks would serve as bookends in state representatives' offices. Some would hold back the doors to entertainment rooms where hairy male beer bellies rose and fell before big screen TV sports events in a more frenetic fashion than the tide that rocks the pleasure boats in Galway Bay.

Inside the modernized church, white oak beams supported a ceiling decorated with heavenly swirls of creamy plaster. The sound system rivaled anything the Chieftains used for concerts. Modern statues of saints that looked more like hipsters hanging at an art gallery opening than emissaries of God replaced the tall, dignified, hand-painted plaster or wooden saints. As the new St. Pat's crowning glory, a $100,000 hand-carved coal altar sat as black shining testament to the deadly shame of the past that killed countless greenhorns with black lung disease they caught after decades of breathing coal dust in the mines.

On opening day for the improved church, the Irish Guys hosted a ribbon cutting ceremony and "all-you-can-drink-for-five-dollars" gala in the social hall. At no time did they think to pay tribute to the poverty of their ancestors or even some of their neighbors by showing compassion to the poor. Greed, free enterprise and bad taste overflowed, creating a petri dish brimming with enough green bacteria to infect all the Trump supporters it took in Wilkes-Barre and Luzerne County to swing the presidential re-election Trump's way in an epidemic of self-deception.

Pulling his unmarked car into the funeral hearse space between church and social hall, Duff stepped onto the lawn and took a quick look around. Marching up the cracked sidewalk, he recalled the old church that coal miner parishioners and their families helped pool pennies to build in 1870.

Generations later, too many poor, old, white descendants spent each day waiting for the last round. More than a few looked forward to that final bell because, in some ways, they were already stretched out face-down on the canvas. In their youth nobody could have counted them out. Now, with nobody willing to help them up, they willingly agreed to stay down.

As for the handful of African-American seniors in town, they died the way they always died, mostly unknown, undaunted, undiscovered and unappreciated. Black men and women usually told no tales, at least not publicly. They just disappeared.

Entering the church, Duff passed one of three fat porcelain fonts brimming with holy water. Catholicism puzzled him with religious rituals that seemed little more than excuses to manipulate people. Believing in goodness and doing good were not the same. Suddenly feeling afraid, Duff pulled his gun from the holster and stepped slowly into the center aisle. Turning to look toward the choir loft, he backed deeper into the church filled with the smell of harsh incense.

About an hour earlier when the phone rang at 7 p.m. during dinner with his mother, Duff was finishing up his leftover broccoli stuffed white pizza and planning to head out to do a few more interviews. With Garrett's killer walking around capable of anything, Duff promised himself to solve this case if it took him the rest of his life.

"Yo," Duff said between bites.

A high-pitched voice squeaked.

"Detective Duffin?"

"What can I do for you?"

"Get your black ass over to St. Pat's."

"Who's this?"

"Catch me and I lead you to a pot of gold."

The voice on the phone no doubt belonged to Pug Mahoney, who also no doubt spray-painted "St. Patrick Sucks Dicks" in a blur of green letters spattered across the wall behind the altar. A splashy drawing of a penis with two small balls accompanied the fighting words. The green paint shimmered in the pale light of a dozen flickering candles burning to light the way for the souls of the faithfully departed. Duff knew nobody gets out alive but wanted so much to feel alive as long as he could, to help others feel alive and enjoy the journey during the time we have on this earth. Duff called for backup on his cellphone, put his gun back in the holster, and took a couple of photographs of the vandalism.

The Irish would lose their minds. So what else is new? The Irish Guys flipped at the opening of their neighborhood's first Chinese restaurant, calling the business an ethnic slur against their heritage, and filed a state Human Relations Commission complaint through their state representative, an Irish Guy. The club awarded plaques a few years ago to three World War II vets from East End who refused to eat "gook" rice pudding at the VA hospital during their combined stays as patients. About a dozen Irish Guys picketed the hospital as a gesture of solidarity against "the Japs" who bombed Pearl Harbor and whom they blamed for opening the Chinese restaurant.

"That's why they call them Orientals," O'Brien told a Times Leader reporter. "They orient themselves and adapt, going from a

Hawaiian sneak attack to 'Nam to making chop suey in coal country without blinking one of their slanted eyes."

When the reporter failed to quote O'Brien in the story, the Irish Guys picketed the paper, accusing management of reverse racism.

Duff expected the Bishop to create an international incident about the ghastly graffiti, give interviews to the press about increasing anti-Catholicism, and gloss over the odious fact that for years he personally covered up for several child molester priests in his diocese.

Lunatic Pug Mahoney remained Duff's only suspect. With the town jabbering incessantly about this teenage kook running amok, Duff called the kid's father. Before hanging up, Mahoney told him he had a wrong number, that the NAACP number was all zeros. The Irish might even defend Pug. Duff could just hear the comments on talk radio about black on black crime that had nothing to do with this homicide. Worse, he could just as easily imagine the word-for-word justification most Irish Guys would offer.

"All he did was bag a coon. Would everybody get as worked up if one of us white guys got killed?"

Duff let his mind drift to a long stretch of beach somewhere in Florida and wondered if he could find a place with black sand. Dark green glass eyes set deep in the last old-fashioned carved wooden statue of St. Pat unnerved Duff. He looked away, listening to his footsteps on the hard marble floor as he backed out of the church.

Duff sensed somebody watching.

Then he saw the body.

To his left another pair of glassy unblinking eyes stared. Bathed in dark shadows, bent half in and half out of the confessional, Father O'Toole bled from a gaping hole in his throat, a wound that left hunks of flesh hanging over his stained and gore-soaked collar. Lifeless pale white hands clutched what Duff thought was a Bible the priest must have been reading when he died. Kneeling to take a closer look, Duff saw the glossy magazine cover that highlighted two toddlers, white, blond, naked, tied to a bed with barbed wire. Their necks, wrists and ankles bled. They looked dead. A man dressed like a priest leaned over their bodies. He wore a devil mask and held a pitchfork.

"Goddamn," Duff said.

WHAT IS WRONG WITH THESE PEOPLE?

Propped up in bed on a couple of foam cushions with a scene from "Riverdance" embroidered on the pillowcases Bridget won in an Irish Guys Valentine's Day raffle, Martin Mahoney read the Times Leader and sipped Paddy's whiskey from a Fraternal Order of Police Lodge 12 coffee mug. The small advertisement in the lower left-hand corner of the obituary page caught his eye. Printed in a decorative square, the ad carried a special dark edging that highlighted the words and photo, making them look like they were encased in an ornate picture frame.

In a way the dead Irish Guy in the picture was better off than Mahoney who had to put up with continuing bullshit until kingdom come. Wearing one of those fat-faced predictable grins you see in a bowling hall of fame group photo, the deceased smiled for the camera that had likely been held by his wife at an Irish Guys dinner of some kind they attended on a festive Saturday night. The man wore a cheap green carnation and a wrinkled Irish tweed cap with a snap brim. Mahoney wondered where the cap was now, thinking he wouldn't be surprised if they buried the poor bastard wearing it.

The paid advertisement read, "Happy 56th Birthday to Our DADDY in Heaven. Sadly missed by sons Ryan (33), Rory (31) and loving wife Mary."

Mahoney stared at the picture until he couldn't take it any longer and threw the newspaper across the room. He groaned with guttural exasperation.

"What is wrong with these people? Who in their right mind puts a picture in the newspaper wishing dead daddy a happy birthday in heaven?"

But he knew. He knew. Oh, he knew. The same people who put similar ads in the paper wishing the dead happiness in heaven on Easter, Groundhog Day and every other holiday or special occasion, that's who.

"Are we completely lost?" he asked, turning his attention to the wall and the picture of the Bleeding Heart of Jesus Bridget decorated with a crimson burning light bulb she kept lit around the clock. "Is there no hope? Answer me you Jew bastard, you."

Taking a long gulp of Paddy's, Mahoney stifled the mad urge to throw the mug at the Savior's image when the telephone rang. Grabbing for the landline receiver, whiskey dribbled from his chin.

"What?"

Errant son Pug's voice screeched on the telephone like a hoot owl mating with a rooster.

"Trump, Trump, Trump."

ERIN GO RAW

At the 2019 Paddy's Day parade, drunk and disorderly by 7 a.m., Pug missed marching with his father for the first time in his life. Alone and staggering his way shirtless through the crowd that lined the street by 10 a.m., he found a hiding place between two buildings to await the politicians' signal to step off on their slow, long slog. When they did, Pug charged, pushing his way through the crowd all the way to the reviewing stand at the other end of the street. When the first wave of the parade arrived to greet the stand full of dignitaries, Pug joined the crowd, straddling the green line painted down the middle of the street.

Even Duff marveled at the brash craziness of this untamed maniac he had never seen before, who spent hours earlier eating a small crate of raw asparagus he stole and guzzling a mix of lime vodka and extra-strength green food coloring that loaded his bladder with a throbbing jade-colored cargo. Fighting to hold his water, succeeding except for a small stream that ran down his thigh, Pug swallowed as much natural vegetable coloring and high-powered green food dye as he could find. Drinking food coloring will not normally impact urine color, but Pug ingested enough to horrify parade goers by pissing the painted line down the middle of the street a deeper shade of green than they had ever seen.

Raising his arms over his head, Pug halted the march of Democratic U.S. Senator Bobby Casey who got re-elected largely based on a rumor his supporters started that vowed Casey's support for a law to register unborn children to vote. Pug also halted the first float called "Cleanliness Is Next To Godliness" comprised of two hands folded in prayer sculpted from 10,000 bars of Irish Spring soap to protest pornography on cable TV. Forward progress also froze for the Quiet Man Club comprised of drunken alumni from four area Catholic colleges who remained in their dull middle age true to their collegial silliness.

By the time uniformed police spotted Pug, he already pulled his member (painted green, of course) from his pants and started to pee. Spraying mightily, he unleashed a stream from a wriggling serpent unlike any St. Pat encountered while driving the slithering creatures out of Hibernia. Pug further stained the green line the city always made such a big deal out of painting each year. Painting the line green is normally a nice, harmless gesture. Pissing the line green is international news and terrible for any mayor's reputation. When Mayor McAnus realized what was happening, he dove at Pug headfirst from the reviewing stand. Despite landing on his face, McAnus' outstretched arms and shoulders took the brunt of the fall with his loose alcohol-lubricated body collapsing into squeeze box form. Surprisingly, the mayor broke no bones and regained consciousness in time to see the chase pick up steam and disappear around Public Square.

Several members of the Knights of Columbus drew their swords and lost their plumed hats as soon as they spotted Pug's green geyser, courageously charging in the direction of the steady viridian stream gushing from the young devil's phallic fountain.

"The River Shannon flows!" Pug bellowed as he waved his private part like an unconstrained hose wielded by the Dublin Fire Brigade during the 1916 Easter Rising. A melee ensued as the spry troublemaker sloppily held his own against aging grandmothers who rushed him from the sidelines in reaction to such a wanton display of genitalia in front of the wee ones, who laughed and clapped for Pug's wee-wee, cheering the Kelly green font like they were applauding the dancing rope routine at a magic show.

According to surveillance video, Pug pissed the line green for close to 15 long seconds, more if you count the involuntary last ditch squirts and shakes as he began his escape. Spinning and continuing to squirt even after Duff grabbed him, Pug fought all the way to the transport wagon, spitting and clawing and calling Duff "nigger" a half dozen different ways. When Duff slapped a nonviolent come-along restraint on Pug's arm, people in the crowd immediately turned on the cop. No matter how awful Pug's transgression, a black cop manhandling one of the local white lads on Paddy's Day was simply too much to take.

"Hey, Sambo, how about the content of his character?"

"Looks like excessive force to me."

Sensing support, Pug began to chant.

"USAUSAUSA."

Perfectly willing to overlook the fact that the kid was blitzed out of his mind and waving his willy around in the middle of the street on parade day, dozens of men and women, mostly of Irish descent and dressed in the lovely shades of four green fields, responded exactly the way Pug expected.

"USAUSAUSA," they responded, pumping their fists in the air.

Unlike the Irish Guys who were always sure what to do, Duff balked. Then he firmly maneuvered the kid into the back of the "prisoner transport van" and closed the door.

Six months earlier the Irish Guys mounted a successful petition drive to urge City Council to pass a resolution banning the use of the term "Paddy Wagon" in any official police correspondence because of "the deep ethnic stereotypic nature and grievous insult to the hard-working generations of Irish in Wilkes-Barre." At that same meeting, City Council turned down another petition demanding at least one black cop, one black firefighter, and a woman (either black or white) to be employed in both city departments at all times.

"We are colorblind in this city. To us, all colors, creeds and political affiliations look alike," said Mayor McAnus in a short prepared statement O'Brien wrote for him and released to the press.

Mahoney and the Irish Guys went Pug's bail, leaned on the juvenile judge (Irish Guy) to get the kid into a first offenders' program (run by an Irish Guy) with an expunged record after a year, filed a brutality complaint against Duff, and learned nothing of substance from the experience.

After all, Pug was one of their own.

SAVE ME, PUGGY

A snowflake-specked wind swept off the river hard enough to blow loose slate shingles from the roof of the double-block home where Binkee lived with her mother until they both ran away. Mom ran first. Binkee followed in a different direction. Binkee's grandmother lived on one side of the house while she and her mother shared the other side until they split up after grandma died from throat cancer.

"Leaving us wasn't my mom's fault," Binkee told the stuffed animal she carried with her when she felt pressure and stress getting to her. A nondescript creature like Binkee with one ear and no discernable species, the nameless, faceless toy was Binkee's closest friend, sharing each night hunkered down wherever she could crash after fleeing foster home after foster home. "Mommy was sick."

Binkee stood on the corner shivering and mumbling to herself. People in passing cars gawked. Sometimes Binkee licked her lips the way she had seen actresses do in movies. If her mouth looked inviting maybe some men would stop for what a prostitute Binkee knew called a "date." Binkee even sucked cherry Tootsie pops trying to look slinky. Nobody stopped.

Disheveled in a blue corduroy sport coat she picked up at the dress-for-success clothing bank, she looked at her feet. Encased in high top Converse sneaks, they looked larger than ever. Embarrassed, Binkee tried to use mental telepathy power to make her feet go away, then her hands and legs, then her heart and head and body and soul. No luck.

"Help me, Puggy," Binkee said.

Binkee needed her protector. She couldn't do anything right. Even with police alerted to her living as a runaway, they ignored her as they passed the corner. One day a female elementary school principal Binkee knew smiled and just kept driving. What kind of woman would do that? What few customers she did have, maybe one or two a week, complained about the way she serviced them resting her small head in their laps and dreaming she was in a limo

189

with a rock star on their way to a party.

"Don't talk to me," one John said. "Don't look at me. Just suck it. You look like a boy, anyway, an ugly boy. Ten bucks is too much money. Five is all I got."

The cop was the meanest.

"Bill me," O'Brien said after she finished with him one Sunday morning after Mass let out and he spotted her across the street from the church where he passed the collection plate and pocketed envelopes and cash whenever he could. O'Brien once put an empty unsealed envelope in the plate and wrote across the front that the amount of his donation was one thousand dollars. Then he signed his name. The priest included O'Brien's name and the amount in the annual published list of church contributions, marking it the "biggest single gift of the year" and providing O'Brien with an award from the Diocese for his devotion.

"It's okay, detective," Binkee said, afraid and trying to smile. "That's a freebie."

Walking slowly toward the church back door, she knew she'd find refuge in the basement. Binkee needed a nap. Sleeping by the boiler in St. Pat's would feel soothing even after the priest's murder. Sneaking in was easy. Pug showed her how to jimmy the lock. Stealing food, beer and meds got easier, too.

"You're so smart," Binkee told Pug. "Good looking, too."

If she ever had a baby, maybe she could give birth in the basement by the boiler. Delivery shouldn't be too tough. The floor always felt warm. Didn't those native women in Africa walk off and squat in the bush until their newborns slid out? She could do that.

Alone and hungry, Binkee watched a man in a red Dodge truck with a Confederate flag tied to the antenna and a Trump/Pence bumper sticker pasted across the tinted rear window slow and check her out over his shoulder. Rolling down the window, the man yelled, "Take a bath and I'll show you the kielbasa."

Binkee began to cry. Why was everybody so mean? How could he say that? Reaching into the pocket of her jacket, she pulled out the last of the heroin she bought from the dude in the Yankees cap she met under the bridge when she went looking for Pug.

"I'm a Crip," he said

"I'm a Sugar Crisp," Binkee said.

"You don't need no dope, girl," the man said. "You're way too fucked up already."

Stepping into the alley behind the drug store where an Italian-American bouncer at a strip club and his buddies beat a Latino guy to death a few years back in a dispute over drug money, she shook out the powder and held it to her nose. Sniffing, she saw silver stars, which were always wonderful, but Binkee wanted a needle so she could walk on the planets. As her small heart slowed, she passed out.

Ten minutes later Pug found her by accident as he prowled the alleys looking for a happy hour businessman to mug. Pug believed the cops didn't really want to arrest him for taking a black life most white people didn't believe mattered, anyway. Still, he regularly taunted police online.

Becoming a social media influencer excited him. What Pug really wanted was to become a reality television show star like Trump on "The Apprentice." Pug would call his show "The Gimp" and choose hyperactive contestants from the studio audience to compete by holding up their hands and flailing their arms the way Trump used a herky-jerky spasm to mock a disabled news reporter who suffered from a joint contracture disease. Millions of members of Trump's base would tune in each week to vote for whoever could do the best tremorous Trump imitation and win a trip to the Trump hotel in Washington for a free dinner and drinks with Pug and his co-host, Binkee. They would become more famous overnight than Pat Sajak and Vanna White on "Wheel of Fortune."

"Wake up, Binkee," Pug said.

Binkee sighed.

"Hey, Binkee, watch this," Pug said.

He then broke into his spastic dance.

Binkee didn't move.

"Let's do the Gimp, Binkee," he said. "C'mon, Binkee, do the Gimp."

HAVE A NICE DAY, BARACK

Standing in line at the post office on South Main Street, Bop O'Brien wondered where this Pug shithead could be. Mahoney wasn't talking. Even if he hated his kid, the kid was still his kid. Mahoney had his own problems, anyway. Struggling to read the black and white FBI wanted posters from across the room, O'Brien lamented his dismal lack of success in ever capturing an escaped convict. Grabbing a ferocious black radical had always been his dream, a Black Liberation Army leader or Black Muslim jihadist. Such a high-profile collar would have been his ticket out of Wilkes-Barre and maybe even a spot on the Pennsylvania State Police governor's executive protection unit.

"Fucking Wilkes-Barre," Bop said, pronouncing the name of his home town "Wilkes-Berra," as in Yankees legend Yogi, not "Wilkes-Berry," as in huckleberry, the way too many stubborn natives preferred. Nobody knew for sure. Little good comes from living in a town you can't pronounce.

Without warning, Duff walked into the lobby and came face-to-face with O'Brien, who started right in on his partner, lecturing in the menacing tone he reserved for special occasions.

"A white man like me can lose a job for no reason," he said. "You, you get to enjoy minority promotions and affirmative action hires. Before you know it the police department will look like the Sixers."

"I'm the only black cop in the city," Duff said.

"From what I hear, you're only half, like curdled coffee creamer."

Duff stepped nose-to-nose with his partner.

"You really can't give this shit up, can you?"

O'Brien couldn't stop.

"When Obama got elected, the mayor put a letter of reprimand in my file because he worried I was going to get us sued. All I did was stop a hot shit colored lawyer from New York in a brand new Caddy just passing through. He got off the wrong exit. I wished him a nice day and let him go with just a warning.

"Why did you pull him over?"

"Speeding."

"How did you wish him well?"

"I said, 'Have a nice day, Barack.'"

"I take it his name wasn't Barack."

"How was I supposed to know that?"

"What warning did you offer?"

"I told him, 'Come back to Wilkes-Barre and you'll wish you stayed in Kenya.'"

No, O'Brien couldn't stop.

"After Obama won the first time I thought you people would love being called Barack. Give some inspiration to your dark lives. Some hope that guys like me would change. Hope and change, right? But you know what, Barack? Guys like me don't change. Sometimes we get worse."

Stepping around O'Brien, Duff mailed his letter to Florida and split.

O'Brien went back to brooding. After all these years on the job, O'Brien was just another goof waiting to buy stamps in the post office. When his turn came, he tossed a ten and a five on the counter.

"I want a book of stamps," he said.

Without thinking, the woman slid him Kwanza celebration stamps left over from the holiday.

"Do I look like I'm celebrating my black heritage?" O'Brien said, pushing the stamps back so hard they flew off the counter. "Save them for Joe Biden and his buddy Mandela."

"Yes, sir," the clerk said. "I mean 'no sir.' I am so sorry, sir."

The woman gently slid a booklet of American flag stamps his way.

"Call me when you get more of them Ronald Reagan ones," O'Brien said, picking up the stamps and his change.

O'Brien couldn't wait to get out of America.

Respect no longer mattered.

The time had come to emigrate.

THE GREEN MAN

Overwhelmed by his release from the hospital psychiatric ward, Franny looked out the window of his room and watched the eastern horizon turn dark pink. The sky reminded him of sweet, crisp candy apples he used to buy on the boardwalk in Atlantic City. Turning and walking a few steps to the bed, Franny strained against the pain of aging to get on his knees. Rather than pray silent prayers to a God in whom he no longer believed, he offered sentiment instead to the natural forces that unite everything in the universe, summoning Celtic powers he read about over the years, superstitions that kept him going because he believed sincere communion with the past worked. He called his prayers "the green magic."

Keeping the faith of his childhood had been more and more difficult each year. With his back bent and head bowed, Franny sensed dawn cast its amber welcome against the stained yellow walls of his room. Despite sour smells in the musty space, the place still held character from better days when single female secretaries, librarians and teachers stayed in the building in the 1920s, when responsible landlords kept the little rooms spotless and in good shape. Tiny as it was, this monastic cell offered whatever sanctuary the roomer created. Franny considered himself a spinster in the best sense of the word if such a sense existed. For now the place contained everything Franny needed.

On his own for too long, he often wondered why his sister had sent him that terrible letter, like a pink slip termination letter telling him how ashamed she was of his failures. Enough was enough, she said with finality. Getting arrested for such a perverse act in their hometown had been a disgrace to the memory of their mother and father, fine people who would never have understood his filthy offense. Time to cut bait, she said. Both the social worker and counselor thought Franny would do better continuing to live on his own. Of course, Franny had his doubts.

Opening his eyes already afraid, he started each morning with a few of the same prayers of old to help his resolve and make it through the day. Focus, he told himself, contained the key to enlightenment. Today, though, as a brave act of rebellion, he altered his prayer routine and said only three Roman Catholic prayers instead of his usual seven. Since his arrest, Franny had been too humiliated to attend Mass or confession. Priests must get bored listening to his same sappy sins that never changed, anyway. Penance for an Irish snake charmer should have been simple for the normally dull priests who routinely forgave mostly venial behavior. Franny never did anything wrong.

Catholicism let him down, not the other way around. Franny didn't leave his religion; his religion left him. In all the time he spent hospitalized, not once did any priest ask how to help or what he needed. The Church just piled on more requests for submission. Absolution only came to those who begged. Raising his bowed head from another dull Apostle's Creed, Franny said, "No more. From here on, I stand my ground."

Franny Finnerty would beg no more. Rising from his knees with bold courage for the first time in years, Franny decided to take charge.

"I am the Green Man," he said, christening a daring new incarnation with an identity borrowed from an ancient Celtic deity who could handle anything life or death threw his way. The Green Man, also known as "Cernunnos the hunter," was a horned force of nature, trees and other growing things of this Earth. Known to all Celtic areas in one form or another, this leader of the underworld was the great father. Often portrayed sitting in the lotus position, with horns or antlers on his head, he sat naked holding a spear and shield. The god of crossroads and reincarnation, the Green Man ruled. Franny would rule his own destiny.

Easier said than done, Franny fought an onslaught of fear as he plodded to the tiny bathroom sink that sputtered brown water from the faucets. Filling a stained kettle for tea and spraying air freshener, he inhaled the pine scent that filled the room with a hint of ancient forest and fragrant boughs. The chemical mist came as close to nature as the poor soul could get. How Franny yearned for a long walk in the old country among flowing hills of purple heather or a deep drink from a cool Maam mountain stream. Better yet, a pint and the smell of peat fire smoke at Joe Keane's Pub by the bridge he read about in a travel magazine sounded grand.

Mostly, though, Franny longed for love.

Taking a seat at the tiny table by the streaked poster-sized window, Franny lit his pipe, waited for his new hot plate to boil water and tried to enjoy the morning. After swallowing two fast cups of Lipton with sour milk and three sugars, he grabbed his Irish walking hat and sweater that he called a jumper the way the real Irish did and descended three flights of frayed carpeted steps. Pushing open the heavy metal side door to the apartment building, he headed to the river.

Wide with grass and thick trees, the riverfront shone as the most beautiful part of the city. Few people utilized the spacious greenery nowadays the way mustachioed men and women in wide-brimmed hats did while strolling the Victorian promenade during long-ago times now portrayed only on antique postcards. Ambling along, Franny breathed mindfully, enjoying slight warmth that would soon get warmer amid the changing season. Focusing on his breathing the way the doctor instructed him, Franny tried to concentrate his thoughts and forget the panic that usually kept him prisoner indoors. Feeling nervous like his insides were yellow elbow macaroni swimming in a boiling pot, he told himself his new Irish powers would make everything better and beautiful again.

On South Franklin Street he noticed a crowd gathered around the orthodox Jewish synagogue. Most watched with dead eyes as three men scrubbed three swastikas drawn in green paint on the three wooden doors that led to the inside of the temple. Another man kneeled on the sidewalk, scouring the words "PUG LIVES" and "IRISH POWER" that decorated another sidewalk.

Franny froze and didn't move until he heard the voice behind him.

"You all right, sir?" Duff asked.

When the decrepit wanderer turned to face him, Duff reached out, worried the feeble man might collapse. Recognizing Franny immediately, Duff patted Franny's shoulders. Regaining some self-control, Franny steadied himself.

"I'm sorry," Franny said. "I thought they might blame me."

"Just get him out of here," said one of the workers. "Before he pulls out his snake and pisses on us. We called 911 as soon as we saw him. They should have never let him out of the vegetable bin."

Duff stared hard at the worker. He put his arm around Finnerty and walked him to the other side of the street. Ten minutes later, Duff had Franny back in his room where the faint smell of forests, pipe tobacco and strong tea soothed their uneasiness. The old man never meant any harm to anyone. He just suffered from the disease of loneliness. Duff's problems paled in comparison.

"Thank you, detective," Franny said.

When Duff's cell phone rang and he answered, Franny watched the man's eyes narrow and close.

"I'll be right there," Duff said.

Looking at Franny he said, "My mother's sick."

Franny put his hands over his mouth trying to evoke some of the pagan power he hoped might help him stay calm. Drawing from the almighty emerald energy force he now knew he possessed, Franny sought the peace of mind he needed to make it through another difficult time.

"Get some rest, Mr. Finnerty," Duff said as he forced a smile and left the room.

Franny hung his hat on a nail he hammered into the wall. Picking up the kettle he tramped to the bathroom for water. Packing his pipe, he took a seat and lit the bowl with a stick match. In the short time it took the kettle to whistle, Franny wiped away tears for the polite police officer and his mother. Franny wept for his whole depressing town that seemed to be sinking deeper and deeper into a poisonous green fog.

Maybe he couldn't save anyone.

Not even himself.

PLEASE FORGIVE ME, PADDY

Not one city official attended Delores Duffin's funeral.

No cops showed up, either.

Cookie represented the whole white race in the worn black church where so much life passed unnoticed by most of the people in the city. Heartfelt hymns of resurrection sung by the somber children's choir comforted modestly dressed mourners who came to grieve the passing of a woman whose gentle kindness touched them all. Small bouquets packed the floor by her polished mahogany coffin trimmed with a red satin interior.

Mayor McAnus meant well. The massive flower arrangement he sent towered over the casket in the shape of a trumpet. Yellow mums spelled out "Hello Dolly." McAnus got the buds, blossoms and bright clusters for free after the high school jazz club's tribute to Louis Armstrong.

Duff sat dazed in the front row of the once extravagant now chilly church, what most white people still called "the nigger church," that needed countless repairs the congregation could not afford. Water often leaked from the ceiling. Paint chips from two walls sometimes fell during services and clung like dandruff flakes to the shoulders of worshippers. Colors in the chipped main stained glass window seemed to fade. A bird had given up on a partially-built nest on the head of the Lord hanging from the cross. Space heater coils glared red and hummed from two corners of the spacious room.

The last service Duff attended there was for a 14-year-old girl who died when a 15-year-old boy put what he thought was an unloaded gun to her chest and pulled the trigger.

"You dead, baby," he said, dropping the hammer while posing like a gangster.

Many of the children now singing had played with that dead child and raised their voices in solemn reverie at that tragedy as well. Watching their faces as they sang the same hymns, their small bodies swaying left and right, Duff tried to guess who among them would be the next to fall in a war of ignorance that framed the broken battlefield on his beat. Which child among them would kill with a too easily accessible gun? Which child would succumb to drugs and live the life of the walking dead? Which child would die next?

Before the service the pastor asked Duff if he planned to say a few words on behalf of his mother. Duff politely declined. Truth was he doubted he could make it past his first few words without breaking down.

"She was easy to please," Duff said. "The 23rd Psalm would be nice. That verse was her favorite."

Sitting in the hearse waiting for the ride to the cemetery, Duff looked across the street and noticed the new Chinese restaurant the children of Vietnamese refugees owned and operated with their children. The boss and his wife stood respectfully outside the front door with their hands over their hearts. Duff waved and nodded, appreciating their silent tribute to his loss. These American citizens knew from their family's immigrant past the peril of walking through the valley of death. But white Wilkes-Barre pretty much shunned them the way they shunned anybody the natives decided didn't belong. Duff wished Cookie was sitting next to him in the big empty limo, but she said she would drive her own car.

Thankfully, she stood beside him at the gravesite, briefly placing her hand in his. Although it didn't strike Duff as terribly significant at the time, her move was not lost on the 22-year-old white grave digger who spent most of his next happy hour at the Coal Hole railing against mixing the races and swearing to God he'd never eat another Aladdin hot dog.

As quickly as the funeral began it ended. Turning away from the freshly turned earth, Duff pulled Cookie to him and hugged her to his chest. As he reached for her hand and started across the thick carpet of grass, the undertaker cleared his throat.

"Excuse me, Mr. Duffin," he said. "A long time ago your mother asked me to make sure I personally placed this envelope in your hand as soon as the service to mark her passing had concluded. She was some woman, your mother. I mean that, young man."

Duff stuffed the large manila envelope under his arm and

thanked the funeral director.

Duff again pulled Cookie close. Closing her eyes, Cookie felt happiness for the first time in a long time. A bright red cardinal whistled as it flew above the tombstones. Low clouds seemed puffier than usual. As much as she hated to admit it, Cookie knew she was in love.

At Tony P's tiny Italian restaurant where they went for lunch, Duff ordered a double Courvoisier over crushed ice. Cookie had a ginger ale, no ice and a cherry.

"I'm driving," she said.

Duff had unconsciously carried the envelope into the restaurant and placed it by his feet under the table. Leaning to pick it up, he tore open the sealed flap and pulled out several folded Times Leader newspaper clippings. The first detailed an incident involving a young police officer named Brendan O'Brien who had been reprimanded many years before after wrecking a police cruiser while under the influence of alcohol. O'Brien argued a cop hater slipped him a "mickey" while doing undercover surveillance on a "government mission" he refused to disclose. Several other small news items described bar fights in which O'Brien played a role both on and off-duty, all disposed of as self-defense.

Loosening his necktie, Duff felt his heart pound through the fabric of the last white shirt his mother would ever iron for him. He slid the clippings across the table to Cookie. Next he unfolded the letter his mother had written in meticulous handwriting and dated the day he took the oath of public service to protect and serve the people of Wilkes-Barre.

The letter said this: "My dearest Paddy, please forgive me. I am so sorry, more than you will ever know, a thousand times sorrier than the hatred you carry for your first name. A sad reason exists for your suffering. You are half Paddy, half Irish. Your people on that side knew oppression and hurt as much as anyone. Another place and time the ancestors of the man who fathered you and my family might have understood each other's pain. Not in Wilkes-Barre. That man will never understand what it means to come from bondage. Agony can teach freedom. But your father remains a slave."

Duff's breath caught in his throat at the words "your father." Watching Duff's blood pulse against the smooth skin of his temples, Cookie stayed cool. Without looking up, Duff kept reading in silence.

"Never forget good can be born from bad. You're the best good born from the worst bad I ever knew. You belong to me, not to him. Your heart is my heart, not his."

Worrying he might pass out, Duff fought to finish the letter.

"Wilkes-Barre Police Detective Brendan 'Bop' O'Brien is pure evil. I wasn't strong enough to stop him. He was young and strong and left me for dead when he finished. He didn't care I was alive. I wasn't a threat because he knew I wouldn't talk. Nobody would have believed me, anyway. I lived scared my whole life, worried for me but mostly worried for you. He eventually forgot about what he did because I didn't matter. O'Brien saw me a few years ago, looked right through me, and didn't recognize me. I thought about ending the pregnancy but didn't know what to do. So I carried you. I loved you. We loved each other. I never got to be a nurse but I was a good mother. I was a decent person. You're a decent person. Keep being nice. Be the better man. I raised you right, Paddy."

Duff slid the letter across the table and sat motionless, blinking the wet blur from his eyes, looking from floor to wall to ceiling while Cookie read.

"You never had a clue?" Cookie asked when she was through.

"Never," Duff said.

"You're sure he doesn't know?"

"If he knew he would have shot me a long time ago."

Duff heard mention long ago of a dog attack. But he never asked for details and would never know the false story his mother told her parents about how a loose Rottweiler mauled her. She told the same lie to nurses and police in the emergency room, about how a wild dog took out her eye, breaking three ribs and two teeth dragging her into the street as she walked home alone at night from work at the 7-Eleven.

For whatever the reason, nobody questioned Delores' account. Nobody investigated. In Wilkes-Bare, probable cause allows a white cop to order a young black woman into his squad car for no reason. She must obey. Spent, O'Brien threw her out like a sack of chestnut coal near the old wire rope factory parking lot. Delores knew he picked her because he could. A white bowling alley janitor on his way to work called 911 when he spotted Delores crawling along the curb at six in the morning, telling the dispatcher he was reporting some welfare queen coming home from a drunken night out courtesy of hard-working taxpayers like him. The dispatcher laughed.

Delores' faith in God deepened as her life went on. She worried less about herself and always about her baby. If Duff ever found out, he might kill the cop and she would lose the best life would ever provide. So she protected them both, keeping the secret with every ounce of discipline she possessed.

Now Duff knew.

He ordered another double cognac.

Revenge sounded like a tempting chaser.

BABOOM

Arriving at ground zero Martin Mahoney, self-appointed national commander of the newly established Mar-a-Lago Militia, pulled his battered Volkswagen camper to within inches of the knees of the young cop standing guard by the barricade at the base of the divine grotto.

"Hiya, champ," Mahoney said. "I'm here to power wash the Blessed Mother so she stays immaculate."

That made sense to the young cop because Mayor McAnus was bonkers with all the out-of-town media starting to show up asking questions about these demented Pug Mahoney videos and live internet feeds that spread as viral as the new strain of Chinese germs. McAnus was all over town with his own ramped up re-election campaign, working for Trump's re-election, and trying to shine one bright, holy light on the tourist attractions in his city, capitalizing on "Trump Town" as the Trump-centric capital of the world.

"We slid him into office," McAnus told a reporter for the BBC. "We plan to keep him there."

"McAnus, that's an old Irish name, right," the reporter said, trying hard to keep a straight face. "I'd love to see your family crest."

McAnus radiated thick ethnic pride as the English reporter visualized a pudgy puckered bum.

Over the years litterbugs left everything at the shrine from empty pint liquor bottles with pornographic poems tucked inside to heartbreaking mementos donated by mothers of children dead from cancer. Disabled vets occasionally showed up looking for miracles, as did addicts and the usual naive Catholics craving help. A rapidly deteriorating population ruled by the Church, wracked by illness, hopelessness and loss often had no place left to go. Most essentially gave up on the Blessed Mother and went with Trump. Virgin wool in your Aran cabled fisherman's sweater was as close as you'd get to chastity nowadays. Abstinence makes the heart grow fonder, but Trump was a dick you could count on.

"Sorry, sir, nobody's allowed to go through," said the stern patrolman, scratching himself through a hole in the pocket of his uniform pants.

"You realize who you're talking to, don't you?" asked Mahoney.

The cop had no idea, but any voice of authority scared him. All the rookie knew was the man in the green beret and olive drab raincoat acted just like every other crazy Irish Guy who showed up at the grotto at all hours drunk or sober, weeping and blessing himself to make outrageous demands of Mary's visage of purity.

"Make it quick," the cop said, stepping aside and pulling a wooden sawhorse from Mahoney's path.

Jumping back in his van, Mahoney steered carefully with his head out the window until he pulled within a foot of the statue. Hopping from the van, he looked both ways and placed a wide purple vase of flowers at the base. Pulling a white cloth handkerchief from his pocket, he spit on the rag and washed Mary's face with the quick ease of cleaning his glasses.

"Baboom," Mahoney said quietly as he secured the explosives firmly planted in the flower pot loaded with a big bunch of white carnations Mahoney stole from a fresh grave in the cemetery. The bomb sat snug against the Blessed Mother's toes, tickling Mahoney to no end at the thought of the upcoming eve of destruction.

"All done," Mahoney said as he pulled past the distracted cop who ignored him to flirt with a group of Catholic tenth-graders wearing plaid uniforms and knee socks who had come to pray for their teacher Mr. Dunn who was dying from liver disease before heading to the "What's Dunn Is Dunn" fundraiser the Irish Guys were holding in his honor.

All Mahoney had to do first thing in the morning was blow the divine statue to smithereens and blame the Trump haters. Vowing revenge in the name of the all that's holy Mar-a-Lago Militia, Mahoney would become a national hero to the Trump base.

Keeping America great was going to be a blast.

IRISH FREEDOM

Nervously looking this way and that, Balor hid in the shadows.

Blending with the night and trying not to whimper, he jumped when his stomach rumbled, yelping in a cry so timid the snivel bewildered him. Being on the run had its moments, of course, but now he questioned if maybe he'd be better off with the screen door at the Coal Hole hitting him in the ass dozens of times a day and the lushes feeding him booze soup and peanut butter crackers.

Born into real Irish freedom as a pup, he ran and tripped clumsily over paws too big to handle his speed and enthusiasm. Reveling in nipping at sea spray and chasing gulls at first light, Balor loved running back to the cow house to lap fresh milk from puddles collected near buckets full of the sweet stuff. Then Irish-American tourists appeared like marauding Vikings, grabbing him by the scruff of the neck, abducting him the way similar poltroons had snatched St. Patrick himself, forcing him shackled and petrified to live in another land.

All these years later, alone and afraid, the poor mutt wandered the streets of Wilkes-Barre looking for his new friend who had come out of nowhere to offer warmth and well-being. For two whole weeks, food, milk and a deep rub behind the ears taught the massive pooch that man could be kind. At the end of each visit, the giant animal would stand and shake his bulky head and body, refreshed and strong once again. Franny Finnerty would imitate Balor, shaking his small bony behind and scratching himself behind the ear. He swore he made the big hound laugh and, in turn, laughed as well.

After just a few days, the great dog sensed he might get bigger and better than ever. Just listening to his benefactor's voice made Balor feel robust. Willing to jump through fiery hoops for his protector's approval, the dog finally had a master he loved.

"You and me will lick this rotten world together," Franny said one night. "Good dog. Good boy. Good lad."

Then he'd place his face close to Balor's, who would plant two or three of his best sloppy kisses, climbing over Franny until his weight pushed the small fellow to the ground.

Today, though, Balor worried something awful had happened to prevent his friend from coming to play. Rising to full height, Balor took a tentative step into the darkness and began sniffing his way down the alley, trying to catch a familiar scent that might lead to Franny. At the end of the back street, he peered around the abandoned bartending school and continued south on River Street. He made it to Ross Street and then to Main and then to the front of the rooming house where he smelled pipe tobacco and tea that made Balor's nostrils flare.

Looking up, Balor saw the chipped steel bottom of the fire escape hanging about ten feet above the ground. In one smooth motion that began somewhere deep in his gene pool, Balor sprang with jaws wide open. Catching the bar in his mouth, he clamped his teeth around the thick metal and hung on. As his weight brought down the ladder, Balor put his paw on the first step and pulled himself to the second. Putting his paw on the second step he climbed to the third and on to the next, the next and the next rung.

Peering into small dirty windows as he climbed, he continued skyward. If Balor was lucky, he'd find his buddy behind one of the dozens of filthy panes. Looking into a window on the third floor, Balor saw him, a skeleton standing in blue pajamas decorated with tiny Celtic crosses. Franny ate one piece of salt water taffy after another, seemingly drugged and so very, very unhappy. Rising to full height, Balor knocked against the window with his brute head. In an awkward motion, the dog stretched the skin around his mouth to show his teeth in a weird doggie grin of affection and recognition, his attempt at a human smile. If nothing else, Balor would show Franny how happiness and friendship could prevail no matter what. Already surprised, shocked and embarrassed at the day's turn of events, the old man awakened from his stupor, spotted Balor and tried to respond. After spending so many years fighting depression, battling to maintain, regain and retain sanity, Franny had lost control again. Drowning in doubt and self-pity, regression overruled optimism. Worst of all, seeing Balor shamed him.

Balor kept smiling.

With the ease of a haze lifting from a sparkling lake, Franny's gloom began to clear. Grunting and straining to open the window, he battled frenzied emotion he worried he couldn't contain. In the midst of self-absorbed despair, Franny had almost forgotten his best friend. But his best friend had not forgotten Franny. A perfect pup at heart, Balor leaped, knocking Franny backward into the cheap mattress where his rubbery skin stretched over brittle bones had grown sore and chafed as he stared for days at the ceiling. Between a gentle breeze from the pooch's tail, an extraordinarily cold nose and a dozen wet kisses, man and dog realized they would never be alone again.

BUGS IN YOUR TV

Cookie heard the bell and opened the door to find Binkee passed out on the small front porch of the one-time company house she rented for $600-a-month in the Heights section of the city. After dragging her inside, Cookie cradled Binkee's head in her lap and wiped her face with a warm wet wash cloth.

"Poor Binkee," Cookie said. "Everything will be all right."

Thinking Duff was at the door when she heard the bell ring again, Cookie opened the heavy windowless oak slab that came with the original house built for factory workers by the wire rope executives who owned and operated the company housing. Thank God. No way could she handle this by herself. Worried about Duff, anyway, Cookie needed a hug.

"You better have beer," Pug said as he pushed his way past Cookie and scanned the foyer leading to the living room.

"We need to call an ambulance," Cookie said.

"No way," Pug said, slamming the door behind him.

Stepping to Binkee's side with the uneasy gait of a father preparing to view a daughter's body at the hospital morgue, Pug kneeled and slowly reached for her hand. Raising her fingers to his lips, he noticed her fingernails, filthy, bleeding and chewed deeply into the cuticle. Leaning to put his face to her cheek, he mumbled into her ear.

Awakened, Binkee rolled her head from side to side and nodded. Trying to speak, she whispered, puckered small lips and blew a weak kiss to Pug. Cookie tried to ignore the drama, to give them some kind of bizarre privacy so they might settle down. She worried Binkee might die from an overdose of any number of unknown toxic substances she ingested. She worried Pug would kill Binkee, her and then himself. The 911 call was out of the question. Cookie had to manage the madness with whatever mental triage she could muster.

"There's Rolling Rock in the refrigerator," she said to Pug.

"Pug need beer," he said, rising from Binkee's side, beating his chest like an ape and lumbering into the kitchen. "Pug must drink."

Sitting cross-legged on the floor, Cookie looked into Binkee's feathery blue eyes.

"You think you love him?"

"Yeah. I can save him, too. I'm the only thing he doesn't want to kill."

"He's killing your spirit."

"I'm a Virgo. I'm down to earth. I put everybody before me. Puggy's a Sagittarius. He likes to explore. He's adaptable. He likes change."

"You got a feeling inside your belly that jiggles like jelly?"

"Yeah, grape jelly."

"That's not jelly in your belly, though. Your little tummy is showing more than usual."

"How can you tell when I can hardly tell myself?"

"When you've run through the jungle as much as I have you can smell a pregnancy from a condom away."

"I don't wear condoms," Binkee said. "I know I should but I don't."

Cookie closed her eyes.

"Does Pug know?"

"Nope."

"Want to tell him?"

"Yep. But I'm afraid. You tell him."

"Do you two consider yourselves a couple, as in a relationship?"

Binkee looked puzzled.

"I don't know about relationships, but, we're like engaged," Binkee said. "That just happened now. When I woke up he proposed. I accepted."

Cookie imagined a wedding reception with chain saws.

"Puggy says he wants us to get ring finger tattoos before we move to the beach. I want a ladybug. He wants a bedbug. Pug says he wants to have children with horns on them. I'm going to name my first baby Casper because he's the friendliest ghost you know, and my baby can learn witchcraft to disappear so no demons can hurt him because they won't be able to see him if he doesn't want them to. Isn't that cool, Cookie?"

"Christ, Binkee," Cookie said. "You're still high. Life has twisted your brain into knots. Pug doesn't know you're pregnant, right?"

"Noper."

Pug shuffled in taking alternating swigs from two bottles of Rock.

Cookie spoke softly.

"Guess who's going to be a daddy?"

Pug drained a beer and dropped the bottle on the floor. Binkee looked joyful. She pointed at him.

"Surprise, Puggy," she said.

The world stopped at that instant. Beginning anew, Pug started squawking like a pirate's parrot, jumping around like a mosh pit punker in heat, falling to his back, obscenely writhing, thrusting his hips into the air, pumping balled fists and screaming, "AHH-AHHH-AHHHHH."

"You happy?" Binkee asked.

Pug leaped to his feet without using his hands like an All-American gymnast and did his jig.

"You're silly," Binkee said. "I love you. Casper loves you."

Pug stopped dancing.

"Bugs are crawling out of your TV, bitch" he said.

"Pug, please," Cookie said. "Let me help you turn yourself in. See a doctor. You're guilty but mentally ill. With the right medication and the right attitude, you'll get better. Raise this little baby the right way. Duff can help. Before it's too late."

"It's already too late," Pug said, turning and diving without warning through the living room window, hitting the porch in a shower of glass, rolling and rising in a smooth motion before disappearing into the parking lot behind the take-out pierogi restaurant.

Binkee struggled to her knees and called after him.

"We don't have to get married if you're scared," she said. "We can just live together."

Bound for Hell, Pug fled.

A SURPRISE VISIT

All the Paddy's Day parade bribes came in early. However the lads did it they did it. By Friday afternoon, the Irish Guys were back to boozing in the Coal Hole after twisting every arm and cutting every corner it took to get the parade up and running. But the best news came out of nowhere, another great lie courtesy of a longtime leader of the band.

"Mr. Trump's people called. The president is marching with us in the parade," O'Brien said.

The crowd roared.

"Right here in Wilkes-Barre, to really put us on the map for something good rather than that basket case kid running around like that dwarf leprechaun in the movies. But first, let us bow our heads and offer a moment of silence for Father O'Toole, if you please."

The assembled men removed baseball caps, tweed caps and bricklayers' union skull caps. They bowed their heads and closed their eyes. After two seconds, O'Brien broke the silence.

"Morale is bad all over," he said. "We need a victory march in Trump Town. Mr. Trump wants to thank us for putting him in office."

The Irish Guys blinked and stood there, waiting to be told what to do next. O'Brien dripped brilliance in his knowledge that the lads would follow orders even if his malarkey took them over the edge of reason, exactly what this long walk to nowhere was designed to do. Good soldiers never question. They follow orders. As history teaches, loyalty has its drawbacks.

O'Brien explained how the Paddy's Day parade would garner international media attention. The club would benefit. Trump knew better than anyone he would not have been elected in 2016 without them.

Mikey Hoyle jumped up and down behind the bar.

"We need a grander float than ever to lead the parade," he said. "What do we got?"

To a man the membership hated the press and would take

every chance they got to denigrate media outlets. Hoyle proposed an "Enemies of the State" float with reporters portrayed by store mannequins dressed as prisoners in chains with the words "Press" and "Traitor" emblazoned across the backs of their black and white striped uniforms. Hoyle also proposed using real reporters they kidnapped from the Times Leader and Citizens' Voice newsrooms.

"Think of the coverage we'll get if we hold a couple of those bastards hostage. Geraldo might even come to town," said an increasingly excited Mikey Hoyle as he washed beer glasses. "On second thought, I'd rather get Bill O'Reilly. Geraldo's a Jew. Remember when I got home from the Army and we rooted for Saddam Hussain to drop a SCUD missile on his head during the Gulf War?"

With the Paddy's Day parade right around the corner, already organized and paid for, the Irish Guys jumped into last-minute action, raising even more money, making last-minute phone calls telling people a surprise emergency had arisen, and leaking the surprise all in the same breath. This was HUGE, as their man would say. Fueling their passion for an incredible America drove them digging deeper and deeper into the congested bowels of the Trump base for cash.

By tapping into the bottom level of their Paddy's Day parade donor list and promising ten times more than they could deliver, the Irish Guys put the arm on even more people who expected favors and jobs and special interest treatment. To their credit, no matter the odds, the Irish Guys never gave up. Their phony hustle reminded O'Brien of those cubic zirconia diamonds he bought on the Home Shopping Network and sold on-duty as the real deal.

Like Trump the parade would make history, even if he lost re-election, which no Irish Guy seriously considered. They were shocked he won to begin with, but never confessed to harboring a single doubt. So the Irish Guys hawked what they were calling an "official state visit" even though nobody thought to confirm the visit. They simply took O'Brien at his word that Trump would show up. Slapping each other on the back until they started coughing and hacking and chugging beers to clear their pipes, they christened the parade "our" parade featuring "our" president the same way they affectionately referred to blood relatives as "our" Joe or "our" Tara.

What an extra cash goldmine it would be since the club was already rolling in the pre-Paddy's Day dough. With early payment of registration fees and kickbacks for prime marching positions, they had more money than ever. With this additional parade infusion they'd have extra greenbacks on hand for any number of projects, including a "Home Of The Irish Guys" flashing neon sign outside the Coal Hole.

Mr. Trump would be so proud he'd probably accept an invitation to visit the Coal Hole when the parade ended. The Irish Guys would stay open all night. Trump's 13-year-old was even welcome. The club would make a fuss over the kid, make him an honorary member, slip him a brew or two, and talk to him even if his old man wouldn't.

Not one business refused to pony up.

Extra checks and currency came in primarily from fast food restaurants, beauty schools, and more than two dozen neighborhood saloons in exchange for prime marching positions at the front of the parade as well as from "Lock Her Up" ads in the printed program. After depositing the money in the special parade bank account O'Brien controlled, he cashed out the account and sat home counting the windfall. O'Brien placed the new bills in a large police department evidence envelope and stored it in the closet at home he told Agnes he booby-trapped.

Another whopping couple of grand in receipts from the illegal "Irish Guys Sweepstakes" money filled a duffel bag O'Brien kept under the bed. He had all the money he needed, including cash contributions from the dumb-ass Irish-American vice president at the right wing news talk radio station, a couple of bigger restaurants, corrupt public office-holding politicians, and their crooked benefactors. The grand total came to $87,957. Not counting the coffee money O'Brien clipped from the police station on a regular basis, he figured the haul would get him started quite nicely in his new life in Ireland.

O'Brien already entered into a secret agreement with an assistant city clerk to cash out his pension. A small bribe here and a bigger bribe there would provide him with a monthly check deposited in a County Mayo bank account for the rest of his life. Ireland would never extradite him. Figuring the Republic of Ireland boasted similar wheeler-dealer hustlers like himself, particularly bankers and real estate speculators who killed the Celtic Tiger, all O'Brien had to do was pay off the connivers over there the way he bought comparable pirates over here. The Irish crooks likely had relatives in Wilkes-Barre and Scranton.

All that remained in the official Irish Guys financial portfolio was a few bucks from the new rubber machine the men hung without fanfare in the Coal Hole men's room as a gesture of solidarity to younger members who were becoming fathers like every day was Fathers' Day and all the kids were free. The club got the machine from the last of the Pittston City mob-connected vending outfits. If all went according to plan, at the same time Donald Trump failed to show up for the Irish Guys parade down South Main Street, O'Brien would be on his way to a soft Aer Lingus landing at Shannon Airport in time to toast the Ennis morning with a half dozen creamy pints of stout.

Bop O'Brien's fantasy drew closer to coming true.

There he was sitting in his first pub, telling his favorite lies, buying round after round of drinks, and settling in for the rest of his life. Wilkes-Barre was history. No more kissing ass and looking over his shoulder. No more Tinkerbell son. His only regret would be missing the pusses on the Irish Guys when they discovered he bailed with their pot of gold.

O'Brien would want for nothing.

He'd even find himself a colleen with red hair so thick he could mop the floor with her.

Trump would understand.

KISS ME I'M IRISH

Thrilled with his newfound sense of control, "Death Wish" Duggan clipped his toe nails on the couch.

"Hey, SueReen, c'mere and gimme a kiss."

"Ewww."

"What, you don't love me no more?"

"I'm watching my stories on TV."

"Bet a whole bunch of other girls would give me a kiss."

"So call them."

"I'll do better than that," he said. "I just had a great idea."

"I thought I heard a fart."

Death Wish jumped to his feet and glared.

"I detect a tone in that voice," he said.

"Whatever," she said.

"I'm going to have my own float in the parade."

"Your bladder always floats in the parade."

Death Wish cracked his knuckles.

"I'll show all these so-called experts that China virus or no China virus, real American men do what we want. My old man and the Irish Guys will love it."

"So what's the float?"

"A 'Kiss Me I'm Irish' kissing booth float. I'll swap spit for free with dozens of plastered girls on the parade route. With the big marches cancelled in New York and Philadelphia because of the disease hoax, revelers will be coming in to party from all over."

SueReen gaped at the man in her life.

"So what do you say, lass, how about a little smootch?"

"I'd rather kiss Mike Pence's mother."

LOVE IS GRAND

After banging down four shots of Irish Mist and five pints of Guinness at the Coal Hole, O'Brien staggered to his car. At the first traffic light he caught himself daydreaming about sitting in Burke's, the Clonbur bar and restaurant he read about online, slurping Galway oysters on the half shell. Behind the wheel and waiting for the light to go green, in his mind he counted out each one of a freshly shucked dozen culinary treasures, some sprinkled with lemon and horseradish.

Behind him a driver pounded his horn. Coming quickly from his reverie, O'Brien realized he must have idled through two cycles of red, yellow and green lights. He instinctively raised his middle finger and waved it over his head like a maestro conducting an orchestra, deciding to purposely wait through another cycle of lights. O'Brien watched the driver behind him step from the car and close the distance with the fury of a linebacker blitz.

Duff's face suddenly appeared at the driver's side window. Standing casually beside O'Brien's car, Duff dropped to one knee and waited patiently for O'Brien to lower his window. Snorting a mouthful of mucus from deep within his nasal cavity, blowing out his cheeks as he cleared the phlegm from his throat, Duff gathered the snot into a molded ball of yellow ooze and hocked the loogie into O'Brien's face. With thick, slimy spit clouding his vision, O'Brien grabbed for the door handle. The raging bull charged. But as O'Brien began to lunge and Duff danced backward to brace himself for the collision, an iron grip encircled his arms and lifted him off his feet. Another pair of thick forearms snared O'Brien.

O'Brien's son, Michael, and his boyfriend, Tommy, had seen the event unfold as they waited to cross the street in front of the YMCA where they had been working out. Seeing the color of his father's face and hearing his war cry, Michael knew Duff could die. Duff could kill, as well. Both men might die as could people caught in a crossfire.

"Relax," Michael said.

Duff relaxed.

Easily controlling O'Brien, Tommy said nothing.

"Get your filthy hands off me, you fucking queer, you," O'Brien screamed.

"It's a pleasure to meet you, too," Tommy said. "Michael has told me so much about you."

"It's cool," Duff said. "It's cool. I'm all right."

Michael sensed the agile in-shape black man meant what he said and loosened his grip. Why he and Tommy stepped in to stop anyone intent on killing his maniac father was beyond Michael's imagination. But he always tried to do what was right. This looked like serious business. As always, his conscience guided his behavior. Duff lowered his head, got back in his car, and pulled away.

As soon as he saw O'Brien's puffy face in the driver's side window, Duff knew he'd never draw his gun, let alone murder this fiend. He had already informed his lawyer and turned over his mother's letter. With his mother dead and the statute of limitations run out long ago, he had no hope justice would be served. No, Duff would not kill O'Brien. That's why he spit. He had to do something foul to respond to O'Brien's sadistic behavior. Delores would not approve. Or would she?

Back in front of the Y, O'Brien strained against Tommy's restraining hold until he felt he might pass out from lack of oxygen. He fell gasping for breath against the fender of his car when Tommy finally released the simple Brazilian Jujutsu chokehold he had applied.

"You fuckers is history," O'Brien said.

"We're getting married and moving to Brooklyn," Michael said. "Mommy's coming with us."

Tommy put his hands on his hips.

"You really need to take up yoga or meditation, dad," he said.

A SICK UNHOLY DEMON

Pug went home to say goodbye to his mother.

Licking superficial wounds he received from jumping through the window that miraculously failed to cut him severely only increased Pug's taste for blood. From where he sat behind the bushes Pug enjoyed a clear view to his parents' front door.

Over the weekend Pug called home three times. He hung up each time his father answered. On his fourth try his mother finally picked up the phone on the first ring. Bridget normally slept fourteen or more hours a day as depression ate holes in her heart and she did nothing but drink during her few waking hours. Closing his eyes, Pug listened to her slur, "Hlow, hlow?" until she dropped the receiver and eventually hung up. Pug wanted to hear her voice because he loved his mother but no longer recognized her as human.

"Blue extraterrestrial microbes ate your mind, Ma," he said into the receiver when she dropped the phone. "Outer space coons sucking out your brains."

Black people, blue microbes, why did everything bad have to be colored?

Binkee, too, right before his eyes, recently contorted into a grotesque anthropoid, a bisexual ape robot that squeaked when she talked because devil bacteria were eating her voice box to keep her from speaking in tongues and telling the truth about the end time. Pug knew to be careful. Forms could take new shapes and become anything. Animals could become people, and people could become germs, and germs could destroy his power just by crawling up his nose and laying eggs that would hatch in his head and make his brain waves create disease globules. If that happened, maybe he'd be lucky enough to get the Chinese virus so he could infect everybody but Trump supporters. Pug's formula was simple. The base deserved to live. All others deserved to die from the pandemic. The "Pug Plague" could help him destroy the world.

While he waited in the bushes for his father to leave the house Pug went over his plan. With money he saved rolling homos and breaking into cars and houses during his time on the lam, Pug had enough cash to buy two bus tickets to California where maybe one of those devil cults would accept him, Binkee and their baby. With some coaching, Binkee would come around. Spending time with a baby might be fun. The thing would be a boy who looked and acted just like him. Maybe he'd love the warped little troll.

Feeling spaced and happy, an enflamed spirit of the jig took hold. Emerging from the bushes and bouncing like a runaway pogo stick, Pug bent his knees. Kicking his legs as high as he could, spinning fast, he smashed into a telephone pole, ramming headfirst into the hard wood. Crawling to his feet, he stood and jumped up and down. Kicking higher, he made an effort to keep his arms straight by his side. Leaping at the pole on purpose this time, his shoulder caught a low metal rung used for climbing, spun him around and knocked him on his back. Hitting the ground hard he bit a deep wound into his tongue. Resting in the dirt, Pug sucked hard on the rusty metal taste of his own salty blood.

When his father's van engine came to life with a sputter, Pug looked up in time to see his father pull away. Leaning on his right arm, Pug sat up and brushed himself off. Adjusting the black watch cap he wore pulled tightly over his ears he stroked the new pointy red goatee that adorned his chin. Pug looked like a chip off the old block if the devil had sired an unholy demon.

Sick St. Pug, the patron martyr of mayhem, squeezed tight against his house, hugging the aluminum siding as he crawled to the door. Sliding his key in the lock, he strolled into the house like he never left, like the family breakup never happened. In other cities the cops would have been all over him. In Wilkes-Barre the cops pulled the stakeout after two days of haphazard surveillance. It wasn't like he killed a cop or a financial advisor. As always, home smelled like stale cigarette smoke and burned oven grease. Walking to his room, he went to his underwear drawer where he kept a collection of state maps he received after writing letters to state capital visitor and tourist offices when he was an overly curious 10-year-old. Thrilled when the thick packages came in the mail, Pug often sat up past midnight looking at maps and colorful brochures, noting the different shapes of the states, trying to memorize city names that seemed important or that he heard about on TV, cities he wanted to visit one day when he grew up, places where he might live and get famous playing in a death metal band. Imagining driving through Arizona and Texas, Pug envisioned searching for Indian arrowheads and gold when he reached New Mexico.

Now Pug needed his California map for when he and Binkee got there. Pug's first map had been Idaho, the potato state he got interested in because he thought the state had something to do with being Irish. When his mom told him everybody Irish was related and that everybody named Mahoney was his cousin, Pug felt important, like he had some kind of super power and friends all over the world.

Life brimmed with innocence.

Next Pug hit the bathroom. Opening the medicine cabinet, he grabbed a tube of his mother's green pain salve and smeared a shamrock on the mirror, in the middle of which he wrote, "ILUVU-MOM." He could hear his mother in the next room breathing heavily through a boozy barbiturate haze. Pug tiptoed to her side. He kneeled by her bed. He kissed her on top of the head. Bridget never flinched, even when Pug spoke.

"Would you like me to tuck you in, Ma? Put a pillow over your head. Put you out of your misery?"

Leaning down Pug gently kissed his mother's cheek.

"Goodbye," he said.

Bridget stirred slightly when she heard the back door slam.

WHAT IF TRUMP WINS?

Snuggled beneath Mrs. Duffin's puffy quilt on her comfy double bed, Cookie and Duff dried their eyes on starched white pillowcases.

"I wanted to kill him," he said.

"But you didn't."

"I knew it was wrong."

"Thank your mother. She knew, too. That's why she raised you the way she did. That's why she told you the truth."

"Then out of nowhere O'Brien and I are both saved by Michael O'Brien and his badass fiancée coming to the rescue like a couple of gay superheroes. You can't make this shit up."

"Michael is a gentleman, Duff. He used to be our paper boy."

"How rational can he be with all them crazy cracker genes running through him?"

"Listen to you. You have the same genes. He's your half-brother, Duff. You're the good seed part of a bad man. So is he. His mother is a saint. Just like yours."

"Brothers," Duff said. "Damn."

"Your mother loved you so much," she said.

"I called the newspaper," Duff said. "Maybe we can't go to court but we can lay out all the facts in public. My mother's letter will embarrass me but should wake up some of these people who run the city. Maybe the feds will come and take a look at the police department. Maybe the Justice Department will get interested. They got a Civil Rights Division. We got an uncivil rights community."

"Can I ask you a question?"

"You don't need permission," Duff said.

"What if Trump wins again? He'll still be in charge of the Justice Department."

"You think he can win?"

"Yes."

"I do, too."

"So what do we do, Duff?"

227

"The Irish Guys have been running life in Wilkes-Barre for more than 150 years. It's time they face opposition. Decent people have to act if only to take an honest look in the mirror. Make a move. Let their white daughters marry black men maybe."

"I love you, Duff," Cookie said.

"Is that a yes?"

"Was that a proposal?"

"What do you think?"

"I think we have a future."

NOBODY'S GONNA PAY FOR IT

A few days before the Paddy's Day parade the Irish Guys played the 2016 election night video where McAnus stood high atop the bar, raised his arms, and stilled the crowd when all the returns were in.

"We did it," he said. "Trump won because of us."

Election Day always came and went as a boisterous affair at the Coal Hole, but this day evolved unlike any other. The Second Coming would pale in comparison. Wilkes-Barre pushed Trump over the top in Luzerne County, Pennsylvania, which helped push Trump over the top nationally. More people in this leaky cave of piss-poor democracy, particularly renegade Judas Democrats, voted for Trump than anybody expected. The conservative uprising of fools was led by local news talk radio buffoons and other Trump apologists who in their smug ignorance denied racism and misogyny had anything to do with the win, then went back to bashing women, African Americans, immigrants and the poor, including working-class whites they deemed to be white trash who likely didn't vote for anybody. This cold-hearted pecking order, accompanied by wealthy local Republicans and other comfortable middle-class bigots who considered themselves blue collar champions, provided an imperfect storm of socially impaired bad citizens. They now identified as victors.

Wisconsin, Michigan and Pennsylvania gave Trump the election. About 77,000 votes did the trick even though Hillary pulled three million more and won the popular tally. Pennsylvanians cast 44,292 more votes for Trump than for Hillary. Unthinking, unblinking Wilkes-Barre and Luzerne County voters went mad for Trump. For that they will forever stand alone on the slag heap of history as the Rust Belt capital of the uncivilized world. There, sheer thick-headed stupidity took a final stand and came out smelling like a neglected toilet bowl loaded with ballots cast by shit-for-brains dullards.

Press from around the world, print and broadcast, flocked to

Wilkes-Barre to cover Trump's first hurrah. Devoted village slugs honestly believed reporters interviewed them for their political genius rather than their limited vision and gullibility. Even second-rate local yokel reporters came away from interviews wondering if any hope would ever exist for common sense in the future of this town and region. Most agreed any chance for positive change and progress finally died and got a headstone. Nobody who voted for Trump in Luzerne County made a more disgraceful showing than Irish Americans who lived in the city of Wilkes-Barre.

None of them thought of their win as white power.

They simply considered the victory the way life was meant to be.

Packed on election night with out-of-control carousers ready to riot to celebrate the new cutting-edge republic, the Coal Hole walls shook from the noise. At about 1:45 a.m. the video showed a close-up of McAnus again leaping on the bar and hushing the crowd.

"More good news," the mayor said. "We will officially take applications for full time jobs at the first Trump Coal Mine which will open here as soon as possible."

A deafening cacophony of whoops served as backdrop in the video to McAnus passing out applications he ran off that morning on the City Hall copy machine with the words "TRUMP COAL MINOR APPLICATION" printed across the top. The misspelling paid Freudian homage, perhaps, to a time when child labor made backbreaking pain profitable for bloated plutocrats throughout the coal fields.

"This is incredible," the mayor said. "Incredible. Your chance to personally make us great again by one day sending your offspring back into the Northeastern Pennsylvania mines like their great-grandfathers before them. You younger men who are out of work, laid-off and fired, without good cause, of course, now have opportunity staring you in the eye."

McAnus missed the countless blank stares that greeted his announcement. Nobody in the room displayed enthusiasm at the prospect of digging into a reopened hell hole as a way to make a living. Working for low wages in short sleeves in an air-conditioned warehouse, retail store or office was bad enough. But a coal mine? Had McAnus and Trump lost their minds? Nobody dared suggest lunacy, however. The men wanted the mines open. They just didn't want to work in them.

"We start hiring in two days," McAnus said. "So get here early. We expect a line out the door and down the block. You might want to pack a nice lunch in a metal pail like our forefathers took with them down the mine. Nothing better than thick meatloaf sandwiches on white bread wrapped in the front page of the Times Leader. That's all the press is good for anyway."

Everybody howled.

The election party continued until about 5 a.m.

Two days later, when an always hazy and hungover Mikey Hoyle unlocked the doors at 8 a.m. to open the bar and start the application process, 17 undocumented Mexicans carrying shovels rushed the door. Grinning and laughing, smacking each other on the back like the Irish, Italian, Polish, German and other immigrants who mined coal in times gone by, they showed up ready to do whatever it took to make a living.

"No speakee Engleese," said Benito, who identified himself as the leader of the work crew.

Screaming, "USAUSAUSA," Hoyle slammed the door in the man's face.

Running to the jukebox, Hoyle pulled out a five, slid the bill into the receptacle, and punched in a couple of Irish numbers so the music would drown out the sounds of cumbia and ranchero music blaring from the Mexicans' uninsured cars and dilapidated pickups parked outside on the street. While corridos blared from speakers, the Mexicans sang along at the top of their voices and drank warm cans of Tecate beer.

Hoyle knew these men shaped the vanguard of a mean hombre army of rapists and murderers who wanted to take over his country. He trembled at the thought that he might one day become a minority.

No Irish need apply.

TIRED OF WINNING

From where he stood in the doorway to "Danny Boy" Duggan's bedroom, O'Brien marveled at the décor. Wilkes-Barre's tough guy cop had outfitted the room with the flair of a Vatican interior decorator, hanging rosaries made from a variety of beads (wood, rhinestones, multi-colored glass and, of course, anthracite coal) from every available lamp, chair and bedpost. Pope John XXIII blessed one pair of rosaries that glowed in the dark. Crucifixes, dried palm fronds, several St. Brigid's crosses, and numerous scapulars bearing a variety of holy inscriptions in Gaelic and English also adorned the room, looming over what Duggan called in a reverential tone "the death bed."

"Jesus, Danny Boy," O'Brien said. "What did you do to your hair?"

"I dyed it yellow," Duggan said. "So I look like President Trump."

"Is that a silk Trump brand bathrobe you're wearing?"

"Junior bought it for me at the outlet mall in the Poconos," Duggan said.

"You look like Hugh Hefner," O'Brien said.

Duggan frowned.

"Please, Bop. This is not the Playboy Mansion."

"You don't look so good, pal," O'Brien said.

"The doctor says I can go at any time."

After missing Duggan at the bar and at work for a week, O'Brien's curiosity got the best of him. When he stopped by the house to check Duggan's condition, his former partner's pallor came as no surprise after a lifetime of guzzling alcohol for breakfast, lunch and supper and happy hour in between.

"Why do you want to look like Trump?" O'Brien asked.

"After all these years, that leprechaun routine was getting to me," he said. "The sicker I get the more I identify with Trump. He's one of us, Bop. Trump means more to me than that little fighting Irish prick ever did."

"So you're terminal," O'Brien said.

"You make me sound like a bus station," Duggan said. "Have a little respect for my liver."

"Sorry, Duggan."

"Call me 'The Duggan' like in 'The Donald.'"

"Er, sorry, 'The Duggan.'"

"I'm going downhill fast," Duggan said. "After I got Junior that motorcycle and the 'Bikers for Trump' position, I quit while I was ahead. I got the sick time coming and didn't want to announce the cirrhosis. I bought a whole new Trump outfit for the wake and funeral, a nice blue suit, a white dress shirt with cuff links, and an extra-long red tie. Ah, Jesus, Bop, won't I look grand?"

"That you will," O'Brien said.

"I'm born again, you know."

"Once wasn't enough?"

Duggan glowered.

"I've accepted Jesus Christ as my personal savior just like President Trump. I was ashamed of some of the things I did in the past, that I could do anything I wanted because I'm a star. People let me do whatever I wanted. Just like Trump."

"You cast your absentee ballot yet?"

"Three times."

O'Brien punched his fist into the air.

"We're winning so much, I'm tired of winning," he said.

"Yeah, please, please Mr. President, It's too much winning! We can't take it anymore," Duggan said.

As Duggan closed his eyes, he stepped onto a heavenly escalator to that big Trump Tower suite in the sky. Satan, wearing a red MAGA baseball cap, stood at the top.

"You got the wrong staircase, Duggan," the devil said. "We're going down."

GET READY TO MARCH

The first cop on the scene at the grotto frantically radioed the dispatcher that the Blessed Mother had been annihilated. When the smoke cleared, calmer first responders realized that most of whatever exploded had fizzled.

Mahoney's homemade bomb got wet from the watery cow manure he drove all the way to farm country to retrieve, moistening the device he studied diligently online to make. The watered-down cow pies dampened the M80s he bought at the fireworks tent that stays open all year and taped to three lit railroad flares that fell over and burned harmlessly into the dirt. The improvised explosive device smoked and petered out shortly after Mahoney lit the fuses and ran laughing into the woods behind the grotto.

All that really blew was a cluster of Roman candles left over from when the Irish Guys stopped at Ft. Pedro at South of the Border in South Carolina on the way back from last year's golf trip to Myrtle Beach. The fire department extinguished the grotto blaze in about seven minutes, dousing the smoking heap and putting an end to Mahoney's sacred sortie.

Although city officials agreed some malcontent definitely tried to blow up the Blessed Mother, nobody but Mayor McAnus seemed overly concerned.

"Who would do such an awful thing?" he asked, moaning into the reporter's mic as lights from the action news television cameras bathed his face in a halo of confusion. "Do terrorists walk among us?"

"Would you relax," said O'Brien, bodily pulling the mayor away from the interview. "You sound like a mental patient. Our parade sponsors will go nuts if they see that interview. Not to mention your campaign committee. We're trying to lure tourists to Wilkes-Barre not drive them away. We can bring busloads of Catholics here now. All we got to do is make the Blessed Mother look great again after this horrible attack on her virginity and all that's holy."

McAnus perked up.

"You think we can doll her up and pull it off?" he said.

McAnus' thoughts turned sober.

"Only one man is capable of this anarchy. This is the work of our wild colonial boy himself. Mahoney went rogue. He did this. The attack has Mar-a-Lago Militia written all over it. He's been sending me threats. Who else would try to blow up the Blessed Mother? Other than Mahoney's psycho kid who would first post a video of himself humping her on a live Facebook feed."

"We'll have Mahoney in custody within the hour in a body bag," O'Brien said.

"What if he talks? Calls in to that loser white nationalist radio station? "

"Mahoney's already lost it. He's been calling the bar threatening to blow everybody up if we don't hire white Americans."

Indeed, Martin Mahoney took advantage of going underground to burrow deeper into strategic preparations for his one-man armed revolution. In one week he drank six cases of beer and called in 13 bomb threats to ethnic businesses in three counties, including Chinese restaurants, Jewish delis, a Japanese sushi spot, the two Arab hot dog joints in town, a Mexican place and, by mistake, the Coal Hole. He asked the same question every time.

"You hire illegals, don't you?"

When the inevitable answer came back negative, Martin would threaten to level the establishment unless the owner promised to hire nothing but white male Americans.

"I know that's you, Mahoney," Mikey Hoyle said when he took Mahoney's call. "You're calling the wrong place. You can't be illegal if you're Irish. We're Irish here. Real fucking Irish. So go shit in your hat."

Neither Mahoney nor Hoyle knew or cared about the 50,000 or so undocumented Irish who live and work in the United States without government permission. They're different, Hoyle would later explain, the way John Kennedy and Bobby Kennedy screwing Marilyn Monroe were different and not even close to adultery.

"We're talking about Marilyn Monroe here," Hoyle said. "What would you do? I mean, Marilyn Monroe."

Before his blasphemous offensive went bust, Mahoney fully expected to successfully atomize the Blessed Virgin and blame it on deep state Jews and liberals. Then he planned to travel the country recruiting future low-intelligence Mar-a-Lago mercenaries, staying in the mansions of rich and famous fascist sympathizers and maybe even get a presidential medal of freedom the way Rush did. Trump would appreciate the great civic service Mahoney offered his country and the sacrifice he withstood to keep America great. So what if Mahoney's behavior was improper, violent and felonious? Just as Mr. Trump reeked of bogus authenticity and self-destruction, so did Mr. Mahoney.

When Mahoney's anonymous telephone threats made the papers in Hazleton, Wilkes-Barre and Scranton, Mahoney started a scrapbook. Word in the Coal Hole was that FBI agents had already started asking questions about him and his nutcase son. Mahoney hoped he would soon be full time on the run and loving it like the genuine 21st Century patriot and freedom fighter he had become.

"You're right," O'Brien said. "Mahoney might talk."

McAnus pondered his next move.

"Unlike us, Mahoney is not a team player. That's what's wrong with this town and this country. Nobody plays by the rules anymore. So it's up to us to straighten them out," he said.

"Look, we already put out an all-points bulletin describing Martin as armed and dangerous," O'Brien said. "Our guys hate him and will shoot to kill even if they catch him sleeping off a drunk or if he tries to surrender. Best practice for our kind of cop is to claim self-defense no matter what happens. Blinking is considered life threatening behavior. That's the new normal. Shoot first. Don't ask questions later. If you think for a split second your life is in danger, your life is in danger even if your target is white."

Blessing himself and kissing his fingertips, McAnus said, "Blue lives matter."

"So just relax and keep your big yap shut," O'Brien said. "I'm going home to get ready for the parade."

"We step off at 2 p. m.," McAnus said.

"I still can't believe them pansies up in Scranton postponed their parade because of that flu that's going around," O'Brien said. "Boston, Philadelphia, Chicago, Ireland, too."

"No illegal germs are going tell Irish Guys in Wilkes-Barre what to do," McAnus said. "Millions of Americans are dead and dying from alcoholism and you don't hear the bleeding hearts belly-aching about cancelling the beer commercials on TV. What would our ancestors say if we let some Chinaman with a bug up his ass cancel our parade because him and his family invented this egg roll pestilence in their restaurant?"

"You showed what you're made of by refusing to cancel our parade, Mayor," O'Brien said. "That's what makes you great."

"I didn't even have to think about it," McAnus said.

"Like all the rest of your decisions," O'Brien said.

McAnus radiated pride.

Clearly pleased with themselves, these two Irish Guys in good standing shook hands. McAnus pulled a white handkerchief from his back pocket and blew his nose in a honker that could have won first prize in a Canadian goose mating call contest. Getting emotional, McAnus quickly wiped tears from his eyes and again blew his nose in a noisy nasal blast before stuffing the hankie in his front sport jacket pocket like a fashion puff.

"I can't believe our day's almost here," McAnus said. "We'll be practicing for next year's inauguration parade. When we Irish Guys show the world we're winners."

"Oh, we're winners all right," O'Brien said.

"Like the founding fathers."

"Promises made," O'Brien said. "Promises kept."

Walking away, O'Brien couldn't get over the level of superficiality to which his peers had plummeted in a short two or three generations. Of all the ethnic groups to scratch and claw their way ashore, the Irish were the worst. With chummy banter and bourgeois mediocrity, they morphed into the very oppressors they fled in Ireland. Had the sordid Black and Tans immigrated to Wilkes-Barre their descendants would hold all elected city offices.

Privilege doomed Irish America.

Liberty made them lazy.

NOT FUN ANYMORE

Saturday shaped up as a truly fine day for a parade.

Heading into Aladdin's for breakfast, Franny Finnerty left his do-it-yourself protest sign outside, propped against the wall. Franny scribbled "Make America Hate Again" in black Magic Marker on a white poster board he bought at the Dollar Store.

Despite his battered tweed cap cocked at a jaunty angle, he looked like he should be engaged to a Rose of Tralee winner. Romance had long ago passed him by. Franny never squired anyone on a date, never closed his eyes for a first kiss. After shaving and dressing that morning, Franny called his counselor and his caseworker, who both granted permission to go to the Paddy's Day parade. He didn't mention the protest sign targeting the cheesy barbarian who campaigned for re-election at the world's expense. The new century was already shot. Self-conscious as he entered the restaurant, Franny tipped his cap to Cookie who curtsied in response.

"My, my, Mr. Finnerty, you surely do look grand," she said. "Isn't that what they say in Ireland?"

Shy Franny struggled to reply because Cookie was always so nice.

"Tis," he said.

After a pause he added, "Grand."

"Did you hear about Martin Mahoney trying to blow up the Blessed Mother and blame it on Jewish people and Democrats? "

"Bernie's a Jew but he isn't a Democrat," Franny said. "The Blessed Virgin Mary's son is a Democrat."

"I'll bet Jesus wants a woman president," Cookie said.

Franny stood looking at the tips of polished black shoes he shined for half an hour the night before. Mustering his courage to speak, he turned and looked at Cookie.

"People fear truth," he said.

Taking his seat in a booth, Franny ordered only tea.

"I'll hate this parade," he said after sitting awhile in silence.

"Me, too," Cookie said. "They should have cancelled. But the

Irish Guys rule. They put Trump in office and now they put us in jeopardy from this virus."

"I'm ruined," Franny said. "Trump might conquer us again. I don't want to go back to the hospital. But I don't feel good. I don't even feel good about being Irish anymore. It's just not fun being Irish anymore, especially now. Especially here."

"I know the feeling," Cookie said.

When Franny got up at five this morning to wash his underwear in the sink, the thought crossed his mind that he might just call it a day. Sneak into St. Pat's before the parade Mass and loop his belt around his neck, tie the other end to the communion rail, and pitch forward until he blacked out for good. Thoughts of Balor stopped him from leaving his only friend alone.

Cookie looked at Franny.

"Wilkes-Barre's a tough town, Mr. Finnerty," she said. "You can't let them beat you. We can't let them beat us. We can make it. We have to make it. We've invested too much time in this madhouse to do anything else."

"We'll rejoice one day with a woman in the White House," Franny said.

"Yes," Cookie said. "No men need apply."

A MIRACLE

Greeting an antagonistic press, a combative platoon of hungover Irish Guys, and a smattering of hostile bar flies, Mayor McAnus took his seat at the pre-parade and re-election fundraiser breakfast. Tri-color streamers hung from the ceiling and Irish reels blasted from a boom box set the stage in a dingy back room of the Coal Hole to kick off a full day of bedlam.

McAnus led with a prayer.

"Dear God and all the saints in heaven, we come together today with open hearts and wallets to dig deep to do what's best for ourselves and our community. What St. Pat did for Ireland, Donald Trump does for America, and I do for Wilkes-Barre. No matter what the haters say, God willing, we'll live to one day see future generations, your grandchildren, digging coal for the rest of their lives in a local Trump mine."

Cheers interrupted the mayor's benediction. Adjusting an orange, white and green satin sash emblazoned with the words "Irish Guys for Trump/McAnus" that kept slipping from his shoulder like an actor's bra strap on the set of a softcore porn movie, McAnus continued.

"As you know, an explosion rattled our Mary in the wee hours of this most revered morning, the day of our blessed Paddy's Day parade. But that won't stop us from making history today. Marching in the face of pestilence means everything to us sons of Erin gathered here. Means everything to our girls, too," he said.

Sweeping his arm in an arc to include the dozen or so wives, mothers and other women standing at the back of the ballroom bloated and sweating from medication, alcohol or both, he continued.

"That's why I'm proud to offer each female in attendance a free Bloody Mary courtesy of my re-election campaign in honor of the Blessed Virgin."

As a rule, the lads banned women from almost every club event, the biggest exception being the annual "Irish Guys Ladies' Night

Out" in May when Mikey Hoyle performed as an exotic dancer for two hours and allowed the girls to stuff dollar bills down his briefs while he gyrated to Bee Gees songs from the "Saturday Night Fever" soundtrack. Last year, though, Hoyle's mother threatened to publicly expose the video she discovered while cleaning his room after seeing with her own eyes hard evidence of how the girls plied Mikey with alcohol and enticed him to remove his shorts. To make matters worse, they stole and hid his leopard skin bikini bottom while he desperately covered his private parts in a fedora with a goose feather in the brim he used in his performance. Mikey's mother almost couldn't watch the ending she re-wound and watched three times that showed several elderly ladies trying to grab the fedora while jabbing Mikey's privates with swizzle sticks and chasing her only child around the bar.

As expected, Irish Guys' wives broke into polite applause with one or two hooting at 8 o'clock in the morning. The girls always did as expected. Even the strongest female political candidates dared not defy the Irish Guys. Women who knew better acquiesced. They did as they were told. Making waves hurt any serious candidate and aspiring public officeholder from working her way into the long line that led to the political system. Waiting your turn helped more than demanding civil rights. Being a good girl might one day convince men to at least grant access to a low-level political office.

Maybe not, though.

Daddy's permission still controlled the lives of too many otherwise bright, independent young women with Irish roots, even those with law degrees. Ultimately, for both men and women, playing the game according to the rules was all that mattered in Wilkes-Barre and Scranton, for that matter, where bald-faced political corruption was actually worse.

Mayor McAnus cleared his throat. Reaching for a pint glass of water spiked liberally with two shots of Jameson, he continued, "Like I was saying, we live in a time of great turmoil. Our youths are misguided and searching. Our lives are impacted by outside forces beyond our control. We must rely more than ever on powers greater than ourselves."

Three Irish Guys roared when Mikey Hoyle picked up two bottles of Powers whiskey from behind the bar and raised them over his head.

"Greater than ourselves," Mikey Hoyle yelled.

Despite the mayor's clear-headed tone, the crowd laughed and lost interest as they began to pile scrambled eggs and burnt wrinkled sausages on plates pulled from a pile at the buffet arranged on a shuffleboard below a framed likeness of Pope Francis made from colorful floor tile and presented to the Irish Guys by the incarcerated former president of the local tile layers' union.

Bolstered by beatitude, McAnus plowed forward.

"Our sweet Mother of God has prevailed. She is no worse for the wear except for that enormous crack in her arse. As hard as this might be to believe, and we have this confirmed by the UGI company, we have traced the source of the explosion to a natural gas leak that erupted through Mary's backside and caused the minimal damage."

As you might expect, a stunned crowd bought the blarney. No way was the mayor going to credit Mahoney with heading up this violent Trump-centric militia intent on blowing up the Blessed Mother and blaming the libs in a false flag attack. Jesus, Mary and Joseph, a Wilkes-Barre based national secret society on the warpath led by an Irish Guy would make the city and McAnus' administration look like a haven for every crackpot radical group in the nation. The Rotary Club was bad enough, but a pistol-packing Mar-a-Lago Militia would lure the worst of the worst.

Life for McAnus was going too well to screw it up now. In due time, McAnus' police department would deal with Mahoney in their own way and stuff him headfirst into a storm drain. In the meantime, the Paddy's Day parade was set. Nervously checking his watch, the mayor clenched his jaw when his cellphone rang. Quieting the crowd he said, "I believe this is the call we've all been waiting for."

"Hello. Yes, yes, yes, Mr. Trump," he said. "Oh, I'm sorry, Mr. Trump. Yes, yes, yes, goodbye, Mr. Trump. Or should I say Mr. President."

The crowd caught on to the ruse at once and a glass smashed behind McAnus' head.

"That wasn't President Trump on the phone. That was Mikey Hoyle you little shit, you," said an already inebriated "Death Wish" Duggan.

"Yes, it was, too," McAnus said. "President Trump said he can't make the parade because there's an emergency in China, but he wishes us well."

At that moment Mikey Hoyle ran into the room on cue. Out of breath and looking like he was about to keel over, he fell to his knees. Looking around to make sure everybody was watching, he spoke in the voice of a senior class play leading man.

"It's a miracle," he said. "A miracle, I tell you."

The room went silent.

"Mary's healed," Hoyle said. "The crack in the Blessed Mother's arse has healed all by itself. A miracle, I tell you."

Seven devout members of the Legion of Mary, three men and four women, immediately fell to their knees. Blessing themselves, they mumbled prayers of thanks to the forces of light and goodness led by Trump's call perhaps or, if nothing else, his national leadership that came their way and inspired hope for the best.

"A goddamn miracle," Mikey repeated with a wink to the mayor.

"Yes, a miracle," McAnus said. "Praise be to God and Donald Trump. Without them nothing would be possible."

Looking skyward, he repeated the message for full effect.

"A heinous crack in Mary's posterior part has healed," McAnus said.

Leaping to his feet, the chairman of the Irish Guys Pro-Life Committee, wearing a rugby jersey with "I'm a Child Not a Choice" printed across the front and back began to weep.

McAnus' re-election looked better than anybody could have predicted. The breakfast ended with only one unrelated fist fight between two Irish Guys who disagreed over whether buying condoms in a business establishment displaying the Pope's picture constituted a mortal sin. Five minutes later McAnus announced the parade was about to begin. The mayor was ready to march.

"Gentlemen, and ladies, start your engines," McAnus said.

It's a wonder nobody got killed in the mad rush for the door. A truly great day for the Irish Guys and Trump finally dawned on Wilkes-Barre and its Luzerne County residents, hard people in hard coal country who pushed a world-class bollocks into the White House because they believed he watched over them.

"Trump, Trump, Trump," the men chanted as they made their way into the street.

Yes, it truly was a great day for the Irish Guys.

TOO BAD ABOUT THE BABY

"Puggy, you're back!"

"I couldn't stay away."

Within minutes of Pug's kicking in the door to Cookie's place, the two wild teenagers rolled on the floor licking and slurping each other's faces like starving children attacking rainbow-colored snow cones. Pug and Binkee squealed and moaned and grabbed at each other.

Excited enough to show off and do his jig Pug stumbled to his feet. Putting unstoppable energy into upright movement, his prancing looked passable as traditional step dancing. Pug was getting better at tradition. Weak but thrilled to see him, Binkee clapped and tried to whistle like she thought the Irish did at ceili dances. Pug gave up quickly and dropped to the floor. Lying still, he imagined giving his son an Irish name. "Feral" sounded good. Maybe he'd teach the kid to dance.

Grabbing Binkee by her bony shoulders, Pug screamed in her face.

"Where's that whore, Cookie?"

"Working. And don't you call her that. Cookie's my friend," Binkee said.

Binkee never got mad. But the stress was just too much. Cramps hit Binkee in the belly, sending her screaming into a fetal position. Lifting the hem of the threadbare peasant skirt she bought for five dollars at the farmers' market and wore with all the pride of an ancient goddess, Pug saw dark blood drip from between her thin legs, covering her pale thighs and reminding him of grape licorice.

"Ahh, shit," Pug said as his voice rose in pitch.

By the time he called 911 and EMTs arrived, Binkee was unconscious. Thinking quickly, the two women paramedics stopped the bleeding and stabilized her vital signs. Pug listened through the closet door in the dining room where he hid drinking warm beer.

"Too bad about the baby," one medic said.

"She's young," her partner said. "She'll make more babies if she kicks the drugs."

The medics wheeled Binkee out the door.

Pug sat in the closet on the floor reciting lyrics from a song he composed on the spot. Throwing back his head, he contorted his face and sang.

"Paddy's Day in Trump Town. Where all the drinks are free. We're unlike any other place I'm sure you will agree. But when the party's over your life is not carefree. Paddy's Day in Trump Town is where the end will be."

Finally seeing for himself the bloodthirsty fairies of death buzzing around his head like fruit flies, Pug sat alone, hyperventilating in the dark closet, losing and finding his breath as great gulps of air seemed to catch in his throat and block the flow of oxygen to his brain. So he sang and he cried all at the same time.

"Paddy's Day in Trump Town is where the end will be."

KISS ME I'M DYING

One lone hungover bagpiper wearing droopy green knee socks stood at the center of South Main Street. Stuffing his air bag beneath his arm, he launched into a depressing off-key hymn designed at first decibel to draw tears at weddings or wakes. A livelier tune would have been better suited for the day, but the hymn was the only song the big lug knew.

Behind the piper, turncoat Democrat and self-appointed (in the wake of Father O'Toole's passing) Grand Marshal Mayor "Spuds" McAnus began his slow waltz up the green line. Aligned immediately behind the mayor, Luzerne County and Wilkes-Barre city elected officials, including many traitorous Democrats who embraced Trump with the welcomed exuberance of free penicillin injections at a venereal disease clinic, stepped off all teeth and titillation, waving at anything that moved along the route. Next came three dozen Irish Guys of all ages, shapes and sizes in their creased stained berets and off-white gloves, paired with a variety of outfits ranging from sneakers to brown dress shoes to leather slip-on bedroom slippers, black pall bearer topcoats to zip-up professional sports team jackets, and an alarming number of too big or too small Notre Dame parkas and windbreakers. Their women followed behind a "Girls Just Wanna Have Trump" banner that stretched from one side of the street to the other, followed by the float they had worked on all year that had a 100 percent chance to win the parade grand prize.

"Micks Don't Let Micks Drive Drunk" was a masterpiece comprised of a crushed vehicle on the back of a flatbed truck surrounded by a dozen handcuffed men (actually four Italian Americans, four German Americans, three Polish Americans and one white Puerto Rican) who had been charged in the city with driving while intoxicated sometime during the past year and were sentenced by an Irish Guy judge to community service which meant helping the Irish Guys with their float. As you might imagine, the judge routinely tossed DUI charges against countless Irish Guys due to lack

249

of evidence.

"Where's O'Brien?" asked McAnus. "Anybody see O'Brien?"

At that very moment, 11.8 miles north at the Wilkes-Barre/ Scranton International Airport bar, O'Brien absentmindedly stirred a whiskey sour with his thumb, creating a little whirlpool in his glass. With everybody wondering where the hell he was by now and the parade picking up steam, nobody would break free to go look for him. Looking forward to a new life in a new land, O'Brien sat alone feeling warm inside when he noticed his heart beating a little faster than usual. Just excitement, he thought.

Spinning off his stool, he grabbed his cash-heavy suitcase and headed for the ticket counter to check his bag when the ache shot up his left arm. Hot pain shot down his right arm. A force greater than anything O'Brien ever knew seemed to pull his heart through his chest. Boozy saliva dribbled from his soon-to-be-turning-blue lips and triple chin as he clung to the suitcase and dropped face-forward to the floor hard enough to break his nose. Fighting to hold onto the bag loaded with money, he stared into space and saw bright lights, brighter than the lights at the professional baseball stadium right up the road.

"Not now," he gasped through tiny blood bubbles that frothed from his nose like the last spurts from an empty beer tap.

Not even Trump could save him now. In Bop's brain, the loud-speakers in the departure lounge announced his son's name. A scene from the past swirled in Bop's head. The homecoming game when star player Michael scored three touchdowns as a senior. That's where Bop imagined he was with Michael's hair blowing in the wind as he removes his helmet at halftime and walks to the center of the field. Agnes looks so beautiful and happy when homecoming king Michael pins a rose to his mother's dress. A hint of burned wood left over from the bonfire smells like smoky peat and the deep rich smell of the bog Bop often dreamed about after seeing a special on the TV. Michael kisses him on one cheek. Agnes kisses him on the other. Shrugging them both off, O'Brien raises his hands over his head like Rocky. Dozens of Irish Guys in the stands cheer and whoop it up, chanting his name instead of Michael's, cheering for Bop like he's the king, like he's the star player and not his son, like Bop is the greatest Wilkes-Barre hometown football hero of all time. Victorious among his own kind that night, Bop began to cheer for himself.

"Bop O'Brien, Bop O'Brien."

With consciousness slipping away, O'Brien tried to cheer one more time.

"Bop-O," he said. "Bop-O."

Starting to lose consciousness, he fought to stay alert.

Agony erupted from every nerve ending. Looking toward his toes, all he could see was his massive beer belly swelling beneath the edge of the gray cable knit sweater Agnes gave him one year for Christmas.

"The Aran Islands is where they wear these sweaters," she said in all her naiveté. "To identify the fishermen's bodies when they drown."

Bop hated her so much that day he wished he could drown her in the Shannon.

Now his breathing got shallow in his chest. He couldn't feel his legs. People leaned down and whispered. He heard voices in the distance, like an echo. A hand unloosened his necktie, the one he wore under the sweater, the one with tiny shamrocks on it. Another hand undid the top button of his shirt.

"His head's going purple like an eggplant," a ticket agent said.

Strong hands lifted O'Brien onto a gurney and pulled a white sheet to his chin and then over his head as O'Brien's eyes locked in the open position.

"There's still a pulse but it has all the power of a piss ant," one paramedic said, pulling the sheet back to O'Brien's neck. "You know him? He looks familiar."

"Yeah, just like a thousand other fuckers whose hearts blow up before we wheel them to the morgue," said the other EMT. "They all look alike when they're dead."

After loading O'Brien into the ambulance, the emergency medical technicians tossed the fat suitcase in with him.

"Jesus Christ, that weighs a ton."

Checking his watch, the driver said, "We're fucked if we don't get our ass back to the parade. The mayor will kill us if we miss our place in the procession."

The other EMT nodded.

"This fella's gone, anyway."

With lights flashing and siren open wide, it took eight minutes for the duo to make their cleanup position at the rear of the parade. Their job was simple. Toss thousands of shamrock-shaped green cards from the driver's side and passenger side windows as the crowd began to disperse. Printed in orange, white and green on both sides, the political message was loud and clear.

"Vote For McAnus" the card said. "Spuds For Everybody."

By the time the ambulance sped past South Street, though, the parade crowd was on the verge of making all the major networks. Riot cops stood arm-in-arm along a two-block stretch of South Main as about a hundred drunken Wilkes and King's College kids burned an Italian flag thinking it was the Mexican flag. Marching remnants of the 70s Mafia-sponsored Italian-American Civil Rights League took immediate umbrage and, throwing heavyweight punches, waded into the crowd of young knuckleheads, now called customers rather than scholars by university officials.

McAnus stood on the roof of a fire truck with a bullhorn trying to quell the mayhem.

Nobody spotted Pug as he ran from between two buildings and took up his marching post in the center of the street. But even the drunks knew something spectacular was about to happen when Pug began to wail his grief and sorrow. Tears slid from his eyes as he moved bawling his way down the middle of the street wearing nothing but green war paint from the top of his big bald head to the soles of his dirty bare feet. Waving his shotgun in one hand and his shillelagh in the other, he began to jig. A couple of drunks in the crowd hooted and began to clap in time. Bulbous and bobbing from side to side, Pug's penis stood at attention, almost erect, looking like it wanted to talk, like it had something important to say. A luminous hue of green spray paint extended from neck to navel to his pubic patch, around his balls to his thighs, and down to the tips of his toes. Like a frenzied ancient warrior charging into battle stained with dye to petrify the enemy, Pug used four cans of paint that morning for three coats that magnified his appearance into a specter of folklore run amok.

The capital letter "T" he recently carved into his forehead had begun to heal. A smooth red scar rose above his eyebrows crusted green with dried spray paint. Pug's head glistened in the sunlight through a thin mixture of blood and Vaseline he rubbed on his dome after shaving it clean with a couple of nicks in Cookie's bathroom. The shamrock tattoo at the base of his noggin flashed like a birthmark as he strutted in the street.

A few blocks away, doctors had already removed the fetus from Binkee's womb. Because Pug had to steer clear of the emergency room for fear of being captured, he had abandoned Binkee to stretch out for a breather in Cookie's tub with a bottle of Baileys Irish Cream Liquor he found in the cupboard and the last of the multi-colored pills he swiped from his mother. Lucky for Cookie she hadn't come home. Pug had been looking forward to sacrificing her to the unchecked insanity that now ruled his brain. But she probably rushed right to the hospital after Binkee or doctors called and the cops located her at the grease pit where she worked. Pug's loaded shotgun leaned against the wall the whole time he soaked in the bubble bath. He had ripped up his poems which marinated among the toilet paper and dark water of the commode he clogged when he tried to flush bloated words about his past life deep into the sewer.

How could Binkee have lost their unborn prince? Obviously a space feminist sent to destroy King Pug, a black hole pod vagina from the mother ship sent to drill into his manhood, collect his semen then blast off to another galaxy with his jizz floating around the space ship in zero gravity, hanging there like UFO slime tinsel on a cosmic Christmas tree. If only he could have alerted the United States Space Force. Had they known of his plight, Commander Trump would have fired laser beams out of his ass and hit Binkee right between the eyes. Warped visions of satellite carnage danced in his head. Green lights flashed in his eyes. In the sky he saw Moses

Garrett dancing a jig with Father O'Toole in the clouds. Like them, in order to make the universe great again, Binkee had to go.

"Trump, Trump, Trump," Pug screamed as he stopped dancing in the street. Turning his head from side to side, he faced the masses on both sides of the parade. Not surprisingly, a large number of drunks along the route now took up the chant.

"Death Wish" Duggan stood with fifteen or so motley "Bikers for Trump" who had already rolled through the route, parked their bikes, and assembled to watch the rest of the parade.

"I guess Trump's not coming," Duggan said. "I thought he'd surprise us."

The gang seemed deeply hurt. To make matters worse, they now faced off against a grim green barbarian who did show up. Was he with them or against them?

Pug marched on. Nearing the Square, he saw Binkee's face in each store window. In one, a halo encircled her head wrapped in a pale blue shawl, making her look like a Muslim Virgin Mary. Pug could stand no more and bellowed through his pain.

"Muslims suck. Muslims suck."

The bikers, drunken college kids and assorted other believers took up that chant, mostly white male Trump backers of limited intelligence earning limited income who thought Pug's part in the parade made the march the best one ever. "Death Wish" almost went hoarse screaming whatever xenophobic slurs he could squeeze like inflamed whiteheads from his limited vocabulary.

Drawing their pistols, panicked city police crouched beside the open doors of their cars.

Pug kicked into another jig.

"Drop the gun," said a SWAT captain wearing a "Trump Digs Coal" pin on the side of the baseball cap he wore backwards.

Pug continued to dance as a thin stream of urine dribbled down his leg. In his eternally loyal mind's eye, Pug saw "The Molly Maguires" playing on the old TV while his father drank beer and he and his mother sat side by side on the couch eating burned popcorn. He wondered how many times a teenager can be expected to watch "The Quiet Man" and Darby O'Gill without getting traumatized.

Pug felt like a fish sandwich.

"Drop the gun now," the Irish Guy cop demanded, using officer discretion to decide it was okay for the freak to hold on to the Irish stick. After all, it was a Paddy's Day parade.

"When you pry it from my cold dead fingers," Pug said.

The crowd roared.

Pug heard the siren. Running later than expected, the ambulance crew careened into the parade route. As soon as the driver saw the turmoil unfolding before him he braked. Steering with his knees and trying to organize the mayor's political literature, the ambulance slid sideways, jumping the curb and going up on two wheels. Grabbing the wheel, the other medic jerked the vehicle to the other side of the street where it slammed head-on into the kissing booth Duggan allowed the Irish Guys Ladies' Auxiliary to operate when he quickly tired of his own brilliance.

In the seconds before the ambulance slid to a stop, the back doors burst open and out flew O'Brien. Bouncing along the sidewalk, cushioned only by the thick knit of his gray Aran Islands cable knit sweater, O'Brien drew his last breath. Watching helplessly as his suitcase bounced over his head, O'Brien expired as the only witness to a thin hand reaching for the suitcase handle from under a dying hedge and pulling it back beneath the bush.

Like a double-jointed carnival act, Pug stretched his long arms and hands behind his back, pushing the shotgun barrel against the base of his skull. Wiggling his tongue back and forth in an obscene fashion, Pug began to squeeze the trigger when a massive weight crashed against his body. Balor, the great dog of Paddy's Day parades past, had seen Pug coming. Earlier, after watching the parade from his hiding place in a stairwell, the poor dog fell asleep. Waking abruptly to pandemonium, Balor immediately recognized Pug from better days at the Coal Hole. Despite painful memories of pulls on his tail, the beast always liked the little hooligan who occasionally gave him drunken belly rubs.

Instead of a direct shot into Pug's brain, the slug sailed off course and through his jaw, shattering decaying teeth and strong bone in a burst of red and white gore as he blew a significant hunk of his scalp into the air and onto a manhole cover. Pug's nose disappeared but his eyes remained. The shamrock tattoo survived. Before he passed out, recognizing chunks of his goateed chin on South Main Street, Pug wondered if Binkee still loved him.

How could she resist?

MY BODY MYSELF

SueReen pooled every penny she saved from cashier jobs at the earring pagoda at the mall, tending bar, and working at Walmart to buy a one-way bus ticket to Santa Maria, California, a mostly Mexican town she had seen on the news during the Michael Jackson trial in 2005. The town seemed clean, otherworldly from what she knew, and sat on the furthest edge of America she could find without falling off.

SueReen needed to get away.

Escape was her plan even before meeting "Death Wish" at the rally that night she was so messed up. Trying her best to belong, to fit in, to be part of something, she cheered Trump and cheered this biker hunk cheering Trump. The next morning, lying in the parking lot like dog dirt in a red MAGA cap felt worse than she ever felt alone. In bright daylight, the word "hunk" took on new meaning. SueReen knew she had hit bottom by thinking a Trump rally one-night stand would be better than methamphetamine sprinkled on vanilla cupcakes. Oh, yeah. She now knew better all right.

Feeling good about herself when she got on the bus, SueReen wore a dandelion in her hair, stepping on board with one suitcase stored in the undercarriage and her backpack loaded with snacks, books and her five favorite CDs, all Madonna all the time. She didn't really understand how young millennials listened to music on their phones and wasn't up on technology. A couple of community college courses to learn about computers would be nice when she made it to the West Coast. So would a skinny illegal boyfriend to whom she could give sanctuary once he bounced over the wall like a Mexican jumping bean. SueReen polished the button she pinned to her denim jacket that said "Nasty Woman."

Nirvana had appeared to her with the ease of a refrigerator light coming on. Maybe the yoga she had started to practice kicked in. Or the carrot sticks and yogurt she now ate for lunch. Maybe the green tea had something to do with her enlightenment or maybe just realizing she had one last chance to get out of town because she had nobody to depend on but herself.

Women didn't matter in Trump Town. Women just existed like fresh red meat on a bone to be dumped when the primitive gnawing was done.

SueReen decided to go when "Death Wish" got so carried away the day after the Trump rally that he called a press conference and made a big production out of slapping her on the ass in front of a FOX television crew that captured what he called "the Trump tap." For the next three days producers ran the segment as a political human interest feature about consensual sexism among Trump's dumb female base.

"I can't help myself. I just do it," Junior told the news crew. "Sometimes I just start slapping them on the ass. They let me do it. When you're president of "Bikers for Trump," they let you do it," he said.

When they got back to Death Wish's place that night, he got so drunk he berated SueReen for having "Obama ears" and pulled them until she cried. The police came that night. A woman from the resource center showed up the next day. Why SueReen hadn't previously figured out the "violence of paternalism" and the "curse of patriarchy" (phrases she made up on the bus out of town and wrote in her journal), she'd never know. Probably just afraid she had nowhere to go and no way to get there without a man.

SueReen had enough money saved to last her about a month, including what she needed for an abortion if she was pregnant. Most people in California understood a woman's right to terminate a pregnancy. Trump said women who choose should be punished. That threat is why SueReen would consider a safe and legal end to an unwanted pregnancy. Strong women needed to stand together, SueReen thought as the bus pulled out. SueReen would live as a strong, independent woman now and forever.

Passing a "Trump" banner tacked to a tree and left over from the rally, SueReen put her palms together in the Buddhist expression of gassho that notes interconnectedness. Bowing slightly, she let the past pass in a cloud of exhaust fumes and memories of pierogis, lousy bar bands and married men. SueReen suddenly clapped her hands for no reason and for every reason.

"Goodbye Wilkes-Barre," she said. "Good riddance."

YOU'RE FIRED

A six-man Irish Guys honor guard flanked Brendan "Bop" O'Brien's casket.

Standing at awkward attention at his head and feet, they fought to stay awake in the heat of what locals still called the corpse house, slang for funeral parlor. Sneaking out for cigarettes and swigs from flasks so often their vigil could have been mistaken for professional tag team wrestling, the men watched over O'Brien's coffin for what seemed like an eternity. Sweating and hung over from an old-fashioned three-day viewing sapped their strength. Resenting the sense of shallow duty that had driven them there, true to local code they still did as they were told.

They didn't yet know about their money, the small fortune O'Brien liquidated and cashed in from parade contributions, bribes, gifts, kickbacks and other sources of under-the-table revenue. Nobody even tried to explain O'Brien's absence from the parade or what the Christ he was doing at the airport when he took the header into the afterlife.

So the fellows struggled with silence and nausea as a long line of politicians, crooked cops and other phony mourners streamed through the room with all the aplomb of a polluted trout stream overflowing steep banks. Wearing chipper green berets and white gloves most of the contingent had stolen from their wives' underwear drawers, the men did their best to appear alert. Turtlenecks sagged at various degrees of disarray. None of their green blazers could be buttoned across the wide expanse of beer belly fat that had not seen a fresh vegetable in decades. But they meant well as they swayed in the blustery heat that blew from vents in the ceiling and caused the pancake makeup on O'Brien's face to melt and run down his cheeks like a mudslide.

Because of gross brush burns on O'Brien's cheeks due to the spill from the ambulance, the undertaker overcompensated. Between the black hair dye and cheap cosmetics dripping down his sideburns, O'Brien looked more like a damaged Elvis mannequin pulled from a wax museum fire than a stiff who looked like himself.

A wreath of green carnations molded into the obligatory shamrock the size of a life preserver on a cruise ship loomed over O'Brien's head. A flimsy gold harp the florist made up carried an inscription across its strings. "Irish Guys Go Bra" read the epitaph meant to be a take-off on the famous slogan "Erin go bragh," which means "Ireland Forever" in Gaelic.

Wife Agnes, son Michael and his fiancée Tommy sat on wooden folding chairs quietly holding hands in the front row.

Blessing himself, Mayor McAnus held up the line as he stood by the coffin and refused to move. Staring at the dented detective badge O'Brien clutched in his fingers, with its dull sheen picking up the overhead lights, instead of symbolic justice all McAnus saw were dollar signs. How could all the money disappear that quickly without a trace? If O'Brien had heisted the dough as some people were mumbling, then where was it?

Nestled deep in the bushes outside, Mahoney peeped through a side window. Pulling the balaclava mask over his head, he prepared to pounce. Reclining unseen behind the forsythia bushes beside the embalming room, Mahoney patiently waited for all the mourners to exit and move on to St. Pat's where a requiem high funeral mass was planned.

During the night, Mahoney had built and planted his latest bomb, a real bomb this time after checking on the internet to make sure he had all the right ingredients. Getting even with these chicken shits would be his last act of chauvinistic, nationalistic, jingoistic revenge against hooligans who tried to steal his honor and turned their backs on the real rebel Irish, an elite band to which he would belong until his dying day. After all his years of sacrifice for the Irish Guys, for his family and for the church, he deserved something special in return. When the heroic deed was done, the Mar-a-Lago Militia would take credit. Mahoney would come out of hiding, throw himself on the mercy of the White House and walk away a hero like Patrick Pearse or some other great Irish patriot of old. That the British executed Pearse did nothing to deter Mahoney.

Checking his watch, Mahoney ran his fingers along the buried line of Cordtex he bought from a biker buddy of "Death Wish" Duggan, a disgruntled Iraq War veteran with access to the National Guard armory. Mahoney hid the thin, almost invisible ultra-sensitive, indestructible military grade detonating cord under dirt, sticks and leaves he scattered all the way to the doorway. Inside, attached to the funeral parlor wall with duct tape, the pentrite-filled cord worked its way under the carpet, up the leg of the folding cart upon which O'Brien lay stretched out in repose, into the green satin comfort of the cheap bronze casket, and finally up O'Brien's pants leg and under his Notre Dame undies. Mahoney secured and tightly inserted the final bit of high explosive primer cord packed with a handful of blasting caps directly and deeply into O'Brien's puckered rectum.

"Wrecked him? It nearly killed him," Mahoney said out loud with a chuckle.

Then he made the call.

"A live bomb stuck up the hole of the deceased Wilkes-Barre detective," the 911 operator repeated. "Is that correct, sir?"

Sirens wailed within three minutes. Squad cars screeched to a halt. Bomb dogs and a robot arrived. The stiff was wired and ready to go.

"You're fired, loser," Mahoney said to O'Brien.

As soon as he triggered the high-speed fuse Mahoney realized he had unknowingly wrapped the charged cord around his ankle. Tripping as he tried to run, Mahoney went up in a gory blaze of glory, going to pieces at a sad event made sadder by his own pathetic display of failed domestic terrorism carried out by a fizzled freedom fighter. Anatomized ass over elbows, a shower of dismembered body parts, guts, bowels and vitals poured down like a warm spring shower.

No rainbow appeared.

O'Brien's remains also did not remain. Symbolic of his well-known temper, O'Brien went through the roof, bringing down the corpse house in the shambles of a historic collapse.

Two days later, Bridget cremated what was left of her Martin, stuck a "For Sale" sign in the yard in front of the house, and moved to a room in Old Forge, a scrappy little town that billed itself "The Pizza Capital of the World." Bridget loved her pizza and figured she could get a job in a restaurant, go into rehab, and visit Pug on Sundays for the rest of her life in a state prison hopefully not too far from home.

FAKE NEWS

General consensus held that Pug, not the parade, put Wilkes-Barre on the map. Even though most Irish Guys and people in the East End neighborhood abhorred rather than adored Pug, he was still one of their own.

The kid had Irish mental problems, they argued, so the courts should go easy on him. A politically correct society pushed the troubled teenager into the abyss, they said. International news reported the events as yet another bizarre American exercise in gun violence and pathology masquerading as freedom. The Irish Guys issued a statement attacking the press.

"Fake news," McAnus said at a press conference CNN, FOX and MSNBC carried live. "Trump and I will win re-election because we tell the truth. The press makes up shit about good people and tries to ruin our lives. The press is the enemy of the people. Fuck you, Anderson Pooper."

Cable stations bleeped McAnus, but the hometown crowd assembled in the parking lot by police headquarters behind City Hall roared its approval.

At General Hospital, doctors continued to marvel how Pug survived, despite severe facial damage from the shotgun blast. With emerald green paint still vibrant on his body days after the event, Pug breathed through tubes as a physician explained how basic plastic surgery would fix most of his face, but prison doctors would never provide a high-class makeover courtesy of taxpayers.

"At least you'll look better than Michael Jackson," the doctor said.

When Pug lunged at the doc despite wearing handcuffs, a guard knocked Pug out by smacking him with a tactical LED flashlight on the side of what was left of his head. Heavy medication injected into Pug's veins clouded his brain and sent him sailing into a vivid hallucination.

In a diabolical fever dream, Pug looked in a mirror at his newly rebuilt self.

Donald Trump Jr. looked back.

THE FUTURE IS FEMALE

A mile or so down the road from Pug's hospital room, a soft rose sunrise broke behind the black coal mountain that stood as testimony to the history of personal struggle. For hundreds of thousands of people in this valley, life started and ended here in a dirty battlefield of anthracite. For them no other place on earth mattered as much. Such uniqueness created simple goodness and high-intensity evil which, together, built the desolate legacy of hard coal country support for the president.

Parked at the base of the culm mountain, Cookie and Duff hugged beneath a blanket.

"The Clearwater Beach sunset will be nicer," Duff said. "I promise."

Watching the new day from the back of Duff's new steel gray Subaru Outback, they pondered their next move. Neither had serious reservations about leaving and had come to this desolate coal peak the night before to sit and park, necking like teenagers, listening to the radio, and before they fell asleep, remembering how far they had come in a town that shunned anyone not willing to believe in the worst tradition offered.

The Times Leader once billed the Wyoming Valley in Luzerne County as "The Valley with a Heart," but that motto marketed by public relations media pitchmen only hyped romantic deception and played into the quaint notion of the Golden Rule. Too many people in Wilkes-Barre did unto others all right. Then they did it again, this time with a vengeance.

Rubbing his eyes and checking his watch, Duff asked, "What time did you tell the county Children and Youth people we'd be picking up Binkee?"

"Nine. Just with her drug use, running away and miscarrying, I never thought the judge would let us have her. I couldn't believe how quickly her mother wrote her off. Binkee has nobody else. The county doesn't want her. The group homes and foster homes don't want her. Nobody knows that better than our Binkee."

Cookie looked worried.

"She knows we really want her, right?" she said.

"She knows," Duff said.

"You think we'll be good parents?" Cookie asked.

"Better us than her," Duff said. "Little girls don't need little babies. The miscarriage was a very scary blessing. We'll get our stuff together and then turn it over to the movers. I'll rent out my mother's house. Drive straight through to Clearwater. Find a pastel apartment near the Gulf. Then maybe one day we'll buy a house. By that time Binkee's adoption should be approved. Binkee's smart, too caring for her own good. She'll adjust. She'll handle it. She knows Pug is sick and dangerous. Hurtful, she calls him. Counseling will help her. A regular life is what she says she wants more than anything."

"Me too," Cookie said.

Duff seemed distracted.

"Paddy 'Duff' Duffin is one real strange name for a brother," he said. "But Duffin is a black name. My mother says it's been in her family for generations. Probably came from a slave owner."

"Probably an Irish Guy," Cookie said. "I can't believe I'm starting college classes for nursing school."

"My mother would be proud of you," Duff said.

"I never thought I could get out of here," Cookie said. "I couldn't believe they agreed to transfer my parole. You tell your new boss about me?"

"The police chief's sister is an ex-offender. He's easier to deal with. Not like people here. He wants me to start as soon as we get down there. With the virus threat it's hard to say when they might stop hiring."

Coal doesn't have a smell. Coal has a presence. The air reeked of old tires and sulfur. Slag and coal debris crunched beneath Duff's bare feet. He looked at one of the remaining black mountains in the coal field. Darkness at the break of dawn pounded his senses.

"Those Irish Guys were right all along," he said. "I never did belong here."

"Me, neither," Cookie said. "Thanks for letting Binkee stick her

Grateful Dead dancing bears bumper sticker on the new Subie. She was so excited. You can't believe how worried I was that something else would surface to hurt her. All her medical tests came back clean. No clap, no HIV, heart murmur, no nothing. Sometimes I wonder if maybe there is a God."

"There's not," Duff said.

Picking up a chunk of coal, Duff put it in his pocket. Then he picked up two more chunks.

Also barefoot, Cookie stepped from the hatchback and watched the sun, imagining what it must be like to live in bright light on what the travel brochures called Florida's Gold Coast. Raising her arms above her head, she stretched. Taking in the early morning air she inhaled deeply, slowly, mindfully and exhaled.

Stooping to pick up her own three pieces of coal power, Cookie remembered reading about how Zen monks around the world sometimes stacked rocks in monastery gardens or mountain paths. Three rocks stacked one on top of the other looked like a seated Buddha's body, shoulders and head. This small hard coal Buddha would sit in a special place in the new Florida apartment, exuding energy as a symbol of devotion to kindness, respect and giving.

Walking to Duff, she stood on tiptoes, wrapped her arms around his back and buried her face deep into the softness of his shoulder. Beneath their feet, tiny chunks of coal tickled their soles.

"We'll go get showers, change and pick up Binkee," Duff said.

Sitting on the bed she made for the last time, kicking her legs back and forth when Duff and Cookie arrived, Binkee held tight to her nameless, faceless stuffed animal.

"I'm sorry for all the trouble I've caused," Binkee said.

"That's yesterday, honey," Cookie said. "Today's brand new. We're going to Florida."

"Yaay," Binkee said.

A week later the new family sang and talked and ate barbecue potato chips on the drive south. Cruising the beltway around Washington, D.C., Cookie told Binkee about the women's marches in recent years when feminists took to the streets of the nation's capital. Even shy women vowed to fight for a new day for America, when women truly mattered in politics and elsewhere. The first march took place one day after Trump took the oath of office, Cookie said, a protest rich with furor over his election and vile disregard of women's rights. More than a million women and their supporters joined millions more women and allies around the world in opposition to the Trump regime, she said.

Binkee took Cookie's hand.

"Can we go to the next protest?"

"Let's hope we don't have to," Cookie said.

PUTIN'S ANGELS

"I'm in a real pickle," said "Death Wish" Duggan.

The gruff stranger on the other end of the telephone listened closely to this big mouth talking too much and giving him a non-stop sad sack-of-shit story about how his father just died and could no longer grease the skids for him in the White House employment line.

"Peekle?" the man said. "What peekle?"

"The security position at Mar-a-Lago fell through," Duggan said. "I flunked the psychological test. They showed me an ink blot and I told the truth. I said it looked like a big bird with a pecker on him, a teeny pecker like Mr. Trump's. I didn't want to insult the president so I told the psychologist I got one just like it. No personal bodyguard gig with Mr. Trump, either, even though I told the Secret Service I'm an eighth-degree Won Hung Low black belt expert, but I made that up," Duggan said. "Looks like tough shit for 'Death Wish' Duggan."

Using the power of his menacing nickname, thinking he was talking to another far less badass biker, Duggan did his best to impress. The caveman on the other end of the telephone line grunted.

"The worst part is Crooked SueReen left me a note saying she was running away with the Mexicans," Duggan said.

More grunts and what sounded like a chuckle.

"The Trump Coal Mine isn't up and running, either. The only job I could get was guarding this coal land the mayor owns where the mine is supposed to open. I'm working the graveyard shift right now sitting here like a clown eating leftover liverwurst sandwiches. Trump promised Wilkes-Barre good jobs. He promised. We believed him."

"Is bad time for you, I can tell," said the man on the other end of the line in an accent Duggan couldn't identify. "My friends and I also work security."

"Bikers for Trump voted me out of the club when I passed out during a TV appearance after only seven shots of Old Overcoat whiskey. Goddamn SueReen drank 14 of them."

"How much you want for motorcycle I see on Craigslist?" the man said.

"Fifteen grand," Duggan said.

"I pay twenty," the man said. "Cash."

Duggan bit his lip to keep from laughing, thinking the dumb sonofabitch of a foreigner had no idea who he was dealing with. After the pounding Duggan gave the bike, he'd be lucky to get five thousand for the piece of shit from anybody who knew anything about motorcycles. Now this alien is offering more than what the scooter was worth when his old man brought it home.

"Sounds like you got yourself a deal, bud."

When the U-Haul truck pulled up to the coal land at midnight, Duggan sat toasting marshmallows, warming his feet by the camp fire he built in the woods. Empty tall boy beer cans littered the site. Ice cubes in a cooler full of fresh beers glistened in the glow cast from twinkling flames. Six industrial cooler-sized men stepped from the truck.

"Comrade," said the leader of the pack. "I am Yegor."

Perplexed, Duggan couldn't shut up.

"What are you guys, Polacks?"

One man looked more menacing than the next. Duggan never saw World Wrestling Federation villains so thick around the neck and shoulders. Wearing combat fatigues and black leather cut-off vests that exposed vein-popping biceps and triceps, their skin showed an array of black, blue and red tattoos. Snarling wolves, nuclear missiles, stars and spiders as well as an assortment of hammers and sickles that Duggan thought were martial arts weapons covered every inch of skin. Yegor wore a drab portrait of Vladimir Putin carved into his neck.

Slowly circling Duggan, the men chuckled.

"Vrooom vroooom," said Yegor, twisting his brick-sized fist as if accelerating.

"Oh, yeah, the Harley," Duggan said. "Here she is, boys."

The slap would have broken Duggan's neck had Yegor not stopped the head from spinning on the second cervical vertebra axis by cupping Duggan's bone head with his other great paw.

"She? Your motorcycle is a girl? We ride men bikes. Do not call us boys."

Spitting blood, Duggan sputtered and spoke.

"Yeah, yeah, what was I thinking?"

Duggan couldn't understand Yegor's reply, but the whispered words sounded like Russian Ivan Drago's lines before he killed Apollo Creed in the Rocky movie. As dumb as he looked, Duggan still sensed danger. These men, KGB-trained combat advisors who served in Chechnya before affiliating with the ultra-nationalist Ukrainian biker gang called the Night Wolves, were on their way to work security at the Russian Embassy in Washington, D.C. and establish a "friendly" presence in the U.S.

One of the beastly commandos wearing a vintage USSR tank driver's helmet and bracelets adorned with sharpened silver spikes jumped into the open U-Haul to drop the ramp so they could wheel the new bike into the truck. Finally free to be themselves, they had to get motorcycles to start their new American outlaw biker gang. This was their first, a righteous time to celebrate. After living and working as bouncers, personal trainers and real estate agents in Little Odessa in Brighton Beach, Brooklyn, for a few years, with Trump as president and lapdog to the Puppet Master, they finally felt emboldened enough to come out.

These six Russkies planned to pick up bikes along the way, stashing them as they went in the back of the truck with what little furniture (including a few Imperial chandeliers, a Cossack-inspired dining room set, a beetroot borscht-colored sectional sofa, autographed posters of the Bolshoi Ballet and recently acquired nude centerfold photos of the new First Lady) they had accumulated during their short time in the United States.

"Your donation to the cause will do nicely for a start," said Yegor, pointing to Duggan's Harley. "Give me keys and papers."

Duggan quickly handed over the works.

In addition to Duggan's motorcycle and ability to breathe, the Russians stole his beer.

"Moral of story," Yegor said. "Don't screw with Putin's Angels."

Teenagers drinking beer in the woods found the body a few weeks later. Police determined the death resulted from a bear attack. For a change they weren't that far off.

DUGGAN WASN'T CAPTURED

Mayor McAnus, while under the influence of alcohol, opioid painkillers and several psychotropic drugs prescribed for a variety of conditions both real and imagined, wrote the following official statement on the death of "Danny Boy" Duggan and posted it on the Wilkes-Barre City Facebook page.

The legendary Daniel "Danny Boy" Duggan could have stood in the middle of Fifth Avenue and shot somebody and never lost support from countless people who loved him. Duggan became quite the local celebrity for his dead-on imitation of the Notre Dame Fighting Irish leprechaun. Sadly, during his last days in the grip of dementia, he needed to be restrained because of all the Fighting Irish merchandise, leprechaun dolls and cards people sent him. Poor Danny Boy's hallucinations made him think the little fellow was chasing him into Hell with blood coming out of his eyes, blood coming out of wherever. Until then Danny Boy always appreciated the applause that greeted his classic imitation. In fact he was doing that imitation for active alcoholic disabled veterans at the VFW when the World Trade Center came down on the TV and he saw thousands of them Muslims dancing in the streets with his own eyes.

A highly decorated police officer, he swore until his dying day he was innocent of them terrible things the NAACP, the ACLU, NOW and other terrorist groups were saying about him. Through it all, Danny Boy stood his ground. He wasn't captured. He liked people who weren't captured.

Lots of people turn to God at times like these. Danny Boy turned to Trump. He worked tirelessly for our champion's election and re-election and will always be remembered by the Trump family as an honorary graduate of Trump University with a doctorate in forensic police work awarded to him following his death by a UPS driver who delivered the official document. As a gesture of his appreciation for Duggan who got him out of at least a half dozen DUIs, the UPS driver picked up the degree at the Staples where his wife works and prints up phony diplomas she sells on the side. I'm sure, as tough as he was, Duggan would have wept had he survived to receive his prestigious graduate degree.

Duggan was preceded in death by his wife, Peggy, and son, Daniel Jr., no relation to the band that performed "At the Hop," whose death was an unfortunate hunting accident. In lieu of flowers cash contributions can be sent to the "Friends of McAnus Campaign Committee" in care of the Coal Hole.

A complimentary BYOB reception to honor Duggan will be held in the near future. Admission is ten dollars.

TRUMP DIGS COAL

"Another cheeseburger, Mr. President?"

"Two."

"Extra fries?"

"With bacon and cheese."

"We're putting together the last few rallies before Election Day, your excellency. This anus mayor in Wilkes-Barre, Pennsylvania, keeps calling the switchboard asking to confirm the date."

"Wilkes wherey?"

"Trump digs coal, remember? Those suckers fell hard for us in 2016 and want us back as the last campaign stop before the election to thank them for their help."

"These hillbillies from shit-hole coal country want me to thank them?"

"Yes sir. Some outfit calling themselves the Irish Guys."

"Incredible."

"What should I tell them, commander?"

"To go grab themselves by the pee-pees."

TAKE ME HOME TO MAYO

From where he sat on Lackavrea Mountain, overlooking the ruins of the 12th Century Hen's Castle where the great pirate queen Grace O'Malley ruled and fought with wisdom and courage, Franny Finnerty surveyed his new Irish domain.

Laid out before him, the land spread like creamy yellow butter bathed in golden honey. Rising in the evening mist, the Maamturk Mountains stood as they have for sixty million years. Casting shadows of comfort across the lush wide valley, they continued in waves of rolling green earth all the way to the horizon. The smell of fresh burning peat lifted across the bog and caressed Franny's nostrils. To him the fiery aroma of turf was the best smell in the world. Inhaling and lighting his pipe, Franny scanned the landscape. The lake, Lough Corrib, splashed gently against a rugged shore, rustling bright wild flowers that swayed in the breeze blowing inland from the western shores of the Atlantic.

Countless people long ago abandoned this haunting beauty in search of a better life, a richer life in places like Pittsburgh, Scranton, Wilkes-Barre, Hazleton, Philadelphia, Boston and New York. Few of the emigres returned.

Franny had come home.

Fifty yards below where he sat, Balor ran and leaped through the meadow with all the active energy of the fat ball of fur he had once been before human clods snatched him from paradise. With his huge head and long legs, the happy beast sprinted with unbridled abandon across the natural splendor of countryside that borders counties Galway and Mayo.

Popping the cap from another warm bottle of Guinness, Franny put down his pipe and reached for the penny whistle he purchased at the airport after landing and renting a car for his trip to the motherland. During many years in and out of the hospital, on the few occasions nurses allowed him to listen to Irish music, he felt so much better than when he took the most powerful drugs, talk therapy or electric current. Traditional music surged through him today, rushing through crackling brain cells, satisfying, pleasing and, for the first time in his life, making him feel perfect. Franny and Balor would stay in Ireland forever. Like his new whistle, he'd play it by ear. Franny's ancestors fled this very place. Returning to reclaim his spiritual inheritance had always been on his mind, even when he was losing it. Franny had mostly been out of his mind. Not anymore.

The suitcase jammed with cash the crash propelled with O'Brien from the back of the ambulance had tumbled directly into Franny's hands as he watched the world fall apart from under a dying bush. Thinking he was doing a good deed, Franny grabbed the handle amid the panic. Intending to return the case to its rightful owner through authorities in the morning, he took it home and stashed it in his room. But when curiosity got the best of him, Franny peeked, discovering he had a sound mind after all.

Now he had a sound bank account.

"Call me King of the Irish Guys," he said to Balor, who barked and galloped like a wondrous gray horse.

Franny played a few sweet notes on the whistle. Swigging from the dark brown bottle, he felt alive knowing a lifetime remained to play music that collected for so long in his head. A hundred yards away, Balor rolled on his back in the rhapsody of puppy life a long, long time ago.

A lamb cried. The night turned purple. Bright planets rose in the sky. A banshee laughed.

Gazing across the magic expanse of his kingdom, Franny took another drink.

Then he took another.

The End

Steve Corbett's author page

theoutlawcorbett.com

Contact Steve at steve.corbett51@gmail.com